D0499583

IN THE
BLOOD

Nancy A. Collins

A ROC BOOK

ROC
Published by the Penguin Group
Penguin Books USA Inc., 375 Hudson Street,
New York, New York 10014, U.S.A.
Penguin Books Ltd, 27 Wrights Lane,
London W8 5TZ, England
Penguin Books Australia Ltd, Ringwood,
Victoria, Australia
Penguin Books Canada Ltd, 20 Alcorn Avenue,
Toronto, Ontario, Canada M4V 3B2
Penguin Books (N.Z.) Ltd, 182–190 Wairau Road,
Auckland 10, New Zealand

Penguin Books Ltd, Registered Offices:
Harmondsworth, Middlesex, England

First published by Roc, an imprint of New American Library, a division of
Penguin Books USA Inc.

First Printing, January, 1992
10 9 8 7 6 5 4 3 2 1

Roc is a trademark of New American Library,
a division of Penguin Books USA Inc.

Printed in the United States of America

Dedicated to the memory of my grandfather:
James Wesley Willoughby, Jr.

The author would like to acknowledge the following people, whose support, criticisms, and input helped along the way: Paul Mavrides, Harry S. Robins, John Shirley, Joe Lansdale, Corby Simpson and, as always, Dan.

PALMER

I am not now
That which I have been.
                        —Byron, *Childe Harold*

1

Where is she?

Palmer looked at his watch for the fifteenth time in as many minutes. She was late. Again. He wanted to believe that it wasn't deliberate on her part, but the truth was Loli enjoyed keeping him waiting.

No, not waiting; twisting in the wind on the end of a meat-hook.

The woman knew she had him: heart, soul, and gonads. Palmer recognized Loli as bad news the moment she sashayed into his office, but the knowledge hadn't kept him from falling hard and messy, like a jumper on the Empire State Building.

She'd hired him to follow her husband, a well-to-do contractor named Samuel Quine, trying to get some dirt on him for a nice, juicy divorce settlement. It didn't take long. Quine was seeing someone on the sly, all right.

They met at a motor court at the edge of town twice a week. It was all very discreet and proper, in a suburban middle-class kind of way. Palmer was all too familiar with the pattern; he'd spent a good chunk of his professional life taking incriminating photos of unfaithful husbands and wives sneaking in and out of hot-sheet joints. What he couldn't understand was why Quine needed to get it on the side when he was married to a woman as sexy as Loli.

Before Palmer could finish that thought, he was dazzled by the high-beams from Loli's candy-apple red Trans Am as it pulled into the deserted parking lot, Bon Jovi pumping out of the speaker system. Palmer grimaced. Loli's taste was dreadful. Except for him, of course. She shut off the engine, returning the lot to shadows and silence. There was still enough illumination from the distant street lights for him to see her slide out from behind the wheel of her car.

She was dressed all in red, from the ribbon wrapped around her ash-blonde ponytail, to the skin-tight red leather stiletto-heeled knee boots that matched her miniskirt. Her fingernails and lips glistened as if she'd painted them with fresh blood.

Palmer's anxiety and aggravation transformed itself into pure lust. It was like being high on a wondrous drug that made rational thought and common sense not only irrelevant, but impossible. He wondered if this was how male praying mantises felt during the mating dance.

"You got it?" Her voice was honey and whisky poured over crystal-clear ice. She raised her corn-flower-blue eyes to his dark brown ones.

He nodded dumbly, his tongue turned into a useless wad of dry cotton. Palmer handed her a manila envelope full of pictures of Sam Quine and his mistress leaving their trysting place, information detailing the days and times they kept their rendezvous, and the name they registered under.

Loli quickly scanned his notes, her mouth set into a predatory smirk. Palmer was startled by the cruelty he saw in her eyes, then shamed by having felt revulsion. But he couldn't help feeling he'd been allowed an unintentional glimpse of the woman Sam Quine was married to.

"Loli, we need to talk."

"I'd like to stay and chat awhile, Bill. I really would. But there's something I need to attend to." She opened the carmine designer purse that hung from her shapely, white shoulder as she spoke.

"Loli, it's about us . . ."

"Now, where did I put that thing? Oh, *here* it is!"

"When will I get to see you again?"

Loli turned to face him, pulling a Smith & Wesson .38 out of the tangled mess of cosmetics and half-read romance novels in her purse. "I guess you'll see me in hell," she replied, leveling the gun at his chest.

Palmer stared in mute horror at the piece of blue steel pointed at his heart. He recognized the weapon as his own, supposedly locked in the desk at the office. He disliked guns, but his clients expected it of him. Damn Bogart.

"But, Loli . . . I *love* you!"

Her painted lips pulled back into a grin that seemed to spread until it bisected her face. "That's sweet of you, Bill. I love you, too."

And then she shot him.

William Palmer woke in a puddle of sweat. Had he screamed? He listened to the other inmates in the prison infirmary, but all he heard were the usual snores and farts. He uncoiled his rigid shoulder and leg muscles. He'd recently taken to sleeping with his arms crossed, corpse-style, across his chest. The prison psychologist had made a big deal out of that.

Palmer sat up, dabbing at the sweat rolling off his brow with the edge of the bed sheet. His hands trembled and he wanted a smoke *real* bad. Hell, he'd even settle for one of those shitty big house

cigarettes, made from Bugler tobacco and a page
from the New Testament. Regular cancer sticks
like Camels and Winstons were hard to get under
these circumstances, much less his preferred brand:
Shermans Queen-Size Cigaretellos.

That dream. That goddamned dream.

How long was it going to keep on? He'd been
having the same dream—or variations on the
theme—ever since he'd come out of the coma six
weeks ago and been informed of Loli's perfidy. The
dreams varied widely, but they were essentially all
the same: they involved him, Loli, and his gun. Each
dream ended with Loli opening fire. Sometimes the
dreams were nonsensical, the way dreams normally
are; he and Loli riding a merry-go-round in the middle of a forest when Loli pulls out the gun and shoots
him. Others were so realistic he didn't know it was
a dream until he was jerked back into consciousness
by the sound of the gun: he and Loli naked in bed,
screwing away, and she pulls the gun out from under
the pillow . . . Palmer squeezed his eyes shut, deliberately blocking the image. That one had been bad.
Worse than the one tonight.

None of the dream-shootings were the real one,
though. He guessed he should be grateful for small
favors. It was bad enough remembering what had
happened in the motel room without being condemned to relive it every night. His right hand
absently massaged the scar on his chest that marked
Loli's parting gift.

She'd called late, babbling that she needed his help
and protection. She'd decided to confront Quine at
the motel, but things had gone wrong. They got into
a fight and now she was locked in the bathroom—
although she'd somehow succeeded in dragging the
phone in after her. Quine had gone crazy, threatening to kill her. She was scared. Palmer didn't realize

what a violent temper Quine had, how brutal he could be.

She'd pushed the right buttons; Palmer was in his car and on his way to the motor court before the receiver hit the cradle.

The door was unlocked when he got there. He wasn't too worried about Loli's husband. Quine was in his late fifties and heavier than Palmer, but not in the best of shape. Palmer knew how to handle himself in a fight. However, he was unprepared for the sight of Sam Quine sprawled naked across the motel room's double bed, his brains splashed across the headboard and nightstand.

Palmer heard the bathroom door click open behind him. He turned in time to see Loli at the threshold, stark naked and holding a recently fired .38. *His* .38.

"Loli, what the fu—"

And she'd fired.

Three weeks passed before he was able to stay conscious long enough to understand what was being said to and about him. Sometimes he wished he could return to the painless gray of twilight sleep and never come out. Anything would be better than the truth.

Loli was dead.

The whole thing was like a bad Mickey Spillane novel. It was typical of Loli, though. The cops kept commenting on the half-baked nature of the scheme. Did she really think no one would question her version of what happened? Didn't she know that forensics could read the splatter pattern left by her husband's exploding head and triangulate the trajectory of the fatal bullet? Did she really think the police were *that* stupid? There was no way she could have pulled it off. It didn't make any sense unless you knew her. Or thought you did.

Loli had never been one to concern herself with

consensual reality. If she said her husband was a brute, a cheat, and a liar, then it was true. That she refused to have sex with him for two years was unrelated to his infidelity. He was the one in the wrong, the one to be punished.

If she told the police that she and her husband had gone to a certain motel to celebrate their reconciliation, and while they were there, her jilted lover broke in on them, blowing her husband's gray matter all over the wallpaper, then that's what happened. It never occurred to her that she would be suspected as well.

When the police began asking her questions, suggesting that she and Palmer had conspired to murder Quine, it proved too much for her. That Palmer had survived the bullet she'd pumped into him was another contingency she had been unprepared for. She kept insisting that she'd wrested the gun from Palmer and shot him in self-defense, but the police suspected Palmer's wounding had more to do with a falling out between illicit lovers.

Frightened and confused upon finding herself, possibly for the first time in her life, in a situation where her sex appeal could not free her from the consequences of her actions, Loli panicked.

A fifth of Everclear and a bottle of sleeping pills provided an escape route from justice, but not before she penned a venomous farewell note, implicating Palmer in Quine's death, and mailed it to the district attorney: "It was all his idea. I didn't want to go along with it."

What she *really* meant was that it was all his fault for not dying. If he'd died like she'd planned, everything would have gone off the way it was *supposed* to. Funny how he was finally becoming adept at understanding Loli, now that it was too late to do him any good.

As soon as the doctors proclaimed him fit, he would be brought before the judge for bail designation. As far as the district attorney's office was concerned, it was a clear-cut case of conspiracy to commit murder; it didn't matter who actually pulled the trigger. His public defense attorney told him there wasn't much hope of making bail.

Palmer craned his head so he could catch a glimpse of the sky through the heavily secured window over his bed. It was still dark out. He remembered his mother insisting, during the periodic hard times the family roller coasted through, how "it's always darkest before the dawn." His mother was a good woman, bless her, but incapable of making a statement that wasn't cobbled together from cliches.

His father had been a great one for cliches as well. His one real effort at imparting something resembling paternal wisdom to his only son had come in the form of a nose-to-nose yelling match when he'd told the fifteen-year-old Palmer: "*Boy, if you don't get your head outta your ass, you're gonna find yourself up shit creek without a paddle!*"

Thanks, Dad.

"Palmer? Somebody here to see you."

Word had come through that morning that the doctors had okayed his transferal to the prison. He was to be placed with the rest of the prisoners the next day. This had not come as welcome news.

"Is it my lawyer?"

"Beats me. The guy says he wants to talk to you." The orderly jerked his head toward the single door leading to the recovery ward. A man Palmer had never seen before was standing at the check-in desk, an expensive attache case in one hand. "You wanna see him?" There was no privacy in the prison infirmary, but the patient-inmates had the freedom to turn away visitors if they chose.

Palmer looked at the stranger for a moment. "Yeah, send him over."

Moments later the stranger with the attache case stood at the foot of Palmer's bed. He was a middle-aged man dressed in an expensive, if drab, silk suit. His skin was pallid, even by today's melanoma conscious standards. He looked like a man who spent a lot of time indoors.

"Mr. Palmer? Mr. William Palmer?"

"Yeah, that's me. Who're you?"

The stranger's mouth smiled, but his eyes did not join in. "My name is Renfield. And I believe I can be of some service to you, Mr. Palmer."

"That so? You a lawyer?" Palmer motioned him to a metal folding chair next to the bed. Renfield lowered himself into the seat; his movements were so rigid and stylized that he reminded Palmer of an animated mannequin.

Renfield's mouth curled into another simulated smile. "Not exactly. I am a representative for a third party who has an . . . interest . . . in your case."

"Look, Mac, I don't know what it is you're getting at. Say what you have to say and get it over with, okay?"

"You are innocent, are you not? Of the crime they accuse you of, I mean. You did not murder, nor did you conspire to murder, Samuel Quine. Is that right?"

"You got it." Palmer wished he had a smoke. This pasty-faced suit was making him nervous.

"Would you care for a cigarette, Mr. Palmer?" Renfield leaned forward, pulling a pack from his breast pocket. Palmer was surprised to see a flat, red-and-white case of Shermans Queen-Size Cigaretellos in the man's pale hand.

"Yeah, don't mind if I do." He eagerly accepted one of the thin, unfiltered brown cigarettes.

"Go ahead, take the pack."

"Uh, thanks." He stared at the cigarettes, then back at Renfield's blandly smiling face. "How did you know I smoke this brand?"

"There is a *lot* we know about you, Mr. Palmer."

Palmer looked up from his cupped palms as he lit the Sherman. "We?"

"Meaning my employer."

"Exactly who *is* this guy interested in my well-being?"

"That is not important—for now. What *is* important is that he can—and will, providing you agree to work for him—clear you of all charges with the district attorney. He can also get your private investigator's license reinstated."

"What is this? Some kind of joke? If so, it's not a real knee-slapper."

"Joke?" Renfield's brow creased. "I never joke, Mr. Palmer."

"I should have guessed. Okay, let me rephrase what I just said. What's going on? Who sent you and what exactly am I to him that he's willing to pull those kind of strings? You're not Mafia, are you?"

Again the smile. Palmer felt a sudden urge to grab the drab little bastard and shake him by his lapels. "I assure you, Mr. Palmer, my employer has no need of such petty power brokers. All I need to know is whether you are amiable to certain terms of employment in exchange for your freedom."

Palmer shrugged. "If your boss can spring me like you said, I'll walk on my hands all the way to Timbuktu, if that's what he wants."

"I doubt that will be necessary. Then you accept my employer's offer?"

"That's what I said, didn't I?"

Renfield nodded and closed his eyes. "It is done." It sounded like a verbal signal. Palmer wondered if the creep was wired for sound. Renfield stood up, straightening the creases in his suit. "You will be hearing from us shortly. Good day, Mr. Palmer."

"Yeah. Sure. Hang loose, dude."

Palmer lay back in the bed, arms folded behind his head, puffing thoughtfully on his cigarette. Who the hell was this Renfield geek? He didn't like the whey-faced bastard, but if he was telling the truth . . . Well, it wouldn't be the first time he had shaken hands with the Devil.

He glanced at the pack of Shermans resting atop the bedside table.

There is a lot we know about you, Mr. Palmer.

Twenty-four hours after his initial meeting with Renfield, Palmer was standing on the street outside the Criminal Justice Building, blinking at the late afternoon sun. It had been over two months since he'd last been outside. He was still a bit weak from the gunshot wound that had creased his heart, but, all in all, he felt pretty damn good. Freedom was an amazing tonic.

I'll be damned. The little wonk said he could do it, and whatever else he might be, he sure as hell isn't a liar.

Palmer hefted the plain canvas tote bag the prison quartermaster had given him before jettisoning him back onto the streets. Inside were what few possessions he could call his own, salvaged from his apartment by his erstwhile public defender before the landlord changed the lock. Hardly the most auspicious of new beginnings.

Palmer glanced at his wristwatch. He'd received a note from Renfield just prior to his release telling him to wait on the corner, but for what? He'd been waiting fifteen minutes already. . . .

A stretch limo, black and shiny as a scarab, pulled up to the curb, its windows polarized against prying eyes. The rear passenger door opened and Renfield leaned halfway out, motioning for him to climb in.

"You seem surprised, Mr. Palmer."

"Dazed is more like it. How did you do it?"

"Do what?"

"Pull that trick with the D.A.'s office? They said something about Loli's diary turning up."

Renfield shrugged. "My employer is not without . . . connections, Mr. Palmer. Besides, what does it matter, so long as you are cleared?"

Palmer wanted to press the issue, but there was something in the way Renfield smiled that made him keep silent. Renfield may have saved him from a jail-house welcome-wagon party, but that didn't mean he had to like the guy. In fact, Palmer felt uncomfortable sitting next to him. He couldn't help himself; there was something inherently loathsome about Renfield that he couldn't quite peg.

"Where are we going?"

"We are going to meet my employer. He is as interested in seeing you face-to-face as you are in meeting him. You should relax, Mr. Palmer; it will be some time before we reach our destination." Renfield leaned forward and opened the liquor cabinet built into the back of the front seat. "Help yourself."

A hour later the limo coasted to a halt. The time had passed in silence, except for the occasional rattle of ice as Palmer replenished his bourbon-and-coke. Renfield drank nothing but bottled mineral water, and that sparingly.

The driver moved from behind the wheel of the car and opened the door for Renfield. Palmer slid after him, feeling a bit more tipsy than he'd realized.

It was dark outside the car—early evening out in the country. At least to Palmer it looked like the country. They were at the end of a long, crushed gravel drive, standing outside a spacious ranch-style house with handsomely manicured lawns and artfully concealed exterior lights. No doubt there was a nice big redwood deck and a hot tub out back. He followed Renfield up the front walk.

Before they reached the porch, one of the shadows detached itself from the shrubbery and blocked their path.

The shadow was a damn big son of a bitch armed with an automatic weapon that looked like a child's toy in his massive hands. He towered over Renfield and Palmer, his shoulders wide enough to block out the sky. Palmer guessed him to be close to seven feet tall, if not an inch or two over. And the bastard was *ugly*, too. The giant's long, horse-like face was made even more unattractive by a complete lack of facial hair, including eyebrows and eyelashes. The guard said something to Renfield in a register so low it was close to subvocal.

"It's all right, Keif. He's been cleared."

The guard didn't take his eyes off Palmer as he made a strangely delicate motion with his free hand that was either sign language or his pantomiming breaking a twig.

Renfield shook his head. "No, that won't be necessary. Like I said, it's been arranged. Now get on with your job. We must not keep the doctor waiting."

The guard nodded and returned to his post. Palmer could feel the giant's eyes on his back as they entered the house.

The living room was right out of a prime-time soap, with a high ceiling, tastefully arranged Danish furniture, and a handful of modern paintings scattered along the walls. It was obvious no one spent any time living there.

"This way." Renfield led Palmer down a narrow

hallway to the back of the house. He stopped outside a door at the end of the corridor and rapped lightly.

"Bring him in, Renfield."

The room behind the door was lined with books and smelled of old leather and moldering paper. Seated behind an antique roll-top desk was a handsome man in his middle years, his dark hair touched with silver at the temples. Despite the dim wattage cast by the Tiffany lamp set atop the desk, the older man wore a pair of green-tinted aviator shades.

"Ah, Mr. Palmer! Pleased to make your acquaintance at last!" He rose from the antique swivel chair and extended his hand to the detective. He was dressed in crisp, white cotton pants, a white cotton shirt, loosened at the collar with the sleeves rolled up past the elbows, and a pair of old-fashioned red leather suspenders. Palmer was reminded of Spencer Tracy in *Inherit The Wind*.

Palmer winced at the strength behind the older man's cool, dry grip. "I'm told I have you to thank for arranging my freedom, Mister . . .?"

"It's Doctor. Dr. Pangloss. Pleased to be of some service." He grinned, revealing pristine bridgework that made Palmer's nicotine-stained teeth look like a demilitarized zone.

"Uh, yeah . . ."

Pangloss motioned for Palmer to seat himself, then nodded to Renfield, who was still standing at the door. "That'll be all for now, Renfield. Have the cook prepare a tray for Mr. Palmer."

Renfield nodded and retreated, leaving them alone.

"You must forgive me for not dining with you." Pangloss smiled. "I've already eaten. Can I offer you a drink?" He pulled a bottle of bourbon, its seal intact, from one of the desk's pigeonholes. Palmer recognized it as one of his favorite brands, when he could afford it. "Oh, and help yourself to the cigarettes," Pangloss added, nodding to a Chinese lacquer box resting on the table next to Palmer's chair.

The cigarette case was, like practically everything else in the room, an antique. A Chinese dragon, looped around itself, adorned the lid. Inside were Shermans Queen-Size Cigaretellos.

Palmer lit his Shermans with a Faberge cigarette lighter, admiring how the light from the Tiffany lamp played across the jewelled platinum scrollwork. "Look, Dr. Pangloss, it's not that I'm ungrateful for what you've done . . . but what the hell is going on? I mean, who are you, and what am I to *you* that you would go so far as to spring me out of jail?"

Pangloss flashed his teeth as he handed the detective the highball glass, but it was impossible to tell if the smile extended to his eyes. "You've got a legitimate right to know, and I respect your forthrightness, Mr. Palmer. I really do. I appreciate men willing to speak their minds. The fact of the matter is, I am in dire need of your services."

"That's flattering, Doc, but there are hundreds of perfectly good private investigators in this country. Some I'll even admit are better than me. I'm hardly Sam Spade, especially in light of the shit both you and I know I've recently been through."

"You underestimate yourself, Mr. Palmer. Or may I call you Bill?"

"Call me Palmer. Everyone else does."

"Very well—*Palmer*. You have tracked down missing people before, have you not?"

"Yeah, sure. I've traced a couple of skips and runaways. Most P.I.s have, sometime or another—it's part of the job. Why?"

"Because there is someone I want you to find for me. A girl. It's very important that she be located. I'm willing to pay you what it's worth."

Palmer sipped at the bourbon. It had been a long

time since he'd been able to afford liquor this good. "Keep on talking, Doc. I'm listening."

"It won't be easy, I'm afraid. She doesn't want to be found and has been highly successful at avoiding my . . . field operatives. She recognizes them on sight and does her best to . . . avoid them." Pangloss's handsome face grew dark. "She's a wild woman, Palmer—crafty, shrewd, fiercely independent, and more than a little crazy. She is also very dangerous. I'll tell you that right now, just to make sure you don't develop cold feet later on."

"This 'wild woman' you want me to find—exactly what is your relationship to her?"

"She's my granddaughter."

Palmer doubted that was the truth. Pangloss certainly didn't look old enough to have a grandchild capable of helling around; but you never can tell, what with plastic surgery nowadays. And while Pangloss hadn't exactly told the truth, Palmer had the feeling he wasn't lying, either.

"I'll pay you a thousand dollars a day, plus expenses. I trust that is satisfactory?"

Palmer nearly choked on the bourbon. "Uh, it'll do."

"There will also be a twenty-thousand-dollar bonus should you find her and successfully deliver this letter." Pangloss pulled a legal-sized envelope from one of the desk's pigeonholes. It was expensive cream stationery, stiff and heavy, and bore an old-fashioned wax seal on the back: a dragon looped around itself.

"Can I ask a question? A purely hypothetical one, that is."

"Go ahead."

"What would you do if I decided not to take the case?"

"That assumes you have a choice in the matter, Mr. Palmer. I prefer keeping the fiction of free will intact, don't you? I find my employees work much better when they believe they have some say in what they can and cannot do."

Palmer stared at Pangloss's pleasantly smiling face, the expensive liquor suddenly bitter in his mouth.

Pangloss slid a companionable arm over Palmer's shoulder, walking him to the door. For the first time Palmer noticed how long the other man's fingernails were. "I have confidence in you, Palmer. I'm sure you'll be a great asset to our team. Now that you're here, why don't you make yourself at home? I've had the guest room specially prepared for your arrival, and I'll see to it that my cook gets your dinner to you. If there's anything you need, don't hesitate to ask."

"There's just one thing . . ."

"Yes?" Although Pangloss was still smiling, Palmer was certain the eyes behind the tinted aviator shades were watching him intently.

"What's the name of this girl you're looking for?"

"How thoughtless of me! Her name is Sonja Blue."

Pangloss opened the door. Palmer wasn't surprised to see Renfield standing on the other side of the threshold.

"Renfield will see you to your room. Oh, and Mr. Palmer?" Palmer glanced over his shoulder; Pangloss was grinning at him, showing way too many teeth. "Pleasant dreams."

2

"Will there be anything else, sir?"

Palmer stared blankly at the bellhop for a double heartbeat before answering. "Uh, no. No, I don't think so." He stuffed a couple of dollars into a outstretched white glove. The bellboy grimaced as if Palmer had just hacked a gob into his hand.

Well, he wasn't going to let some college student's wounded sense of self-worth sour the pleasure of having his very own suite at the Hilton.

Palmer shrugged out of his jacket and plopped down on the couch in the sitting room. He rang up room service and ordered a New York Strip and a couple bottles of imported beer, all courtesy of the good Dr. Pangloss. He wasn't sure what his employer was a doctor *of*, but it sure paid well.

While he waited on his food to arrive, Palmer thumbed through notes scribbled during his time as Pangloss's "houseguest."

1. *Is Sonja Blue really Pangloss's grand-d?*
2. *Is S.B. into illicit drugs? Prostitution?*
3. *Is Pangloss?*
4. *What the hell am I doing here?*

So far he'd failed to turn up answers to any of those questions, although placing a jet flight between himself and his "employer" made #4 seem less pressing than when he first wrote it.

He glanced at the stiff, cream-colored envelope jutting out of the breast pocket of his jacket. No doubt the letter would give him some answers, but that wasn't how the game was played. At least not when he was on the field. Still, for a man supposedly desperate to locate his grandchild, Pangloss had been stingy with personal information concerning the girl. After some questioning, Palmer had finally learned that she might be traced through a boyfriend, if that was the proper word to use, named Geoffrey Chastain, better known as "Chaz."

From what little Palmer had pieced together, this Chastain was an expatriate Brit with a taste for hard drugs and unsavory sex partners. Your basic low-life hustler. Palmer scrounged a pencil from his hip pocket and added to his notes.

5. Is Chastain S.B.'s lover? Connection/Pimp?
6. Pangloss sure S.B. no longer in area, but thinks it good a place as any to start.

Palmer looked at the photograph of the elusive Chaz that Pangloss presented him with before he left the estate. Odd that Pangloss should have a picture of the bad-ass boyfriend but not a single snapshot of his own granddaughter. It looked like a passport photo; either that or a mug shot. The man glowering at him from the other side of the camera was in his late twenties, his hair combed in a rebellious rooster tail. There was still a hint of masculine beauty in the shape of his cheekbones and the tilt of his eyes, but what physical attractiveness Geoffrey Chastain had once possessed had been eaten away by his addictions; the drug hunger was obvious even in a photo.

Still, it was easy to see how a young, impressionable girl might become fascinated with such a sleazeball.

Room service brought him his steak and beer. He always prepared himself for a night on the prowl by eating his fill of red meat. It put him in the proper mood for the hunt.

"You know this guy?"

It was roughly the four hundredth and fifty-seventh time Palmer had asked that question that night. His feet were tired and his bladder ached from too many beers.

The man with the anarchy symbol chalked across the back of his black raincoat glanced first at Palmer then the snapshot. He took a swig from his beer and shook his head.

"Sorry. Can't help ya."

A slightly built youth seated on the opposite side of the man in the anarchist coat craned his head over his companion's shoulder, looking mildly curious.

"How about you? You know this guy?"

"He don't know him, either," snapped the man in the raincoat. "He don't know nobody I don't know, do ya?" This he addressed to the boy seated next to him. It didn't sound like a question.

The boy cringed, smiling nervously at this friend. "Course not, Nick. I don't know nobody."

"Fuckin' A."

Palmer cursed under his breath and headed for the men's room. This wasn't the first time he'd run into such aggressive ignorance. He'd come close to getting somewhere at least twice, only to have the parties in question suddenly clam up on him.

As he relieved himself at the urinal, he heard the restroom door open and close behind him.

"Hey, mister?"

Palmer glimpsed enough out of the corner of his eye to recognize Nick's boyfriend.

"What is it, kid?"

"I know that guy. The one in the picture."

"Do you now?"

"Yeah. Chaz. He's from England."

"How come your friend didn't want you talking to me?"

"Nick? Oh, he's just jealous, that's all." The boy giggled. "He and Chaz crossed swords a couple of times, so to speak. Chaz muscled in on a couple of his boyfriends."

Palmer shook off and made himself presentable before turning to face the boy. The kid couldn't be more than seventeen, his strawberry blonde hair cut short in front with a long, braided rat-tail at the base of his neck. He wore a pair of designer jeans and a Psychic TV t-shirt.

"What's your name, kid?"

"Terry."

"Look, Terry, can you tell me where I could possibly find this Chaz? I'll make it worth your while . . ." He produced a twenty from his pocket, holding it tight between his knuckles. It was obvious the boy was interested, but his eyes flickered away whenever Palmer tried to look him in the face. "Is this Chaz a friend of yours? Are you afraid you'll get him in trouble?"

Terry snorted. "Chaz? A friend? I always thought he was a creep! Always looking at me like he knew what was going on inside my head. Besides, no one's seen him in almost a year. Not since what happened to the Blue Monkeys."

"The Blue Monkeys?"

"Yeah. This gang Chaz used to hang with. Bunch of real hard-asses. Used to dye their hair blue. He was friends with 'em . . . but they only hung with him on account of the blow he always had on him."

"Where can I find these Blue Monkeys?" Palmer handed Terry the folded bill.

"You can't."

"What do you mean?"

"They're dead."

"*Dead?*"

"Well, not *all* of them, but enough got killed off to deep-six the gang."

"What happened?"

"No one's real sure; it got hushed up pretty quick. But there was this gang war, or something, in the back of some bar. Those that weren't killed got crippled up pretty bad. I . . . wait a minute. Jimmy!"

"Jimmy?"

"That was the kid Chaz was seeing. He was the only one that didn't get trashed."

"Where can I find this Jimmy?"

Terry grinned and stuck out his hand, looking like a kid asking his father for this week's allowance. "That's worth more'n a twenty, dude."

Palmer grumbled and produced another bill. Terry's hands moved so fast he couldn't tell which pocket the money disappeared into.

"His name's Jimmy Eichorn. He lives with his mom somewhere over on Thirty-Ninth."

"You're learning quick, kid."

Terry shrugged his narrow shoulders as he turned to leave. "Nick's stingy when it comes to buying nice things."

"Mrs. Eichorn?"

The woman peering at him from the other side of the burglar chain scowled, as if deciding whether she should answer.

"Mrs. Eichorn, my name is Palmer . . ."

"Whatcha want? You from th' Welfare Department? If so, it's too late for a business visit!"

It had taken him a couple of hours to find the right house. Terry's instructions had been off by a few blocks. It was long past Palmer's supper time and his scar was giving him trouble. He'd been forced to climb five narrow, badly lit flights of stairs, the smell of human piss and old garbage pungent enough to make his gorge hitch. He felt his temper start to flare.

"Mrs. Eichorn, do I *look* like a fuckin' caseworker?"

Where Mrs. Eichorn was concerned, there was no such thing as a rhetorical question. He could feel her taking in his shaved temples and narrow goatee, lingering on his wavy, gray-shot hair, combed straight up; a holdover from the days, more than a decade gone, when he used to slam-dance down at Club Lies.

"I'd like to talk to Jimmy, Mrs. Eichorn. Is he in?"

Mrs. Eichorn blinked. "Yeah, he's here. He's always here. Whatcha want with my Jimmy?"

Palmer slid a crisp twenty through the crack in the door. "It's important, ma'am."

Jimmy's mother hesitated then closed the door, taking the twenty with her. A second later the door reopened, allowing Palmer a better view of both her and the apartment.

Mrs. Eichorn was a unsmiling woman with pale, washed-out hair that had once been blonde. Her skin was pasty and her eyes so light a shade of blue they seemed to lack any color at all. Deep lines creased the corners of her mouth. The only color evident on her face was a purplish-red lipstick smeared on her mouth. She wore a much-washed yellow waitress's uniform with the name "Alice" stitched across the bosom in red thread. The few items of furniture in the living room looked as worn and over-used as their owner.

"Whatcha want with my Jimmy?" She pulled a filtered cigarette from her apron pocket and clamped it between purple-red lips. Palmer wrinkled his nose in distaste. Funny how other people's smoking got on his nerves. "You better hurry it up, whatever it is. I gotta leave for work in a few minutes."

"Mrs. Eichorn, was your son a member of a youth gang called the Blue Monkeys?"

The look she gave him was hard enough to cut glass. "You a cop?"

"No, ma'am, I'm a private investigator. I'm not familiar with what happened. I heard there was a gang war—"

Mrs. Eichorn snorted smoke from her nostrils. "You believe that shit?" She gave him another look, this one not quite as hard as the last. "You're not from around here, are ya? Shoulda figured when you asked if Jimmy was in. Not that it matters. People forget things, get the stories wrong, make up stuff because they like the way it sounds. You know how it is."

"There wasn't a fight?"

"Massacre is a better word for it. I'm just thankful my boy was spared, that's all. The rest of those sleazebags you could've flushed and no one would've cared. But Jimmy . . . he was new to the gang. They hadn't had time to mess him up yet, least not much." The creases at the corners of her mouth deepened.

"Can I talk to him?"

"You can try."

She lead him down a narrow, unlit hall and opened a door with a Metallica poster tacked to it. It was dark in the small room, although enough illumination spilled through the window facing the street to allow Palmer a quick glimpse of a narrow child's bed in one corner and heavy metal posters plastered on the cracked and peeling walls.

Jimmy Eichorn sat in a wheelchair, staring at the world beyond the windowsill.

"I left the room the way he had it." Mrs. Eichorn's voice dropped into a lower, softer register, as if she was in church. "I think it makes him happy." She went and stood beside her son's wheelchair, one hand absently stroking the back of his head. "The blue's almost grown out. I hated it when he dyed it. He always had such pretty hair, don't you think so?"

Jimmy's hair was the same mousy non-color as his mother's. Palmer grunted something non-committal. The boy slumped in the wheelchair looked to be sixteen years old, although his slack features made him seem even younger. He was dressed in a pair of pajamas, a blanket draped over his lap. Jimmy ignored the adults standing to either side of him, his attention fixed on the street below.

"Jimmy? Jimmy, look at me, sweetheart. This nice man wants to ask you a question."

Jimmy took his eyes away from the lamppost across the street and tilted his head in order to stare at his mother. After a couple of seconds his lips pulled into a smile, drool wetting his chin. He reached up and clasped his mother's hand. Mrs. Eichorn smiled indulgently and brushed the hair out of his eyes.

"Jimmy?"

The boy's eyes flickered toward the window then shifted to Palmer. They were the eyes of a preschooler; wide and clear and uncertain of strangers.

"Jimmy, I need your help."

"Go ahead, darling. It's all right." Mrs. Eichorn squeezed Jimmy's hand.

Palmer pulled the photo of Chaz out of his jacket

and held it up so the boy could see it. "Do you know where I can find this man, Jimmy? Do you know where Chaz is?"

A muscle in Jimmy's face jerked. Palmer couldn't tell if the boy had shook his head "no" or suffered a muscle spasm. Before he could press the issue, Jimmy gave a weird, high-pitched squeal and began to twitch.

Palmer stepped back in disgust as the boy voided his bowels. Jimmy's eyes rolled in their sockets and then glazed, staring at some unknown fixed point.

"Get out! Go on, get out!" snapped Mrs. Eichorn.

"But—"

"Just get out! I can't deal with him with you in the room!"

Jimmy clawed at his own throat, as if trying to pull an invisible attacker from his windpipe. Palmer glimpsed what looked like puncture marks in the shadow of the boy's chin. He stood awkwardly in the Eichorn's drab front room, listening to the mother soothe her imbecile son. Palmer looked at his hands and noticed they were shaking.

"He was such a happy baby."

Mrs. Eichorn stood slumped against the doorway, lighting another cigarette. Her hands were trembling as well.

"He used to laugh like nobody's business," she continued. "His daddy thought the world of him, because of that laugh. It made him stay around a couple of years longer than he would have if Jimmy had cried like most babies, I guess. When he ran off in '79, Jimmy was just five. Things changed. I . . . I was just fifteen when Jimmy was born. What did I know about bringing a kid up by myself?" She looked at the cigarette in her hand then glanced at Palmer, as if daring him to say otherwise. He suddenly realized this hopeless, washed-out woman was seven years his junior.

"It's not my fault he got like this . . . someone *did* that to him." Her voice tightened and she looked away. "He wouldn't be like that if he hadn't been with the gang that night. I asked him not to go—to break it off. But he wouldn't do it. He said being a Blue Monkey was important to him. More important than anything. You know what they made him do to be a part of their goddamn special gang? They made him suck their . . . their *things*! I couldn't believe he still wanted to have anything to do with them after what they made him do, but he was *proud* of being a Blue Monkey." She shook her head in disgust. "I told him that night I didn't want him hanging around that bar with those scum. I told him that if he went there he better not come home. He cursed me out! His own mama! And he went anyway." Her eyes were bright with unshed tears, but her cheeks remained dry. "I guess we're both paying for our sins, huh?"

Palmer couldn't bring himself to look at her. "Mrs. Eichorn . . . I'm sorry, I didn't realize my questioning your son would . . . *upset* him."

She shrugged. "No way you *could* know. It's funny what sets him off sometimes. But you didn't have to ask him, though. *I* could have told you where to find Chaz."

"You know Chaz?"

"Yeah, I *knew* him. He's dead. Died the same night the Blue Monkeys got into trouble. Jimmy brought him here once or twice. I figured him for a dealer. I told Jimmy I didn't like the kind of trash he hung out with, so he stopped bringing Chaz over. Rumor had it Chaz got himself bumped off."

"You mean it was a hit?"

"That's what it looked like, at least. I wouldn't

have been surprised. Chaz was the kind of jerk who'd cross the wrong people just for kicks."

"Mrs. Eichorn, this is *real* important: did Jimmy ever mention if Chaz had a girlfriend?"

"Not that I recall. But, then, Jimmy and I didn't exactly talk a lot by then."

"I don't want to delay you any more than I already have, Mrs. Eichorn. I appreciate everything you've been able to tell me." Palmer slipped a couple of fifty-dollar bills into her apron pocket as he left.

"You know something?" she said, opening the door for him. "It's funny, in a way, but I can't bring myself to really hate whoever it was that did those things. In a way, I got what I wanted. I got my little boy back. Don't you think that's funny?"

Palmer simply nodded and hurried away. On the third landing he paused long enough to sneak a pain pill. By the time he reached the street, his ribs no longer felt like they were being cracked open with a lobster mallet. He did not look up to see if Jimmy was watching over him.

That night he dreamed he was in a wheelchair, being pushed down a long, poorly lit corridor. The wheelchair needed to be oiled and squeaked whenever it moved. Everything seemed so vivid, so *real*, Palmer thought he was back in the prison infirmary. Then he remembered he'd been released. Confused, he twisted around to find out who was propelling the wheelchair.

Loli smiled back at him, looking both sexy and menacing in her starched white nurse's uniform. Palmer was acutely aware of the erection tenting his hospital johnny.

"Did you miss me, darling?" asked Loli, her lips painted the color of fresh blood.

"Yes. Very much." He hated to admit it, but he

did miss her, no matter what she'd done to him. It made him feel stupid, powerless, and degraded, but his dick was hard enough to cut diamonds.

"I missed you, too. But I won't *this* time!"

Loli halted the wheelchair at the top of a flight of stairs that seemed to stretch, Escher-like, into another dimension. Palmer's head began to swim. He tried to stand up, but his arms and legs were strapped to the wheelchair.

He twisted his head around, hoping to catch another glimpse of Loli. Instead, he found himself staring down the bore of his gun. He knew he was dreaming and knew what would happen next. He also remembered an old wives' tale—or was it a disputed scientific fact?—that if you dreamed you were killed, you'd die in your sleep. Surely even an imaginary Loli couldn't miss at *this* range.

Palmer threw himself headfirst down the warped, endlessly replicating stairwell. Miraculously, the wheelchair remained upright as he caromed through gothic arches and past half-glimpsed crumbling facades. He could hear Loli shrieking obscenities from the top of the stair, along with the sound of receding gunfire. He wasn't sure where he was going, but at least it was away from Loli, with her bleeding mouth and punishing .38.

For a brief, giddy moment, Palmer knew what it was like to be free. Then he saw the massive brick wall blocking his way. And in front of the wall, standing in a policeman's firing stance, both hands wrapped around the handle of the gun, was Loli.

"Fooled you!"

When he woke up, he realized he'd wet the bed.

Palmer looked at the rows upon rows of cold marble and granite, then back at the map the caretaker had given him at the gate. According to what information there was, Geoffrey Chastain, better known as "Chaz," was buried in Sector E-7. Most of headstones in the area were newer models, some even looked machine made. The names and dates were still sharply defined and easy to read; it would be several years before the wind and the rain rendered the inscriptions as vague as those found on the older stones.

It was early February and frost crunched under his heels as he made his way amongst the stones. Palmer was cold despite his anorak, and his mood had not been helped by the nightmare that had jerked him awake, sweating and shivering, at four that morning. He'd been unable—unwilling?—to go back to sleep, his scar throbbing like a bad cigarette burn.

He rechecked what little information he'd been able to get from the cemetery caretaker's files as he trudged along. Chastain's plot had been paid for anonymously—in cash. The only point of interest was that the deceased had originally been interred in Potter's Field, then dug up and replanted in a proper grave, complete with headstone, a month later. Palmer was certain Sonja Blue was behind Chaz's change of address. But why? Was it out of guilt? Sense of duty? Love?

He literally stumbled across Chaz's grave by accident. His feet had become entangled in the faded remains of a funeral wreath, and to keep from falling, he had leaned against a nearby tombstone. When he'd finally freed himself, he saw he was resting his butt on Geoffrey Chastain's monument.

Palmer stepped back and stared at the nondescript granite marker: *Geoffrey Alan Chastain 1961–1989*. There was no other information, sentiment, or religious symbol to be found on its chill face, except for a stonemason's mark at the bottom.

Palmer cursed himself, the self-deprecations rising from his lips in puffs of mist. What had he expected to find out here in the first place? The missing heiress's forwarding address chiseled into her dead lover's tombstone?

Then he saw the flowers. At first he thought they were part of the same wreath he'd originally tripped over, then he realized they were wrapped differently. He bent and lifted the bouquet from their resting place atop Chaz's grave. What he thought were long-dead flowers were relatively fresh roses the color of midnight. Palmer handled the bouquet gingerly, since the bundled stems were full of thorns.

Black roses. With the florist's name and telephone number stenciled onto the ribbon binding them together. Palmer smiled as he pulled the ribbon free, wincing as a thorn bit into the meat of his thumb.

He stared at the bead of blood—as shiny and red as a freshly polished ruby—for a long second before bringing it to his mouth. As he sucked, he glanced up and saw a gaunt young man dressed in a unseasonably light jacket watching him from a few yards away, a lit cigarette dangling from his lips. Palmer caught the odor of burning clove on the crisp morning breeze. When Palmer looked again, the man was gone, although the scent of his French cigarette still hung in the air.

Palmer was sure he'd seen the stranger's face before. Was it possible he was being followed? Pocketing the florist's ribbon, he turned and hurried back the way he'd come. He wondered where the man could have gone so quickly. He also wondered how the stranger could stand hanging around a graveyard on an overcast February morning in nothing warmer than a silk jacket. He stopped and turned to look back in the direction of Chaz's grave. He reached into his anorak and pulled out the snapshot that Pangloss had given him.

Impossible. He could feel the sweat trickling down his back. His scar tightened. It was the lack of sleep doing it to him. And the dreams. Even though it was a perfectly rational explanation, it didn't make him feel any better. He had to do something about the dreams before they drove him completely out of his mind. But not now. It would have to wait until after the case was out of the way.

"Yeah, that's ours, awright," said the florist, studying the length of faded yellow ribbon Palmer handed him.

"I was wondering if you might be able to help me find out who placed the order."

"Look, fella, we sell a *lot* of flowers . . ."

"Black roses?"

The florist pulled his bifocals down a fraction of an inch and squinted at Palmer. "Black roses, you say?"

Palmer nodded. He was on the trail, he knew it. He could feel the familiar, almost electrical, thrill of connections being made, invisible machinery dropping into gear. "A dozen of them. Delivered to the Rolling Lawns Cemetery."

The florist moved to a filing cabinet. "Deceased's name?"

"Chastain."

The florist grunted and pulled a manila folder from one of the drawers. "Yeah, I remember filling that order. Customers usually don't order roses for grave decorations. Mother's Day, St. Valentine's Day, anniversaries, birthdays, sure. And black roses, at that—especially this time of year."

"I take it they're expensive."

"You could say that." He tapped the order form.

"Says here it was a phone order. Long distance. Paid for it with a credit card."

"Could I see?"

"I don't know . . . My partner wouldn't like me letting strangers look at our files."

"Uh, I understand. Say, how much for one of those thingies over there?" He pointed at a large floral display shaped like a horse shoe, GOOD LUCK spelled along its rim in white carnations.

"That runs around seventy-five, a hundred bucks, depending on where you want it delivered."

"I'll take one." He peeled five twenties from the roll in his pocket.

"The order was placed a week ago and was paid for by Indigo Imports of New Orleans, sir."

Palmer let himself grin. He could feel it coming together. For the first time in his professional life he knew he was on a *real* case, like the ones Sam Spade and the Continental Op solved; the kind that cloaked his profession in glamorous clouds of cigarette smoke, whiskey fumes, and gun powder. The years spent staking out hot-sheets joints with a Polaroid in his lap seemed to melt away, reviving the romanticism that had led him to make a career out of detective work that he'd thought died long ago.

As he headed for the shop door, the florist called after him. "Sir? Sir! Where and when would you like the display delivered?"

"Send it to the same place the roses were delivered to. There's no hurry."

CARNIVAL

During a carnival men put masks over their masks
—Xaiver Forneret

3

When Palmer informed Pangloss of his destination, the good doctor assured him Renfield would see to airline tickets and accommodations. Palmer knew that flights into New Orleans during Carnival were booked solid weeks in advance, not to mention the hotels, and mentioned it to his employer. Pangloss laughed and said there was nothing to worry about; he kept an apartment in the French Quarter, away from the serious tourist cruising areas, but still close to the action. He'd call the housekeeper and have the place aired out in anticipation of Palmer's arrival.

He arrived late Sunday evening. The city was swarming with drunken, raucous merrymakers. Still, he had not expected Renfield to answer the door.

"You're here," was all the pale man said in way of greeting, stepping back into the hallway to allow Palmer entrance.

"Doc didn't say anything about sending you to keep tabs on me."

If Renfield noticed the barb, he ignored it. He pointed to the staircase, curled inside the house like a chambered nautilus. "Your room is on the second floor. Third door to the right."

"I thought Doc said he only kept an apartment here."

Renfield shrugged. "In a way. He owns the entire building."

Palmer frowned at the stack of junk mail piled haphazardly on the antique sideboard inside the foyer. Most of it seemed to be addressed to "Occupant" or "Current Resident." Renfield cleared his throat and lead Palmer upstairs. As they made their way to the landing, Palmer could tell by the echoes that the downstairs was empty.

Palmer's quarters were quite spacious, consisting of a bed-sitter, a sizable bathroom complete with a cast iron tub with lion's feet, and a kitchenette furnished with a stocked refrigerator and a microwave oven. There was also a wide-screen color TV, a video deck, a stereo system, and a wet bar. The apartment also came with two of the wrought iron balconies the city was famous for.

The bedroom balcony offered a view of the patio and what, a century and a half ago, had been the slaves' quarters. It was too dark for Palmer to see much, since the patio below was unlit, but a faint reek of vegetable decay rose from the garden beneath his window.

The balcony fronting the sitting room was better, as it overlooked the street, empty now except for the occasional passing mule buggy and cruising taxi. As he stood savoring his Shermans in the pleasant evening breeze, Palmer could hear Bourbon Street—its roar blurred and muted, but still distinct in the otherwise quiet neighborhood. Every now and again a drunken celebrant would shriek with laughter, the echoes losing themselves amongst the ancient buildings.

Palmer experienced a slight twinge of unreality, as if he was dreaming and aware of dreaming at the same time. When he had left for New Orleans that morning, there was still frost on the ground, and in certain alleys where the shadows rarely part, there were still hard crusts of snow and ice to be found. Now he was standing in his shirt sleeves, taking in the fragrant subtropical night air while listening to the sounds of Carnival.

He contemplated going out and joining the party, but jet lag claimed him instead. He fell asleep splayed across the massive four-poster, wisps of mosquito netting fluttering in the breeze from the open French windows.

He dreamed that he woke up. In his dream, he lay in bed for a few seconds, trying to place where he was and what he was doing there. When he remembered, he sat up, rubbing his eyes. It was still dark outside; a pale sliver of moonlight fell through the open windows. There was a table and chair near the foot of the bed. Palmer's dream-self was aware that someone—or thing—was seated in the chair, watching him. At first he thought it was Loli—he could see enough to tell his visitor was female—and he instinctively put his hand to the scar over his heart. The puckered skin remained cool to the touch.

Whoever this dream-intruder was, at least it wasn't *her*.

Palmer wanted to stand up and walk toward the mysterious woman, but he couldn't move.

Who are you?

The dream-woman did not answer but instead got to her feet. She stood in deep shadow, fingering the length of netting draped across the footboard. A spear of moonlight struck her face, but all Palmer could see was his own perplexed frown, reflected in miniature.

Who are you?

The shadow-woman smiled, revealing teeth too white and sharp to belong in a human mouth. *That's funny, I was going to ask you the same thing.*

It was her. The one he'd traveled so far to find. Palmer had never seen her photo, much less heard her voice, but he was certain that the woman standing at the foot of his bed was Sonja Blue. Before he could ask her another question, her attention was drawn to the balcony.

Here? No, not here. But close. On it's way.

She sprinted for the French windows. Palmer opened his mouth to shout a warning that they were two stories up, but nothing came out. He felt slightly embarrassed for trying to warn a dream about breaking its legs. When she reached the open windows, she seemed to expand and elongate at the same time, stretching like a spaceship achieving light-speed, then shot headfirst into the early morning sky.

Palmer was suddenly aware that he was cold and sweating and shaking like a malaria victim. His scar began to burn like a hot wire pressed against his chest.

Loli popped up from behind the footboard like a malignant jack-in-the-box, the .38 leveled at his heart.

"Surrr-prizzze!"

He was unable to control himself this time and woke screaming, his fingers clawing at the scar.

There was no listing for Indigo Imports in either the New Orleans Yellow or White Pages. Palmer hadn't expected one, but you never could tell. Still, if you wanted a credit card, you had to have a phone. It was a fact of life. It was probably an unlisted number, but there was always the chance she relied on a message service to relay her calls. And those *were* listed.

After three hours and eighty-six answering services, he called Telephones Answered, Inc. and asked to speak to the head of Indigo Imports.

"I'm sorry, sir, but this is her answering service. Would you like to leave a message?"

He had her. He fought to keep his voice from betraying his excitement. "Yes. Tell her William Palmer called. It's very important that she contact me. She can reach me at 465–9212," he said, reading the number off Pangloss's phone.

"Very good, sir. I'll make sure she gets the message."

Palmer replaced the phone in its cradle. Sightseeing would have to wait.

The call came at six that evening. He'd fallen into a light drowse, helped by a couple of shots of expensive bourbon he'd found in the wet bar, and nearly fell off the couch attempting to answer the phone before the second ring.

"Hello?"

There was silence on the other end of the line, then a woman's voice. "Mr. Palmer?"

"This is Palmer."

"What do you want of me, Mr. Palmer?"

"I'm a private investigator, Ms. Blue. I was hired by your grandfather, Dr. Pangloss, to find you."

"You work for him?" There was both suspicion and curiosity in her voice.

"In a fashion. Let's say I owe him a favor. All I know is that I'm supposed to deliver a letter to you. Please, I'd like to arrange a meeting with you, if it's at all possible."

"You will be alone." It wasn't a question.

"Of course. You set the time and place; whatever you're comfortable with."

"Very well. Tuesday night at eleven. The Devil's Playground, on the corner of Decatur and Governor Nicholls."

The severed connection droned in his ear like an

angry hornet. Palmer's hands were shaking, his shirt glued to his back. It was the same woman. The one from his dream. He'd recognized the voice. He blinked and massaged his brow with the flat of his palm. Christ, what was going *on*? Was it the acid he'd consumed back in the seventies? If so, it had picked one hell of a time to treat him to a flashback.

Still, so many things had changed since he'd awakened from the coma. Sometimes it felt as if he'd spent the past thirty-eight years stumbling around in a sleepwalker's daze and was only now fully awake. Other times it seemed as if he was on the verge of complete and utter mental collapse.

He'd never considered himself an ordinary schmuck, but before his "accident" he'd never experienced much in the way of nightmares. Not since he was a kid, anyway. He'd had some doozies back then. His parents had disapproved of his discussing the dreams, so he'd stopped.

His father insisted that talking about "things that ain't real and never will be" was pointless and only lead to confusion and, in some strange logic that only his parents seemed to grasp, insanity.

Whenever Palmer pressed the point, his father would threaten him with Uncle Willy.

"You keep fretting about stuff that ain't real, you're gonna end up just like Uncle Willy! He was always worrying about the things he saw in his dreams. Where'd it get him? In the State Hospital, that's where! You're gonna end up sharing a cell with him if you don't lay off this shit!"

Palmer smiled wryly as he reached for the bourbon. *Better shove over, Uncle Willy. Look's like you're going to have company.*

*   *   *

Palmer let the crowd push him along Bourbon Street. It was slow going and intensely claustrophobic, but in spite of the overcrowding, the noise, and the reek of curbside garbage, he was enjoying himself.

It was Mardi Gras and he'd spent the day wandering the narrow streets of the French Quarter, marveling at the costumes and sampling the various local alcoholic beverages. Carnival revelers on the balconies overhead tossed beads and other trinkets at the crowd below. Occasionally a drunken tourist would bare a tit or a backside, causing a brief firestorm of camera flashes from the photographers in the crowd and a shower of hurled plastic beads. The whole thing was silly, trivial, bawdy, and dumb. Palmer thought it was great.

He broke free of the press of body on body at the next intersection and headed toward Jackson Square to watch the costumers promenade past the Saint Louis Basilica. He was amused by a band of masquers dressed as frogs heckling the handful of extremist Fundamentalists protesting the merrymaking by handing out their own bogus religious tracts. Palmer was so impressed he offered to pay for some of their literature.

"Don't bother," the young man grinned from inside the gaping cloth mouth of a frog's head. "We just do it to piss these jerks off. In fact, more people offer *us* money than them, and that *really* gets their goat! They've been out here for the last few years, being a major pain in the butt. There's not nearly as many of them this time, though. I guess their funding got the triple whammy, what with the PTL scandal, ole Jimmy gettin' caught out on Airline Highway, and that weird Catherine Wheele cult-massacre last year. Thanks anyway, mister! Happy Mardi Gras! Remember: Frog Croaked For Your

Sins!" The frog priest laughed, hopping after his departing flock.

"You weren't offering that man money, were you, sir?" Palmer looked down at the florid-faced woman in the "Christ Is The Answer Crusade" t-shirt. Her eyes were so over-magnified by her coke-bottle glasses they seemed to hover in front of her face. "They do the Devil's work, mocking the Lord's word and deed! They shall burn in hell on Judgement Day! Jesus loves you, even if you *are* a sinner! If you confess your sin now, and kneel with me and pray for deliverance of your soul, it may not be too late for you . . ."

Palmer shook his head, too overwhelmed by the woman's conviction and madness to say anything. It wasn't until he'd disentangled himself that he realized she'd slipped a tract into his pocket. The title dripped red ink like slime and read: *Are You Ready For The End-Times?*

Judging from the crude illustration beneath the question, no one was: terrified "sinners" in tattered rags ran from flying insects the size of dachshunds; haggard derelicts tried to slake their thirst at drinking fountains gushing blood; a busty MTV-style Whore of Babylon lolled on the back of a seven-headed Beast, while in the background a 900-foot tall Jesus beamed beatifically at the hundreds of souls zipping skyward from a tangle of wrecked and abandoned cars on the interchange.

Disgusted, Palmer hurled the offending tract to the ground and hurried away in search of a beer.

He passed the next few hours drinking concoctions with so much grenadine in them the back of his throat puckered. Darkness came, and as if upon clandestine agreement, the families vanished from the area, leaving only the hard-core to bid farewell to the flesh.

A shrill, almost hysterical, sense of abandon tinged the masquers' celebrations. Drunken horseplay turned into open brawls. Palmer could not tell the difference between screams and laughter. The eyes of the revelers gleamed from behind their borrowed faces, as if compelled to cram as much as possible into the few hours remaining to them before returning to their real lives.

The *need* Palmer glimpsed in their bleary, unfocused stares was both repellent and fascinating. It was as if he was surrounded by thousands of empty people desperately trying to fill themselves. He was overwhelmed by an image of himself being attacked by the screaming, laughing, empty people, devouring his soul as easily as a lion cleans the marrow from a broken bone.

Gasping, he pushed past a group of masquers dressed as cockroaches and stumbled inside one of the all-hours tourist traps that lined the street. He leaned against a postcard rack and shivered like a drunk with the d.t.'s. There was still an hour to go before he could consider his job done. He'd better lay off the booze if he wanted to be in any condition to talk with the elusive Ms. Blue. Or if he meant to steer clear of the nut house, for that matter.

He could still remember the day the men in the white suits took Uncle Willy away, screaming at the top of his lungs about the worms crawling out of his skin. His father had been quite upset. People on TV didn't have members of their family carted away. At least not on *Leave It To Beaver* and *Father Knows Best*. It happened on the soaps his mom liked to watch all the time, though.

"You awright, mister?"

He jerked his head up and stared at the man behind the cash register. The shopkeeper was the overall shape and size of a small foothill, dressed in khaki pants and a "I Saw the Pope" t-shirt. He chewed on an unlit cigar, eyeing Palmer warily.

"You ain't gonna be sick, are ya? If yer gonna puke, do it outside, fer th' love'a Gawd! I awready cleaned up after three people awready t'night! Jesus!"

"I'm okay, thanks. It was a just a little . . . crowded . . . out there."

"Yeah, ain't that the truth! I'll be glad when ever'-body goes home so's I can get some sleep. I— Hey, is that some friend of yours?" He pointed at the busy street on the other side of the glass.

Palmer spun around, the hairs on the back of his neck erect. A well-fed tourist couple stood and stared at a "life-like" plastic turd stapled to the brim of a synthetic baseball cap which bore the legend "Shithead."

"You mean *them*?"

"No, it was some guy in a suit. You know, dressed like them queers down at the art galleries. He was smokin' a cigarette and wavin' at ya, like he was tryin' t'getcher attention."

"It must have been a case of mistaken identity. I don't know anybody in town."

The shopkeeper grunted and returned to thumbing through his porno magazine. Tourists is tourists.

Palmer stared out into the street. He hadn't lied. He *didn't* know anybody in New Orleans. So why did he feel as if someone had just walked over his grave?

The Devil's Playground was a block off the historic French Market, and the odor of discarded produce was strong on the night wind, mixing with the ever-present reek of beer and urine that seemed to hang over the district during Carnival.

The bar's windows were covered by painted flames. A fiberglass statue of a grinning Mephistopheles, resplendent in his skin-tight red jumpsuit and neat goatee, stood next to the door. The grinning devil held aloft a pitchfork in his right hand, his left fist firmly planted on one hip; the Prince of Lies' jaunty demeanor far more reminiscent of Errol Flynn as Robin Hood than Goethe's demon.

Palmer pushed his way inside, ignoring the looks from a couple of young men sheathed in black leather and chrome chains lounging near the door. The place was packed, the buzz of a half-hundred voices lost under the crash and thunder of over-amplified rock music. He scanned the cramped quarters for sign of his quarry. He made a try for the bar, brushing against a tall, heavyset woman.

The woman turned, smiling good naturedly if drunkenly. Her face was heavily made up, chunky costume jewelry dripping from her fingers and ears.

"Hey there, handsome. You look lonesome." Her voice was husky, her breath redolent of whiskey. She reached up with one beringed hand and patted her hair.

"Uh, I'm looking for someone, actually."

The woman's smile grew wider. "Aren't we all, sugar?" She leaned closer and Palmer glimpsed a hint of five o' clock shadow under the makeup. She placed a large, knobby-knuckled hand on his sleeve. "Maybe I can help you find what you're looking for."

Palmer shrugged. "You might. I'm supposed to be meeting someone here. A woman."

The transvestite removed her hand from his arm. "I see." Interest drained from her voice as she returned her gaze to the mirror behind the bar, readjusting her wig.

"Maybe you know her. She lives somewhere around here. Her name's Sonja Blue."

The transvestite jerked her head in his direction

so hard she unseated her wig. Palmer glimpsed thinning hair the color of wheatstraw.

"The Blue woman? You're meeting the Blue woman? *Here?!*" All pretense of imitating a woman's voice ended. The transvestite stared at Palmer as if he'd just announced he had an armed nuclear device strapped to his back.

Palmer was suddenly aware that everyone else in the bar was staring at him. The music continued to thump and growl like a caged animal, but no one spoke. Palmer felt his armpits dampen.

"Get out! Get *out* of here! We've got enough trouble as it is without you bringing *her* here!" The bartender, a muscular fellow naked except for a leather jockstrap, a rams horn headdress, and a tattoo of a rampant dragon on his chest, gestured angrily at the door.

"But—"

A dozen pairs of hands grabbed him, lifting him bodily over their heads. Palmer recalled how he used to stage-dive at the hard-core concerts, leaping onto the stage for a brief moment of stolen glamor before jumping back into the seething dance floor. He didn't try to fight them and allowed himself to be roughly passed over the heads of the bar's patrons and dumped, unceremoniously, back onto the street. He straightened his rumpled clothes as best he could, glancing back at the doorway. The two young men dressed in leather and chrome blocked the entrance.

"Fuck this shit." Palmer was in no position to take on two guys ten years his junior. Not if he wanted to keep what was left of his teeth. He shoved his hands in his pockets and stalked off around the corner.

He paused halfway down the block, lighting a cigarette with trembling hands.

"Palmer?"

He spun around so fast he burned himself with his lighter.

She was dressed in a pair of faded, much-worn blue jeans, a "Cramps 1990 Tour" t-shirt, a ragged leather jacket a size too big for her, scuffed engineer boots, and sunglasses. Even though he could not see her eyes, Palmer was aware of being watched.

"Sonja?"

"You are Pangloss's agent?"

He shrugged. "You could say that."

"Were you followed?"

"No."

Her lips twisted into something like a smile. "You seem sure of yourself."

"I'm good at what I do."

"No doubt. You spoke of a letter from my . . . grandfather."

Palmer reached into his jacket and withdrew the letter. "Funny, the Doc doesn't look old enough to have a granddaughter your age."

"He's very well preserved. It's a family trait. I'll take that letter now, if you don't mind." She extended a pale, narrow hand toward him.

Palmer handed over the sealed envelope, his fingers accidentally brushing against hers.

There was a sound like a flashcube going off in the back of his skull and his fingertips tingled. He saw Sonja Blue jerk her head as if she'd received a sudden electrical shock. The street disappeared and Palmer found himself in a strange room.

He saw a pool table surrounded by splintered pool cues, scattered cue balls . . . and broken boys. The smell of blood and fear was strong. The fear smell's primal intensity was erotic; the greatest aphrodisiac he'd ever known, and most of it radiated from the frightened boy clutched in his hands. The youth's hair was the color of a Maxfield Parrish sky, his face that of an errant choirboy. There were brief,

*blurred glimpses of rape, robbery, looting, each involving
the same baby-faced miscreant. . . . An orgasm shuddered
through Palmer's nervous system as a hot gush of thick,
salty blood filled his mouth.*

Sonja Blue jerked her hand away from his, growling like a mountain lion. She turned and ran, disappearing into the darkness before Palmer had a chance
to reorient himself. He felt dizzy, as if he'd just
stepped off the Tilt-A-Whirl at the State Fair. He
could still taste the boy's blood. The thought made
him moan, and bile burned the back of his throat.
He didn't want to think about it. Not now, not ever.
He especially didn't want to think about how he'd
recognized the blue-haired boy's face as belonging to
Jimmy Eichorn.

All he wanted to do was get back to the apartment,
phone Pangloss, and tell him he'd fulfilled his part
of the bargain. He'd collect his bonus and go somewhere nice and sunny. Mexico sounded good. He'd
retire to Mexico and sell stuffed frogs playing mariachi instruments to the *turistas*. That sounded *real*
good.

He started back toward Pangloss's house. It was
almost midnight and Bourbon street was jammed
with party-goers determined to wring the few remaining minutes of pleasure out of Carnival. The
noise and excitement was almost enough to make him
forget what had just happened.

At first he thought the tugging on his sleeve was
the wind. Then it spoke his name.

Palmer turned and stared into the pale, smiling
face of a man in his late twenties, dressed in an
expensive, loose-fitting suit. The stranger lifted a
smoldering French cigarette to his thin lips, his eyes
strangely sunken in the fluorescent and neon glare
from a nearby live-sex show sign.

There was something familiar about his arrogant, smirking features—then Palmer recognized him.

He took an involuntary step backward, his scalp tightening as his heart began to race. The street noise faded into an indistinct rumble, as if he was underwater. He prayed he wasn't having a stroke, although that would at least explain the things happening to him.

"You're *dead*!" It sounded like an accusation.

Geoffrey Chastain, known to friends and enemies as Chaz, shrugged. "Is that a crime? I've been tryin' to get yer bleedin' attention all bloody night! Coo! Yer a dense bugger!"

Palmer noticed that parts of Chaz were semi-transparent. The dead man drew another lung full of smoke from his phantom cigarette, causing his midsection to swirl. Palmer wondered if he'd still be toking on his beloved Shermans a year after his own death.

"Look, there's not much time left. Mardi Gras night's one of th' few times th' friggin' spirits of th' dead can corporalize 'n mingle with th' livin'. As it 'tis, it's damn near Ash Wednesday. I know we dead men ain't supposed to be tellin' tales, but I was ne'er one for th' rules. So take some advice from one who knows, eh? Get th' 'ell outta town while yer able. Fuck gettin' yer money from Pangloss. Just get on th' next bleedin' bus outta town and don't look back! Fergit y'ever laid eyes on 'er!"

"Who—?"

"Who th' bloody fuck y'think I mean? Sonja soddin' Blue! The Bloofer Lady 'erself! She's death, boyo! Death on two legs! Pure 'n simple. Not that she can 'elp it, mind you. It's just 'er way. But knowin' that won't 'elp you none when the time comes. An' it will. Look, mate—I was a real pisser when I was like you. Alive, that is. Bein' dead's changed 'ow I see things. It innit pretty, lookin' back an' seein' meself for th' bastard I was. But it ain't bad, really. Actually, I prefer it to 'ow things was when I was flesh 'n blood. So mebbe 'ow she did me weren't so bad. Mebbe."

Palmer's stomach knotted tighter. "Are you saying she—"

"Snuffed me? Aye, that she did. Ain't you th' bright student? She killed me, awright. Just like she did th' lads with th' blue 'air. She was feelin' 'er oats that night. Not that I should blame 'er for it—but I still do. I guess I 'aven't been knackered long enough t'forgive 'er fer that. But I don't 'ate th' lass, if that's what yer gettin' at. Like I said, bein' dead changed 'ow I look at things. I used t'think I 'ated 'er, back when I was alive. Now I see that I loved 'er, that was me problem. Me! *Lovin'* someone! It scared me so bad I got to 'atin' 'er fer it. That's why I did 'er th' way I did. That's why she did *me* th' way she did. Love. Funny 'ow death makes things so much clearer, innit?"

"Then why are you warning me, if you're so ambivalent?" Palmer's fear had abated in the face of this mundane, chainsmoking specter. He was starting to feel more aggravated than frightened.

"Shall we say you 'n me, we're kindred spirits?" Chaz's smirk widened. "That bullet did more'n punch a 'ole in yer skin, ducks. It woke up somethin'. Jump-started it, as it were. Yer what they call a 'sensitive.' 'Ow else y'fancy ol' Pangloss found you, eh? You might 'ave been unconscious th' whole time you was in 'ospital, but part of you was broadcastin' like a bloody short-wave radio! They like usin' sensitives like you—an' me. We make 'andy servants, don't you know? So far you've only 'ad a taste of what it's like—'avin' th' world turn itself inside-out like a bloo-min' magician's sack, an' you bein' th' only one noticin'. But get used t'it, mate. Yer'll ne'er get t'like it, but yer'll get *used* t'it, if it don't drive you mad first. Like it did me mum. An' yer Uncle Willy."

"Wait a second! What do you *mean*?"

"Sorry, luv. Seems me time's run out." The bell in the basilica's tower rang, marking the transition from excess to penance. Chaz grinned as he stepped into the street.

"What do you mean? Who are *they*?"

Second stroke. Third stroke.

The ghost laughed and shook his insubstantial head. "Yer not goin' t'leave it be, are you? Yer in love with 'er already! You don't even know it yet, but I can see it in th' folds of yer brain, mate!"

Fourth stroke. Fifth stroke.

"Why are you telling me these things? *Why*?"

"Because y'put flowers on me grave, *that's* why! Th' dead are a sentimental lot."

Sixth stroke. Seventh stroke.

Halfway up the block uniformed policemen appeared astride horses, riding four abreast, bullhorns held in their hands. Behind them Palmer glimpsed the huge street-sweeping machines, brushes spinning in anticipation of flushing the gutters clean of accumulated filth, human and otherwise.

Eighth stroke. Ninth stroke.

Chaz shimmered with every toll of the bell, like a reflection in a bestirred pool. Palmer tried to push past the throng of revelers, desperate to win one last answer from the smiling ghost.

"MARDI GRAS IS OVER! EVERYONE GO HOME!" bellowed the police as they moved forward, forcing the people milling in the street either onto the sidewalks or into the bars.

"MARDI GRAS IS OVER! EVERYONE GO HOME!"

The sanitation trucks blasted their horns to punctuate the mounted officers' commandment.

Tenth stroke. Eleventh stroke.

A huge, heavy hand closed on Palmer's shoulder, pinning him so he could not move. He looked up and stared into the brutish features of the man he'd seen skulking in Pangloss's shrubbery.

"Renfield say come now."

"MARDI GRAS IS OVER!"

Twelfth stroke. Midnight arrived, ushering in Lent.

Chaz wavered like a hologram projected onto smoke. Palmer watched as one of New Orleans' finest rode through the dead man. He expected the horse, at least, to react to the ghost, but all it did was flare its nostrils, toss its mane, and leave a pile of dung in its wake.

"Renfield say you come *now!*"

The gorilla tightened his grip on Palmer, causing him to cry out in pain. This made the gorilla smile; something Palmer definitely wished he hadn't seen.

He had a funny feeling he was soon going to find out exactly who "*they*" were.

4

Sonja Blue watched as the police and sanitation workers brought Carnival to an end. She knew that the hard-core partying would continue well until dawn, but from now on it would have to be indoors, not on the streets. The harlequin's mask had been exchanged for the sack-cloth of the penitent. She lifted her gaze from the streets, watching the spirits of the dead spiral upward like bats leaving a cave. Neither variety of tourist would be staying to take communion.

She frowned and pulled the envelope from her pocket, turning it over and over as by handling it she could divine its contents. Pangloss. Had it been a decade since they last met? Like most Pretenders, her time sense was distorted. It was becoming more and more difficult for her to distinguish months from years.

She ran her fingers over the wax seal, her mood darkening as she recalled Pangloss's treachery below the streets of Rome.

The seal cracked easily, falling in three separate pieces at her feet. The letter was on expensive stationery that felt like silk and smelled of cologne. The penmanship was exquisitely baroque. No doubt the good doctor favored an old-fashioned quill pen.

My Dear,
Please forgive the method in which this letter was delivered.
I have attempted to contact you on numerous occasions,
through various menials, but you are a difficult woman to
communicate with. I do not hold such rash disposal of my
minions against you. In many ways, I find your gift for
carnage reassuring. It has been far too long since we last
spoke, and I fear that the conditions of our previous meeting
may have influenced you to view me in an unfavorable
light. I have followed your antics with great interest since
we last met. I must admit I found your handling of the
Catherine Wheele situation gauche but effective. You have
a natural talent for atrocity, my dear. It needs refining,
but I believe you have it in you to produce a tableau on the
level of Baron Luxor's Jonestown, Lord Mavrides' Stockton
Elementary School Slaughter, or even Marchessa Nuit's
classic McDonald's McMassacre! But I am not writing sim-
ply to compliment your style. There is much I must tell
you, my dear, and it concerns one who I know you are
interested in. I speak of your maker and my former student,
Lord Morgan. You can contact me through the human,
Palmer.

Sonja looked at her left hand. The hand the private
investigator had touched. She hadn't recognized the
human as a sensitive at first—it was obvious he was
unaware of his own talent—so she'd been unshielded.
She'd received a barrage of sensory images, the most
vivid being that of a scarlet-clad nymph with a
smoking gun, before breaking contact. The exchange
had been unexpected and unwelcome, but she had
gleaned enough information from the jumble to dis-
cern that William Palmer was exactly what he
thought he was: a free agent.

She knew where Palmer was staying—she made
it a point to be familiar with the city's nests—and

wondered if it was time for her to get in touch with the "family."

Renfield sat in an antique chair, his pallid bureaucrat's features breaking into something like a smile at the sight of Palmer in the company of the gorilla.

"Excellent. I assume you fulfilled your part of the bargain, Mr. Palmer. You *did* succeed in delivering the letter?"

"Yeah, I delivered your fucking letter! What the hell are you trying to pull, Renfield?" Palmer tried to jerk free of the gorilla and heard the seams in his jacket tear.

"Pull?" Renfield smiled again. Palmer wished he'd stop. "Mr. Palmer, if you continue struggling, I'll have Keif pull your right arm off and beat you with it."

Palmer didn't doubt Keif could do it and ceased trying to break free. He glanced around the room— empty except for the chair and Renfield—and wondered if the louvered shutters were nailed shut. If they weren't, he might stand a chance of escape, providing his guard let go of his shoulder, and he didn't break every bone in his body jumping from the third-floor balcony onto the patio below.

"I wouldn't recommend trying such heroics, Mr. Palmer," Renfield said, smiling and crossing and recrossing his legs like a bored personnel manager at a job interview. "The shutters are, indeed, nailed in place. Oh, don't look so surprised! Of course I can read your mind, such as it is. It's an open book— although short story would better describe it. You may let go of him, Keif." The vise clamping Palmer's shoulder disappeared. "I can handle our friend from here on. Go and watch the door."

Keif grunted, pausing on the threshold to give Palmer a final, hungry look.

"Go on! Go on! Do as I say!" snapped Renfield, waving at the goon as if shooing a bothersome child out of the kitchen. "You'll get your share, as always!"

Palmer swung toward Renfield, fists balled. "Look here, you mealy-mouthed bastard! What the hell do you think you're doing? If I don't get some answers I'm gonna—"

"You're going to die, Mr. Palmer."

Fire coursed through Palmer's veins, turning his blood to slag. His intestines boiled in their own juices as his bones powdered into ash. His eyeballs exploded and dribbled down his cheeks like egg yolks. He tried to scream, but his lungs were full of burning water.

The fire disappeared as quickly as it descended. Palmer lay on the bare floor, knees draw up under his chin. He could taste blood in his mouth. Had he bitten his tongue?

"Wha—What did you do to—?"

"You died, Mr. Palmer. And you will continue to die until I decide otherwise. Honestly, I can't understand what it is the Doctor sees in you. True, you have *some* talent," he sniffed, "but all this other mental and emotional baggage—empathy, sympathy, the ability to love—it's simply not worth the effort of deprogramming!"

Cold shot through Palmer, spearing his nervous system with a million icicles. His lungs filled with ice crystals and his urine turned to slush in his bladder. He whimpered as his toes and fingers turned black and fell off.

"I have no intention of letting you survive this little ordeal." Renfield was back, only this time his head was wreathed in a strange glow the color of a fresh bruise. Funny how Palmer hadn't noticed that before. "I've worked too long to allow some upstart to turn the Doctor against me!" Renfield's wan features were flushed now. He was drunk on emotions long held in check, his eyes bright and feral as a starved coyote's.

Renfield abandoned his chair, dropping to his knees beside Palmer. "You think I don't notice how he favors you? How he looks at you? He promised me power and life eternal! He said he loved me! *Needed* me! *Me*, not you!" There were tears in the other man's eyes. "He lied to me! But he won't have you. I won't let you take my place! I'll tell him you couldn't handle the deprogramming—it won't be a lie, really—and I gave you to the ogre for disposal. No one will know! Not even the Doctor!"

The louvered shutters shattered inward as Sonja Blue made her entrance, leather-clad arms lifted to shield her face. She hit the bare floor and rolled, distracting Renfield away from his victim.

Palmer felt the numbness in his limbs vanish as Renfield faced the intruder. The reverse-negative halo surrounding his head pulsed, snapping a whip-like tendril in Sonja Blue's direction.

Sonja made a motion with her left hand, as if flicking away a worrisome insect. "You'll have to do better than that!" She laughed.

Renfield looked confused, then frightened. "Keif! Get in here! Keif!"

Palmer got to his feet, surprised to find the recent agonies he'd undergone had left his flesh unscathed. He could hear the gorilla fumbling with the lock. Sonja grabbed Renfield by his lapels, pulling him so close they were literally nose-to-nose. A spiky crown of reddish-black light seemed to radiate from the woman's head, flickering in and out of Palmer's vision like a defective neon sign.

"Where's Pangloss?"

"Do you honestly think I'd tell *you*?" Renfield sneered.

"You've got a point." She let go of his jacket. Renfield smiled hesitantly, straightening his lapels. She moved so fast Palmer almost didn't see it; grabbing Renfield's chin and forcing his head up and back at an unnatural angle. The door banged inward, sagging on its hinges. Keif had grown frustrated with opening the door.

The gorilla squeezed through the doorway, his piggy little eyes moving from Palmer to Sonja before settling on Renfield's corpse. Sonja stepped forward, motioning for Palmer to get behind her. He saw she held an open switchblade in one hand.

"Jesus Christ, woman, there's no way you can go up against that goon—"

She waved him silent, never taking her eyes off the hulking figure filling the doorway. "Keep quiet! I know what I'm doing!"

Keif rumbled deep in his throat and stepped forward, sniffing the air like a hunting dog. Keif glanced at them suspiciously, his nostrils flaring, but did not offer to attack. His attention was fixed on Renfield's carcass. Saliva dripped from his lower lip in thick ropes. Keif emitted a loud snuffling sound, like that of a hog at a trough, and pounced on the corpse. Palmer heard fabric rip as the giant tore at the dead man's clothes.

Sonja motioned toward the door. She moved to follow, never taking her eyes off the drooling goon.

"What's he *doing*?" Palmer hissed.

"You don't want to know. Let's get out of here while he's preoccupied. Ogres aren't very bright to begin with, and when they're hungry they tend to let their bellies override their brains. We're lucky this one hadn't had dinner yet."

5

Palmer sat on the penthouse patio, a glass of bourbon in his hand, while everything he'd assumed was real disintegrated.

Palmer prided himself on his ability to adapt to adverse conditions. He'd learned how to cope when his family kicked him out of the house at the age of seventeen. He'd survived three hellish months on an Alabama work gang, back when having long hair was a criminal offense. He'd watched friends unwilling to admit they were no longer as young and invulnerable as they used to be succumb to overdoses and disease. There was no percentage in denying change. Evolve Or Die. He should have it tattooed on his forehead.

He took another swallow of his drink, glancing over the rim at his savior. She sat on the edge of the parapet, scanning the surrounding rooftops. Palmer was uncertain as to whether he trusted the mirror-eyed woman, but did not see he had any choice.

"Is Pangloss really your grandfather?"

She shrugged but did not turn to face him. "Some would say so. But if you mean is he my *biological* grandfather; no, he is not."

"I didn't think so. He's nowhere near old enough to have a grandchild your age."

"Pangloss is at least fifteen hundred years old, Mr. Palmer."

"So I'm lousy at guessing ages."

"You seem rather . . . calm . . . considering what's just happened."

"After talking to the dead, discovering I possess psychic powers, and being brain-raped by a crazed telepath, being told my employer is a vampire is rather anti-climatic."

Sonja glanced at him. "You spoke with the dead?"

"Actually, it was more the other way around. It was your old boyfriend."

"Chaz?"

He nodded, watching her face for a reaction. If the news affected her in any way, it did not show.

"And what did he have to say?"

"That I should avoid you like the plague and get the hell out of Dodge."

"Death has given him some smarts."

"He said you killed him."

"The dead don't lie. But they don't speak the truth, either. Yes, I killed him. Does it matter?"

"It did to him."

"Chaz was my . . . partner. He was like you—a sensitive. He was a small-time hustler when I met him. We clicked. It was good—for awhile. Then there was trouble. Chaz ended up selling me out. He betrayed me with a kiss. He always did have a flare for irony. I spent six months in a madhouse because of him. I do not expect loyalty from humans, but I do not countenance treachery. His death was not just, but it was fair. I have been a murderer for a very long time, Mr. Palmer. Killing is a habit of mine. It is only proper that I tell you this."

"There was a boy . . ." He felt his throat tighten at the taste of Jimmy Eichorn's blood, but continued anyway. "A boy with blue hair you did something to."

"The Blue Monkeys? Yes, I remember. I take it the boy is still alive?"

"If you want to call it that."

She shrugged. "He possessed information. And I was in need of . . . well, let us say I was in need and leave it at that."

"He was only fifteen—"

"—and already guilty of gang rape, hit-and-run driving, and second-degree murder. Do not waste your sympathy on him, Mr. Palmer. Like I said: what I do is not just, but it *is* fair."

Sonja Blue showed Palmer to a small attic room. A narrow bed was placed where the slope of the roof met the wall.

"It's not much. Then again, I normally don't entertain guests. You'll be safe here. It's another four hours until dawn. I'll be outside guarding the door. Once the sun comes up you shouldn't have to worry about Pangloss's pet ogre."

"Ogre?"

"What do you think the lunk chowing down on dear departed Renfield was? The tooth fairy? They're big and dumb and have some seriously nasty habits, as you might have guessed, but they're pretty much helpless without a handler. Left to themselves, they'll spend their time eating children and wandering around raping and looting villages. They could get away with shit like that back during the Dark Ages, but it tends to attract notice nowadays. So most of them end up signing on as muscle with various vampire or *vargr* big-shots. That way their employers can dispose of the empties without calling too much attention to themselves. That's what Renfield had planned for you, if you haven't figured it out by now."

"But *why* did he do what he did?"

A flicker of sympathy softened her features. "There's no shame in admitting what happened to you. Renfield may not have raped you physically, but the result was the same."

"Yeah, well—" Palmer looked away. He did not know what to say. He doubted he ever would.

"As to *why* Renfield hurt you—he was trying to twist you."

"Come again?"

"In order for you to be of any use to Pangloss, or any vampire, for that matter, he has to make sure you're twisted to suit his needs. That involves a complete and utter destruction of superego and restructuring of the ego. The sensitive's needs and desires must revolve around his master. He must be willing to live—and die—for his master. Sometimes this emotional dependence is reinforced with drugs, or sex. Inclinations to evil are fostered while any vestige of human emotion, except those required by the master, are systematically destroyed. While this may take some time, the initial deprogramming is usually done within a matter of minutes, assuming the attacker is a skilled psionic. If the deprogramming is pushed too hard, too fast, death occurs.

"Obviously, Renfield had orders to twist you; to add you to Pangloss's stable, so to speak. But he was jealous and rebelled. You're lucky he wanted to kill you, or you'd be Pangloss's slave right now."

"Yeah. Lucky."

Sonja Blue squatted on her haunches, listening to Palmer's breathing with half an ear. She doubted the ogre had the brains to come looking for them, but she'd learned the hard way never to underestimate the good doctor. She plucked Pangloss's letter from inside her jacket, flattening the paper against the attic floorboards.

There is much I must tell you, my dear, and it concerns one who I know you are interested in.

Morgan.

Her hands balled themselves into tight fists and she exhaled a nervous, shaky breath. She had spent the better part of twenty years—her entire unlife— searching for the vampire that had raped a teenaged girl, tainted her blood, and turned her into something that called itself Sonja Blue. Now Pangloss, the vampire responsible for Morgan's own creation, was tempting her with information concerning his whereabouts. It wasn't the first time he'd tried it. The last time had been under the streets of Rome, in a catacomb held sacred to the shadow races that manipulated mankind. She had been too proud to agree to Pangloss's "business proposition." She was lucky to have escaped.

What was Pangloss planning this time? It was not in his nature to volunteer information. He wanted— or needed—something from her, that much was certain.

You can contact me through the human, Palmer.

It was obvious that Pangloss meant to lure her closer by using the human investigator, then putting him into thrall once his usefulness was at an end. Pangloss was astute enough to realize she would never allow a twisted sensitive or a Pretender within sniffing distance and allow it to live to tell about it. So what was she to do with Palmer? Part of her, that which she thought of as the Other, *knew* what it wanted to do with him, but she refused to listen to its council.

*   *   *

Palmer moaned in his sleep, shifting uneasily on the narrow bed. Renfield's pasty face, as wide and pale as the moon, filled his dreams. The dead man's eyes were as flat and black as buttons, his lips thin and blue. Palmer could hear Renfield's voice, even though the satellite-sized face's mouth remained caught in a rictus grin.

Like me. Like me. She's going to make you like me. Lap dog. Lap dog. Lap, dog, lap!

Palmer sat up suddenly, the sweat running into his eyes. His mouth was dry, his head aching as if the lobes of his brain were dividing like amoebas. He stared at the circular window set near the peak of the roof. He got up and swiveled the window open on its pivot, inhaling a deep breath of Mississippi River-saturated air. Somewhere on the river, a barge sounded a long, mournful note.

"Will-yummmm?"

No. It couldn't be. He leaned his forehead against the windowsill, trying to find some comfort in the peeling paint pressing against his skin. He was awake. He *knew* it.

"William? Why won't you look at me, baby? Aren't you glad to see me, honey?"

Palmer bit his lip as the familiar burning tore at his chest. His scar throbbed and pulsed as if he'd been branded with a red-hot coat hanger. He wouldn't look at her. She wasn't real. She was a dream. He was awake. He opened his eyes, scanning the world outside the window for proof.

New Orleans was on fire.

The city was wrapped in sheets of flame, yet no one seemed to notice. Burning children ran up and down the streets, smoke and laughter billowing from their lobster-red mouths. Women dressed in crackling aprons swept their stoops clean of ash. Business executives dressed in smoldering Brooks Brothers suits paused to check the melted slag strapped to their wrists before hurrying on their way, smoking attache cases clenched in their roasted hands. On the balcony opposite Palmer's window two lovers embraced, oblivious to the blisters rising on their naked flesh, while the wrought iron bower softened and dripped like licorice left in the sun.

The pain spasmed through his chest, forcing an involuntary cry from his lips. There was no use in denying her. She was going to have her way, no matter how hard he tried to stop her. Groaning, Palmer turned to face Loli.

The smell of the *marui* started Sonja from her brooding. She'd scented it before, but had been uncertain then as to its intentions. The reek of ectoplasm was strong. Then she heard Palmer's stifled cry.

She kicked the door open, growling at the sight of the ill-formed creature crouched atop the sleeping man, its claws buried in his chest. The *marui* screeched in alarm and spread its membranous wings. Her fingers closed on its slippery flanks and the creature's high-pitched squealing became ultrasonic.

"Holy shit!"

Palmer was awake, staring in confusion at the combatants wrestling beside his bed.

"Don't just sit there gawking! Help me!"

"*How?*"

"Grab its neck!"

Palmer took one look at the *marui's* barbed teeth and shook his head. "Like hell I will!"

"Just *do* it, damn you!"

Palmer grimaced as his hands closed on the *marui's* telescoped neck. Its flesh was chill and rubbery, as if the wildly struggling beast was composed of phlegm.

With its biting end under control, Sonja was able to pin the creature to the floor.

"What in the name of hell is this thing?"

"This, Mr. Palmer, is your nightmare."

The beast, weakened by the scuffle, no longer tried to escape. It lay crumpled like a damaged kite, mewling to itself. Palmer stared at the *marui's* twisted, almost human musculature and tattered, bat-like wings. The nightmare creature's neck looked like a loop of umbilical cord; its bald, old man's head dominated by large, fox-like ears and bristling barbed teeth. Just looking at the thing made his scar tighten.

"They're called *marui*," she explained, resting her foot on the brute's neck. "They're also called night-elves, *maere*, and *le rudge-pula*, depending on the part of the world you happen to be in. They batten onto sleepers, manipulating dreams in order to feed on the fear and anxiety born of nightmares. Judging by its size, this one's been feasting on you for some time. They only take on corporeal form while they feed."

"You mean, this thing's a nightmare?"

"Bad dreams exist for their own reasons; *marui* simply benefit from the negative energy released by nightmares. But they're not what you'd call smart." She applied pressure on the *marui's* neck, smiling as it wailed in distress. "My guess is that Pangloss sicced this little darling on you, hoping to make Renfield's job easier when the time came. Isn't that so, Rover?" She applied more pressure to the *marui's* throat. The creature squealed.

"Will-yummm, help meee."

Palmer brought his heel down on the *marui's* skull, grinding it into a sticky paste. The *marui* shuddered once and began to dissolve, the ectoplasm evaporating like dry ice.

* * *

"I trust you slept well."

Palmer put down his mug of chicory coffee and turned to stare at the vampire standing in the kitchen door. She was dressed in a green silk kimono embroidered with tiny butterflies the color of smoke. Her hair was hidden by a clean white towel piled atop her head turban-style. She was still wearing mirrored sunglasses. It had never occurred to Palmer that the undead took showers.

"Never slept better." It was the truth. For the first time in weeks, Palmer's sleep was free of the recurring nightmares. When he awoke late that afternoon, he felt genuinely refreshed and rejuvenated.

"I trust you kept yourself entertained while I was . . . indisposed." Sonja opened the refrigerator and removed one of the bottles of dark red liquid. Palmer had stumbled across them earlier and guessed their significance. "I'm afraid I don't have much in the way of house guests." She cracked the seal and brought the bottle to her lips, then caught sight of Palmer's face. "Oh, I'm sorry—I've forgotten my manners." She put the blood aside, smiling apologetically.

"There's nothing you have to apologize for. After all, it's your house. I'm just a guest. I have no right to judge."

Sonja tilted her head to one side, regarding him with her one-way gaze. "You're quite adaptable . . . for a human."

Palmer coughed into his fist. "There's something I need to say. Look, it's pretty obvious that I'm at something of a disadvantage right now. Discovering everything I've ever known is wrong is unnerving enough, but to also find out everything I've ever been paranoid about is true . . ." He spread his hands in an expressive shrug. "I need help. Big time."

"So?"

"Well, I'd like to make a business proposition. Call it a modest proposal. I need help with this ham-radio set in my skull, right? You need help with Pangloss, right? How about we team up—just for a little while? You could teach me how to use what I got, and I could . . . do whatever it is you need me to do."

"Mr. Palmer, do you have any idea what you're getting yourself into?"

"No. I'll admit that up front. But I know that if I don't get help, I'm going to go mad. I can't handle walking around with other people's thoughts and fears and craziness going through my head." He could feel his hands tremble as he spoke, but he refused to look at them. "Look, I can't lie to you. You scare me, lady. But it's like my Uncle Willy used to say: better the devil you know."

When she laughed he saw her fangs. Even though he knew it was going to be okay, it still frightened him.

Compared to the day before, the French Quarter was practically deserted. Bourbon Street was open for business, as usual, but the barkers were, for once, uninterested in luring the handful of tourists wandering the neon and garbage-strewn strip into their dens of iniquity.

Local merchants swept the remaining debris of plastic cups and busted liquor bottles outside their shops into the gutter with powerful pistol-grip hoses. The overall mood was a mixture of exhaustion and relief, as if the city was recovering from a malaria attack.

Palmer trailed after his new employer, trying to ignore the stares that followed them down the narrow streets. Sonja Blue moved swiftly and purposefully through the clustered shadows, her hands jammed into the pockets of her leather jacket. She seemed preoccupied, but Palmer had no doubt that she was very much aware of the looks aimed at her.

The fear and loathing that radiated from the hustlers, pushers, and other Quarter habitues was strong enough to make Palmer's skin crawl. It felt as if someone had liberated an ant farm in his underwear. He ran through the mental exercises for blocking ambient emotions Sonja had taught him before they left the house that evening, and the horde of invisible ants disappeared.

"It appears you're not well liked around here."

She shot him a glance over her shoulder. "Get used to it. Most humans have an instinctual dislike of Pretenders—and sensitives, for that matter."

Palmer recalled his own immediate, gut-level reaction to Renfield and winced.

"You've used that word before: Pretenders. What does it mean?"

"Ever read Lovecraft?"

"Back in high school. Why?"

"Remember that stuff about Cthulhu, the Elder Gods and the Old Ones? How mankind was only a recent development, as far as the earth was concerned, and that these hideous giant outer space monsters used to rule the world back before the dinosaurs, and how the giant ugly nameless horrors are just sitting around on their tentacles, waiting for when the time is ripe to take over the world?"

"Yeah."

"Well, it's kind of like that."

"I don't think I want to know any more."

"Too late for that. But showing's easier than telling. I can *tell* you anything I want. Whether it's true or not—well, that's up to you to decide. But when you *see* something, can actually smell its breath and body odor, well, that's a different thing entirely. Humans call it witnessing."

"Where are we going?" Palmer was starting to feel itchy again, but it had nothing to do with telepathic intrusion.

"Do you believe in hell?"

Palmer blinked, taken aback by the change in subject matter. "If you mean the Christian hell, where people are tortured by guys with pitchforks and pointy ears—no, I don't believe in that."

"Me neither. But I *do* believe in demons. And that's where we're going; to make a deal with a devil."

"You mean Satan?"

"Are you kidding? He's way too expensive. Doesn't deal for anything less than souls. No, the guy I go to is reasonably priced."

Palmer decided it might be better if he stopped asking questions.

The Monastery was a small, dark bar that had, in a fit of perversity, decided on an ecclesiastical decor. The booths lining the wall had once been pews; fragments of stained glass, salvaged from various desanctified churches, had been soldered together to create a disjointed jigsaw collage on display in the skylight. Plaster saints and icons in varying states of decay were scattered about; a Black Madonna and Child, whether darkened by exposure to too many votive candles or Vatican II's attempt at "modernizing" its appeal, stared at the Monastery's denizen's with flat, robin's egg-blue eyes from its perch over the liquor supply. A battered Rockola jukebox played scratchy Rolling Stones records.

With its cheap prices, slovenly service, and haphazard attitude toward hygiene, it was obvious that the Monastery did not cater to the hordes of Visapacking tourists the Quarter thrived on. A prostitute sat at the bar, sipping a sloe gin fizz while the bartender cleaned a highball glass with a grimy rag. Both watched Palmer and Sonja Blue intently as they entered.

"What if the guy you're looking for isn't here?" Palmer whispered hopefully.

"He's here, all right. He's *always* here."

Sonja's connection was seated in the back booth, where the shadows were the deepest. Sonja's lips curled into a thin, cold smile.

"Hello, Malfeis."

The demon returned her smile, licking his lips with a forked tongue. "Ah, Sonja! Please, call me Mal! There is no need to stand on formalities."

Palmer frowned. Whatever he'd been expecting, it definitely hadn't been a teenaged boy dressed in faded denims and a "Surf or Die" t-shirt. A skateboard, its belly painted to depict an eyeball wreathed in day-glo flames, leaned against the converted pew.

"Kid, are you old enough to be in this place?"

Malfeis lifted an upswept eyebrow in amusement. "Who's the renfield, Sonja?"

"My name's *not* Renfield." Palmer fought the urge to grab the snot-nosed little skatepunk by his rat-tail. "What'd you mean by that?"

Sonja waved Palmer silent. "I'll explain later. After I get through with business. Wait for me at the bar."

"But—"

"I *said* wait at the bar." Her voice was as hard and cold as steel, and as unyielding. She waited until Palmer left before sliding into the booth.

"Quite a change from the last time, Mal." Six months ago Malfeis had worn the body of a young black male wreathed in coils of gold chain.

The demon shrugged, smiling slyly. "I like to keep up to date. I've always been something of a fashion plate. So, what brings you back into my clutches, sweet thing?"

"I think you know that already."

"Do I?"

"Don't play cute with me, Mal. I don't have the time or the patience right now. I need to know what Pangloss has up his sleeve." She pulled the letter Palmer had delivered to her out of her jacket, sliding it across the table.

Mal tapped the folded paper with an overly long fingernail and grunted. "Easy enough. What's in it for me?"

Sonja produced a black ceramic vessel the size of an unguent jar from her pocket and held it up so the demon could get a good look.

"Got it in from Katmandu just last week. The powdered skull of a man who killed six Tibetan holy men, then murdered and raped three missionaries. It's good shit, man; as pure as you'll find it."

Mal's cat-like eyes seemed to fill with a strange fire. His fingers drummed nervously against the table top. "Gimme a taste."

Sonja carefully unscrewed the lid and dispensed a pinch of a fine, chalky yellow powder into Mal's outstretched palm. The demon daubed a forefinger in the pulverized skull and popped it his mouth.

"So? What's the verdict?"

Mal nodded appreciatively. "Yow! Mama, buy me some of that!"

"Deal?"

"Done."

Sonja pushed the jar over to Malfeis's side of the table. The demon brought out a gold-plated razor blade and a flat piece of volcanic glass, quickly arranging himself a generous line of powdered skull. Oblivious to his surroundings, Malfeis lowered his head to the table and inhaled the line with both nostrils, snuffling like a bloodhound. He jerked his head up when he was finished, blowing out his cheeks and shaking himself like a winded stallion. His eyes were too big and the pupils slitted unnaturally, but otherwise he still looked human.

"Coldblooded! True righteous shit!" He grinned, showing a mouthful of shark teeth.

"Glad it meets your approval. Now, about Pangloss . . ."

"No problem!" Mal picked up the letter and tapped one edge between his eyebrows. His eyes rolled up in their sockets, exposing green-tinged whites. A strange, basso profundo gargle rumbled from deep inside his narrow, hairless chest, but no one in the bar seemed to notice. After a second or two Mal reconnected, his eyes dropping back down like the symbols on a slot machine.

"There's not much available information concerning Pangloss, outside of his recent attempts to make contact with you. That much seems up front. There does seem to be a bit of a buzz concerning Morgan, though."

"Really? Were you able to find out what?"

"Sorry, that requires First Hierarchy clearance. I don't have the necessary power to access that information for you, at least not in detail. I *can* tell that whatever it is Morgan is doing, it's generating a great deal of speculation amongst the First and Second Hierarchies. Whether that means they approve of what he's doing is impossible to say."

"Don't you have some connections? I thought your uncle was a Second Hierarch."

"Uncle Oeillet? Yeah, but he's not exactly what you'd call a big wheel. I mean, he's in charge of tempting people to break their vows of poverty, for crying out loud! His star's been on the decline since the Reformation. In fact, most of the Second Hierarchs are pretty redundant, since they were originally conscripted to tempt holy men back during the Dark Ages. Still, a direct hookup with any of them rates a blood sacrifice. At least three quarts. I wish I could cut you a better deal on that, babe, but them's the rules."

Palmer glowered first at the highball in his hand then back at Sonja, still talking with the fresh-faced punk with the funny looking eyes. The Black Madonna stared down at him from her place above the half-empty liquor bottles. The Black Baby Jesus looked like a doll someone had dropped down a coal chute, its chubby uplifted arms ending in misshapen fists since the fingers were rotted off.

"Hey, mister. You looking for someone?"

It was the prostitute at the end of the bar, the one he'd noticed when they entered. He shook his head without looking up from his drink. "Thanks, but no thanks."

"Are you *sure* you aren't looking for someone?"

There was something in her voice that made him look up, and what he saw was enough to push him to the brink.

He could feel insanity yawning like a snake eager to swallow him whole, right down to his Shermans and public library card. All he had to do was let go of the bar and let it suck him deep into its guts, never to be seen or heard from again.

The woman seated at the end of the bar was Loli. And this time he knew he wasn't dreaming. She smiled seductively and moved closer to him. She smelled of sloe gin fizzes and something Palmer recognized but could not name. Her fingers were cold and dry against his exposed flesh, but Palmer was beyond shivering. At her touch, his penis became erect. It was so hard it hurt, forcing tears from the corners of his eyes.

"I've been waiting for a man like you," she cooed into his ear. "I've waited such a *long* time!"

Palmer wanted to cry out, but his mouth had been sealed from the inside. His dick throbbed as if someone had slipped a piano wire tourniquet around its base and was slowly cutting off the circulation.

"Come on, baby. I got a place we can go and be alone." Loli hooked her arm in Palmer's, pulling him free of the bar. She was at least a head shorter than him, but she was strong. Too strong. "When we're alone, I'll fuck your brains out!" The way she laughed made it sound as if the joke was on him.

Palmer didn't want to go with her, but it was as if he was being pulled along by a wire fastened to the end of his dick. Every time he tried to fight it, the invisible tourniquet tightened its hold on his member. They were almost out the door before Palmer felt a second, equally female hand close on his right elbow.

"He's *mine*, you skaggy hell-bitch!" Sonja Blue yanked Palmer in her direction, but the succubus still held firmly to his left arm. The demon-whore hissed like a cat, digging her nails into Palmer's upper arm. He tried to scream, but his mouth was still pasted shut.

Palmer pictured himself being ripped apart like a wishbone as the vampire and the succubus fought over him. Then Sonja produced a switchblade and neatly severed the demon-Loli's hand at the wrist. Momentarily confused by this new development, Loli's grip on Palmer weakened enough for Sonja to wrench him free. Once away from the succubus's physical control, his overinflated sex organ rapidly shrank. It was the first time in his life he'd been relieved at losing an erection.

He stared as Loli picked up her severed hand and tried to stick it back on. To his surprise, the graft took.

"Loli . . .?" It was the first time he'd had the power to speak since the trouble started.

"She's not Loli, Palmer. Take my hand. See as *I* see." Before Palmer could protest, she grabbed his right hand and squeezed.

The thing that had bewitched and tried to kidnap him had three pairs of floppy tits, her arms as long and hairy as an ape's, her legs crooked and a six-inch-long sheathed clitoris dangled between her shanks. Tiny horns grew from the creature's sloping forehead. The succubus hissed, her lipless mouth hinged like a piranha's. She stepped forward, growling a challenge to the mirror-eyed intruder that had dared steal her evening's repast.

"Jamara!"

The voice was as loud as thunder and so deep the speaker sounded as if he was at the bottom of a well. The succubus cringed, automatically turning her flank in submission.

Palmer turned and saw the boy called Malfeis rise from his booth in the back. But now he was no longer a boy. The demon stood well over six feet tall, although the curvatue of his spine made him stoop. The demon was covered in coarse brick-red hair, like that of an orangutan, except for his twin-pronged penis. His features were porcine, complete with curving boar's tusks. His feet were cloven.

Malfeis shouldered Sonja and Palmer aside, jabbering in a language that consisted largely of squeals and grunts. He reached behind Jamara and grabbed the succubus's tail, twisting it viciously. Jamara yelped and tried to break free of the demon's grip. Mal propelled the protesting succubus out the door and onto the street. When he turned back around he was a skatepunk again.

"I'm sorry about that. New girl. Actually, she's family. I promised one of my sisters I'd break her in, but I'm afraid it's just not working out."

6

Palmer shifted in his seat and tried to ride out the nicotine fit.

The flight was under six hours and therefore, according to FAA regulations, smoke-free. Palmer could feel the pack of Shermans calling out to him from inside his breast pocket, nestled against his heart like the picture of a loved one.

Sonja Blue sat beside him, mirrored shades in place, nonchalantly paging through an in-flight magazine. His companion was an up-to-date vampire; no crates packed with native earth for her. She believed in traveling first class.

"We should arrive at the airport within the next two hours. Pangloss said he'd have his car there to meet us. I have no reason not to believe him," she said without looking up from an article on Fun-Filled Florida Family Vacations.

Palmer nodded without saying anything. Personally, he considered Sonja's decision to meet with Pangloss something close to suicidal. At first he thought she'd used a devious form of mind-control so he'd agree to come along, like she'd used on the security guards at the airport. The ones who'd demanded that she take the switchblade out of her pocket.

"What switchblade, officers?" she asked, holding up the ornately decorated knife. Her voice had been steady, without a tremor of fear.

"We're terribly sorry, ma'am. Our mistake. Have a nice flight," the security guards said, in unison, doing everything but tugging their forelocks as they backed away.

Palmer wanted to believe that his decision to become involved had been shaped by forces outside himself, that he had no say in what was happening around him, but that would be lying to himself. Like it or not, he needed her.

Disgruntled by where his thoughts were taking him, Palmer glanced at the night sky on the other side of the window and immediately wished he hadn't.

There were *things* sitting on the wing of the airplane.

At first he mistook them for children, although he had no idea what kids would be doing clinging to the aluminum skin of a DC-10, fifty-thousand feet in the air. Then one of the frail figures stood up, unfurling its bat-like wings as it embraced the jet stream, and shot up and away.

No, not children. At least not *human* ones.

There were at least six of the grayish-white creatures crawling up and down the length of the wing, their arms twice as long as their bodies. Their skulls were long and bullet-shaped, the bodies devoid of hair. As Palmer watched the things scuttle along, bellies pressed against the plane's vibrating skin, one by one they surrendered themselves to the winds. He was reminded of children taking turns on a tire swing.

One of the winged things caught some turbulence and struck the side of the plane near Palmer's window. He grimaced, expecting to hear a juicy thump as the creature hit, but there was no sound and no one else seemed to notice, not even Sonja. The thing peeled itself from the fuselage, peering through the window at Palmer.

The eyes were huge, lidless orbs the color of rancid butter that hovered over a tube-like proboscis that hung from the middle of its face. A long, worm-like tongue whipped out of the thing's snout, tasting the reinforced plexiglass that separated it from Palmer. Satisfied that it couldn't get in, the creature began climbing back to the wing.

Palmer could feel cold sweat running down his brow. He tugged on Sonja's sleeve, gesturing to the window. "Am I seeing things?"

Sonja looked up from her magazine and leaned forward, peering into the dark on the other side of the window.

"There's nothing to worry about. They're real."

"Great." He pulled the plastic shade down with trembling fingers. "That's all I need right now."

Sonja shrugged. "They're just *afreeti*, that's all. Nothing to get upset about. They're a form of elemental. They like hitching rides on airplanes. They're harmless, unless you get a couple of warring tribes arguing over who gets to go first. The few humans who've seen them—or had the misfortune to be in a disputed plane—usually mistake them for gremlins."

Palmer wished he could light up. It was a lot easier to tell himself that this was all part of the rich and varied pageant of life if he could soothe his jangling nerves with a double lungful of nicotine.

Sonja was watching him from behind her reflective lenses. She leaned toward him, resting her hand atop his.

"Look, I know what you're going through is tough right now. But, believe me, you get used to it. I remember the first time I started 'seeing things.' I thought I was going nuts! And I didn't have someone to walk me through it, not at first. I didn't know when I saw something if it was real or if I was hallucinating. You've got to watch out for that. The seeing things that *aren't* there bit, I mean. It's some kind of defense mechanism the human brain sets up to protect itself. Most real psychics end up schizophrenic. Only two percent of all active sensitives manage to stay out of the funny farm."

Palmer found himself staring at her hand as it lay atop his own. This was the first time she'd touched him, outside of saving his bewitched butt from the succubus, since their initial, accidental contact two nights ago. He was expecting her touch to be cold and clammy, like that of a corpse, but it wasn't. Actually, it was kind of nice. Suddenly the taste of Jimmy Eichorn's blood flooded his mouth.

He jerked his hand away from hers and stood up stiffly, trying to control the tightness in his throat.

"Uh, yeah. Excuse me a minute, would you? I gotta go to the john."

Palmer screwed his mouth into a bitter grin as he made his way toward the first class cabin's toilet. *Christ, as if my world isn't complicated enough, I've got a goddamned punkette vampire putting the moves on me!* He shook his head in amazement. *Well, I guess it could be worse. I could have the IRS after me.*

Palmer tried the toilet door, found it locked, then noticed the "occupied" sign. Sighing, he folded his arms and glanced back down the aisle, idly scanning the handful of passengers who could afford to fly first class domestic flights.

His gaze momentarily settled on a heavyset man in a rumpled business suit rooting through the contents of an attache case. Wisps of smoke wreathed the business man's frowning face.

What the fuck? I thought this was a non-smoking flight! How come none of these tight-assed little bimbos haven't ragged his ass? This guy on the board of directors? As Palmer stared harder at the florid-faced man, the smoke surrounding his head shifted and roiled, as if coming into sharper definition. Palmer's heart beat faster as he saw the shape crouched on the business man's right shoulder. It looked like a squirrel monkey sketched by a sky-writer and left to the mercies of a strong breeze.

Palmer quickly looked away, uncertain as to what it meant but certain a cigarette would help him deal with it, whatever it was. The rest room door opened and Palmer dived into its solitude without waiting for the previous occupant to completely clear the threshold. His hands were shaking as he slammed the bolt home and pressed his back against the door. Inches from his knees stood the under-sized, uncomfortable airline toilet, its stainless steel bowl beaded with droplets of sky-blue disinfectant.

The equally tiny hand basin bruised his hip as he searched his pockets for a lighter. He glanced up at the smoke detector above his head and scowled.

They make such a big deal about how we shouldn't tamper with these damn things, so that probably means they're pretty easy to fuck up. Still, the last thing I need is to have the bloody thing go off while I'm messing with it. Then all I get for my trouble is a snoot full of CO_2 and a five-hundred-dollar fine slapped on me. Palmer looked at the packet of Shermans liberated from his breast pocket, then back up at the plastic disc dangling over his head like an electronic Sword of Damocles.

Fuck it.

He stuck the cigaretello in his mouth and reached up to disconnect the smoke detector, giving himself a leg-up on the edge of the toilet seat. As he did so, he found himself staring into the shatter-proof mirror mounted over the sink.

Palmer snorted in self-derision. It was just like trying to cop a smoke in the boy's room at Mater Delarosa Junior High back in Akron. His hair was threaded with gray and he wore a tailored black trench coat instead of a school jacket, but essentially there wasn't that much difference between the fourteen-year-old Palmer who'd been suspended for smoking behind the gym and the thirty-nine-year-old preparing to hamstring the smoke detector. Except for the smoke-monkey perched on the adult Palmer's shoulder like Long John Silver's parrot.

"Yaaah!"

Palmer screamed the moment he saw the apparition, losing his balance and plunging one foot into the toilet. The fear he'd experienced at the sight of the smudged gray thing crouched on his shoulder was replaced by the far more practical terror of accidentally being sucked out through the toilet's little trapdoor. Swearing viciously, Palmer yanked himself free, falling against the door with a thump.

"Sir? Sir! Are you all right? Are you hurt? Can you hear me?" It was one of the stewardesses, sounding both solicitous and suspicious.

"I'm all right! Just had an . . . accident, that's all!" Palmer glowered at the dye staining his lower leg. Luckily, his pants and shoes were dark enough to hide the discoloration. He avoided looking in the mirror as he exited the cramped confines of the toilet, smiling sheepishly at the flight attendants grouped outside.

"Please take your seat, sir. We're preparing to make our approach to San Francisco International."

"What in the name of hell is wrong with you?"

"Huh! What?!" Palmer flinched as Sonja snapped

at him. He'd paused to light his cigarette the moment they were free of the jet's confines, only to find himself staring at a grotesquely thin woman—with a huge smoke-monkey the size of a gorilla riding her back—dragging her luggage through the terminal.

The woman seemed oblivious to the gargantua straddling her narrow shoulders. A filtered Pall-Mall was clamped between her cranberry-red lips.

I've heard of "Gorillas in the Mist," but this is the first time I've seen a gorilla made of mist! Palmer bit back a laugh he knew would sound too high-pitched and brittle to be mistaken for sane. He dropped the match cupped in one hand before it had a chance to burn him.

Sonja shook her head in disgust. "Come on, damn it! You'd think you'd never seen a tobacco demon before!"

Pangloss's chauffeur was waiting for them at the exit gate, holding a neatly printed cardboard placard that read *S. Blue*. They were shown to a stretch limo with tinted glass and a fully stocked bar in the back. Sonja hesitated a moment before climbing into the back seat.

"Something wrong, ma'am?" The driver's voice was as smooth and cold as glass.

"No, I was just remembering a limousine drive I took a long time ago."

The moment the door slammed shut behind them, Palmer popped one of his foul smelling cigarettes into his mouth and opened the liquor cabinet. His hands were shaking.

"What's wrong?"

Palmer snorted, expelling a cloud of smoke. "What's *right*? That bastard tried to turn my brains into guacamole dip, and here we are riding in the back of his fuckin' limo! We're walking into a *trap*, for Christ's sake! It might as well have 'T-R-A-P' spelled out in flashing neon letters!"

Sonja sighed and looked out the window. "Don't worry about Pangloss. I can handle him. He's not going to bother you. He got what he wanted. Adding you to his stable was a bonus—a little *lagniappe*."

"You sound real sure of yourself."

"Pangloss is crafty. I don't doubt he's got his own reasons for bringing me into this. But I don't care what they are. The only thing I'm interested in is Morgan."

"That's another thing: who *is* this guy Morgan, and why do you want his head on a spike?"

She glanced at him, the corner of her mouth lifted into a bitter smile.

"Ever hear of Thorne Industrials?"

"Yeah, sure. Old Jacob Thorne's one of the last 'bootstrap' millionaires, like Getty and Carnegie."

"Do you recall a kidnapping involving Thorne's daughter? Her name was Denise."

Palmer frowned and nodded. "Now that you mention it—didn't she disappear sometime during the sixties?"

"No ransom demands were ever made and she was listed as missing. It was a long time back. Over twenty years. Long before they started putting pictures on the back of milk cartons. . . ." Her voice was wistful.

"But what does that have to do with you?"

"In 1969, while on a vacation to London, Denise Thorne met a man who went by the name of Morgan. *Lord* Morgan. The title turned out to be real enough, but Morgan wasn't a man. He coerced Denise Thorne into taking a moonlight drive in his chauffeured limousine. It was all very romantic. Once they were alone, he raped her and drank her blood. He then threw her from the back of the moving car, leaving her for dead. By sheer luck, she was found and taken to the hospital, where she remained in a coma for nine months. Then I woke up."

"You're Denise Thorne." Palmer stared at her, cigarette smoldering, forgotten, between his fingers.

Sonja shrugged. "That is open to debate. But something in me *used* to be Denise Thorne. Perhaps still is." She returned her gaze to the window, staring at the dim outline of Candlestick Park as the limo sped along Highway 101. "There are a lot of things I do not know. But I *do* know one thing: I will send Morgan to hell, even if I have to take him there myself."

Pangloss's hideaway was in one of the older downtown skyscrapers. Dwarfed by Bauhaus-spawned megaliths like the Transamerica Pyramid, the Dobbs Building dwelt in perpetual shadow.

The limo slid into the underground parking garage, depositing its riders before an old-fashioned elevator shaft secured by sliding metal gates. The driver spoke into a hand-mike attached to the radio, and the elevator car descended into view.

Sonja Blue stepped out of the car, signalling for Palmer to follow. The elevator door opened and the protective gates folded back. The elevator operator, an old man in an ill-fitting uniform, gestured for them to enter. The interior of the car smelled of old leather and cigars.

Minutes later the car halted at the penthouse and the doors opened—to reveal the hulking figure of an ogre blocking the way.

The ogre's massive jaw jutted forward, flaring his ape-like nostrils. Palmer recognized him; the last time he'd seen him, he was chomping away on Renfield's left leg like a drumstick.

Palmer rolled his eyes. "I *told* you this was a bad idea."

The ogre's lips peeled back in a rictus grin, revealing teeth better suited for a shark's mouth.

"Keif! Heel! Heel, damn you!"

The ogre moved aside, permitting a narrow-shouldered man in a nondescript suit and tortoiseshell spectacles, a clipboard clutched to his chest, to step forward.

"I'm Doctor Pangloss's assistant. He's in the gymnasium right now. If you'd like to wait . . ."

"I'd like to see him. Now."

The assistant scowled at his clipboard. "I'm afraid that's not possible."

Sonja Blue stepped forward, pushing her face into his. *"Now."*

The assistant's pale face grew even pastier. "Yes. Of course. Permit me to show you the way."

The gymnasium was larger than most of the apartments Palmer had lived in. Parallel bars and other acrobatic equipment were scattered about, while a state-of-the-art Nautilus machine crouched in one corner like a chromium spider. But what held their attention were the two men, dressed in the mesh faceguards and starched white tunics of professional fencers, dueling with sabers in the middle of the room.

As they watched, one of the duelists drove his weapon through his opponent's chest, neatly skewering the tunic's red heart. The wounded fencer, still clutching his saber, staggered backward, staring at the length of cold steel jutting from his breastbone. A dry chuckle emerged from inside the victor's visor as he turned to leave.

The moment his foe's back was turned, the wounded swordsman swung his blade, neatly decapitating his adversary in mid-stride. The head, still encased in the protective faceguard, bounced a couple of times before rolling to a stop near Sonja's right foot.

Pangloss removed his own visor and tossed it aside, motioning for his assistant to pull the saber free of his chest. For the first time Palmer was able to see his erstwhile employer's eyes; they were the color of garnets, bisected by a narrow, reptilian pupil.

"I'm glad that's over and done with! What a bore! Always going on about those scars he got at Heidleberg. Why, I remember when Heidleberg was no more than a wide spot in the road!" He winced as the sword was removed. Blood the color and consistency of transmission fluid spurted briefly from the wound. "Ah! That's much better—it was starting to itch."

"Is there anything else I can do for you, Doctor?"

"That will be all, Renfield. I will see to our guest myself."

"Very good, sir. I'll have Kief dispose of Herr Gruenwald."

Palmer watched the pinch-faced young man exit the room, then swung to face Pangloss. "You called him Renfield!"

"What of it?" replied the vampire as he unfastened the buckles of his tunic.

"Renfield's dead! I saw him die!"

Pangloss sighed and his pupils flexed. "My dear Mr. Palmer, the world is *full* of renfields! Just like it's full of letter openers and paper clips. You don't christen each and every paper clip you use with its own name, do you? The operative our charming Ms. Blue terminated was one of my renfields. Just as you are one of hers."

Palmer felt his face color. "Hold it, buddy, I don't like what you're implying—!"

Sonja raised her hand for silence. "Stop baiting him, Pangloss. You lost out. You should have known something like that would happen when you sent a loose cannon to twist him."

"I prefer the term 'reprogram.' It sounds so much more up-to-date. Don't you agree?"

Sonja snorted and folded her arms across her chest. "I didn't come here to play word games, *herr doktor*."

Pangloss clucked his tongue in disapproval. "The years have not improved your etiquette, my dear. You're just as blunt as ever. I guess that's what comes of being American." He shrugged free of the bloodstained tunic, revealing a hairless chest as pale as milk and covered with the faint traces of hundreds of criss-crossing scars.

The newest wound, the one piercing his heart, was already puckering into pink scar tissue. Palmer thought the vampire's exposed torso looked like a braille road map. Without realizing it, he touched his own chest, tracing his near-fatal flaw. He wondered for a moment if Sonja's flesh was equally scarred, then hastily pushed the thought aside.

Pangloss strode across the room and removed a green silk dressing gown from a peg near the door. "You still cling to certain human conceits, such as the ludicrous idea that time is valuable. You're far too impatient, my dear! When will you realize that time is the one thing you have plenty of? Then again, I forget how young you are. You are indeed a prodigy, my dear. But, in many ways, you are a backward child. Come, let us retire to more amenable surroundings."

As they left the gymnasium, Palmer glanced over his shoulder and saw the ogre, Kief, enter from another door. As he watched, the ogre picked up the severed head of the ill-fated Herr Gruenwald from its resting place on the floor. The ogre shucked the head free of the fencing mask and grinned, revealing hideous teeth, and lifted the dead man's skull to its mouth. Palmer looked away, but he could still hear. It sounded just like someone biting into a big, crisp apple.

Marble art deco nymphs flanked the hearth while a panther carved from a single piece of obsidian crouched on the mantelpiece. There was a fire burning behind the ornate iron screen, but Palmer couldn't feel it. Perhaps it was just the notorious San Francisco Bay damp getting to him, but he doubted it.

Pangloss stood at the picture window, his back to his guests. The fog was heavy, obscuring what little view was available at two in the morning. The swirling gray mist reminded Palmer of the tobacco demons he'd seen earlier, so he returned his gaze to the fireplace.

"You said you know where Morgan is."

Pangloss glanced back over his shoulder. "I do."

"Well?"

"I would rather speak to you in private. Shall we retire to the patio?" Pangloss gestured to the sliding glass door that opened onto a rooftop garden.

Sonja glanced at Palmer, then nodded her assent. She followed the elder vampire onto the fog-enshrouded terrace. The sea air was sharp in her nostrils, reminding her of blood. The Other's voice stirred inside her head, admonishing her for having subsisted for so long on nothing but bottled plasma. She tried to ignore it; this was neither the time or the place for the Other's yammering to put her off guard. Pangloss was dangerous. She'd learned that the hard way over a decade ago.

Pangloss stood with his hands clasped behind his

back, staring into the fog bank. "You've changed, my dear. Matured. I noticed it the moment I laid eyes on you. You're not as angry as you used to be."

"Me used to be angry young man, me hidin' me head in the sand."

"Beg pardon?"

"Let's just say I've discovered how to work within the system since the last time we met. I've learned to . . . focus myself. Enough idle chatter, Pangloss. Now, about Morgan . . ."

Pangloss turned to face her, and for a brief moment she was looking at an unwrapped mummy with red coals banked deep in its empty orbits. The vampire reached into the voluminous pockets of its dressing gown and retrieved an ivory cigarette holder with dry twig fingers. The first time she'd glimpsed Pangloss's true self she'd come close to screaming. But now, fifteen years later, his desiccated appearance seemed almost normal.

"Ah, yes . . . Morgan. It always comes back to Morgan, doesn't it?" His voice was melancholy. "He was my greatest mistake, just as you are his. However, in my case I created him with full knowledge of what I was doing. Or so I thought." Pangloss frowned and his features were once more those of a handsome man in his early middle-age. "It can be lonely for beings such as you and I. I'm certain you've discovered this for yourself by now. Alliances with humans are, by their very nature, destined to be brief.

"Speaking of which, I congratulate you on claiming Palmer as your renfield. He's much better spoken than that piece of trash you picked up in London. Tell me, does he still imagine himself the captain of his own will?"

"That's none of your damn business!"

Pangloss held up a hand in supplication. "You're

quite right, my dear! That *was* rude of me! Now, where was I? Ah, yes. When I was younger—younger than I am now—I longed for companionship. At the time, I fancied myself quite ancient—I was seven or eight hundred years old, which means it must have been either the eleventh or twelfth century. I was the same age as Morgan is now, if that means anything.

"I had grown bored and wished to have an equal as a companion. Since I was forced to recruit from serfs and peasants, with the occasional yeoman thrown in, the basic templates were far from the first quality. Most of my broodlings were unsuited for any intellectual pursuits beyond hunting down their next meal. Then I met Morgan.

"At that point, I was working for the Church as a gelder. The choir masters sent their most promising sopranos to me for alteration into *castrati*. I was renowned for having a low mortality rate, at least by the standards of the day. It was a good cover, allowing me access to the byzantine jealousies and in-fighting created when human sexuality is subverted. I fed well at the Vatican's expense for the better part of twenty years. But Morgan's arrival changed all that.

"He was only twelve when I first saw him, but I knew I had found what I had been searching for. He was the fifth son of a nobleman and had been forced into joining the Church. The original intention was for him to become a priest, but his excellent singing voice had drawn the attention of the choir master. Instead of castrating the boy, I took him with me when I abandoned my identity.

"It was the closest I had come to experiencing genuine passion since my resurrection.

"Morgan accepted me for what I was. His intellect was astounding and he proved himself an apt pupil.

We traveled Europe in the guise of uncle and nephew for several years. He longed to be transfigured, but I withheld my benediction until I was certain he was seasoned enough to survive the change intact. When he was thirty, I remade him in my image.

"My faith in his innate superiority was justified. Within ten years of his resurrection, Morgan had evolved beyond the crude revenant stage. I was proud of him! For two centuries he was my constant companion. I was his brood-master, but I never abused my status. I allowed him far more liberty than I've granted any of my by-blows, before or since. In the end it cost me dearly.

"Morgan turned against me. I'd underestimated the strength of his will. And his guile. He came close to killing me—just as you did." Pangloss opened his robe and pointed at a long, ragged scar in the middle of his chest. Although she knew the wound had to be at least ten years old, it still looked fresh. "I nearly died from that silver blade of yours. It still hurts, even now."

"If you're expecting me to feel guilty, forget it."

"I know better than to expect pity from you, or from any of our ilk."

"So why are you telling me this?"

Pangloss's smile was bitter. "When you love someone as much as I loved Morgan, and find that emotion betrayed . . . You see, my dear, I hate him as much as you do. And for far better reasons. It is in my interest that Morgan's plan be foiled."

"Plan?"

The elder vampire chuckled, shaking his head in admiration. "The fool's ambition is boundless, if nothing else. He is plotting on revolutionizing Pretender society, although I'm uncertain as to how he expects to do so. Something about creating an army of silver-immune vampires."

"Don't you know anything else?"

"He's screened himself quite well. It took me five years to trace him to this city."

"Here? You mean he's *here*? In San Francisco?" Sonja felt her stomach knot. She'd been hunting for so long, traveling the world in search of the vampire who had made her into something beyond human. To be told that she was in the same city with him, after twenty years . . .

"He's operating under deep cover. Has been for well over a decade. I don't know what name—or face—he's wearing, but I have succeeded in tracking down the name of someone who does. His name is Russell Howard, a human real estate agent. He knows who—and what—Morgan is. I suggest you start your inquiry with him."

"Why me? Why are you telling me this? If what Morgan is planning on doing will disrupt the nature of things in the Real World, why aren't the other vampire nobles taking an interest in what's going on?"

Pangloss grimaced as if he'd sipped tainted blood. "The ruling class—those known as the Combine—are convinced his efforts are folly, that he's gone mad. It happens sometimes—vampiric senile dementia. But they don't know Morgan as I do. They are too preoccupied with their own blood-feuds and atrocity exhibitions. I can understand Morgan's disgust with their narrow-mindedness, but what he's proposing . . . It's too dangerous. For both the human *and* the Real World! What is required is a free agent, such as yourself. You're unorthodox, but no one can deny your effectiveness. And what better weapon to turn against Morgan than one of his own making?"

"Flattery will get you nowhere, *herr doktor*. I still don't see why you haven't intervened if Morgan's scheme is so damned hazardous to your health. Unless you're afraid of him."

The vampire's smile faltered.

"I know you're scared of Morgan, just as I know you're scared of me. You've been frightened of me since you first saw me. Why is that, *Herr* Pangloss?" Sonja removed her mirrored glasses. "What is it you see when you look at me?"

There was loathing in the old vampire's wine-red gaze, but he did not avert his eyes. "I don't know. And that's what scares me."

7

Pangloss's driver dropped them off at their hotel, a couple of blocks from the famed dragon gates of Chinatown. The place catered largely to students and Asian businessmen, so it was both inexpensive and clean. As they exited the back of the limousine, a homeless person shuffled forward, gesturing and muttering unintelligibly.

The old man, dressed in several layers of cast-off clothing, his feet wrapped in old newspaper like dead fish, looked no different than others of his kind. He smelled of piss and cheap wine and reminded Palmer of a cross between his Uncle Willy and a pigeon. Yet Sonja seemed genuinely startled by the old man and hurried past him into the lobby. Perplexed by this unaccustomed display of fear, Palmer glanced back at the ragged figure as it returned to the fog-shrouded doorway it had shambled from. In the diffused light from the street lamp, the old man's eyes glinted gold.

By the time he reached the front desk in the lobby, Sonja was once more in control of herself. The night clerk, an elderly Chinese gentleman who moved with the grace of a *tai chi* master, did not seem terribly surprised by their unconventional appearances. After all, it was San Francisco.

Sonja asked for and received connecting single

rooms. Palmer would have preferred separate floors, but said nothing.

After he'd stowed his suitcase in the shallow closet behind the door, there was a light rapping on the connecting door. He opened it halfway.

"What is it?"

"We need to talk."

Palmer glanced at his wristwatch. It was close to four in the morning and here she was, wanting to talk. He'd once fancied himself a night owl, but now he realized his previous estimation of his nocturnal stamina had been naive.

"About this Morgan guy?"

"That, and what Pangloss told me."

Palmer grunted. "Okay. But let me get cleaned up first, okay? I feel like a pile of dirty laundry."

"You got a point there."

"I know. That's why my mama made me wear a hat."

She laughed, and Palmer liked the sound of it. That disturbed him.

Twenty minutes later, after toweling his bristling mane dry and slipping into a clean pair of jeans and a loose-fitting sweater, Palmer knocked on the door between their rooms.

"Sonja?"

No answer.

He knocked a little louder, and this time the door swung open on its hinge.

"Uh, Sonja?"

Palmer stepped over the threshold, squinting into the darkness. From what little he could see, Sonja's room was identical to his, only reversed. Not yet adapted to the gloom, he jarred his hip against the dresser bureau opposite the double bed. Cursing under his breath, Palmer looked up, expecting to see his grimacing face reflected in the mirror. Instead, he found himself staring at a blanket. He touched the bed linen draped over the upright mirror.

Vampires cast no reflection.

It was one of the rules he remembered from the movies of his childhood. The films his father had condemned as junk and Palmer had consumed with uncritical eagerness and a sense of wonder so sincere it bordered on epiphany.

For a brief moment he could see his old room, circa 1965, in all its preadolescent glory. He could smell the chemical stink of airplane glue as the Aurora models of Hollywood monsters dried on his desk. He could glimpse the stacks of *Famous Monsters of Filmland* and well-thumbed *Dr. Strange* comic books stashed in the back of his closet. The flashback was so sharp, so immediate, Palmer had to steady himself. His hand dropped to the top of the dresser and touched something smooth and cold. His fingers closed on the object before he realized what he'd done.

She left her glasses.

It felt weird, standing there holding her sunglasses. They were so much a part of her, it was like he'd stumbled across her severed ear, like in that movie.

"Don't turn around."

Her voice was at his shoulder. She'd come up right behind him without his being aware of it. Sweat broke out on his brow and upper lip. He wondered what her eyes looked like. He recalled Pangloss's reptilian, red-rimmed pupils and how they'd flexed, and fought to repress a shudder.

Sonja's bare arm reached around and plucked the glasses from his grip. He could hear the quick rustle of material as she pulled on her robe.

"Okay, it's safe to look now."

Palmer turned around just as she switched on the

lamp next to the bed. The vampire sat with her back against the headboard, her legs curled under her like a cat. She was wearing the same kimono he'd seen in New Orleans. Her hair, still damp from the shower, was plastered against her milk-pale forehead like feathers. She was beautiful and she scared him.

"Sorry I walked in on you like that. I knocked . . ."

"Forget about it." She motioned for him to be seated in the room's only chair.

"Uh, you said you wanted to talk?" Unsure of what else he could do, he lit a Shermans.

Palmer alternately blew smoke rings and frowned while she told him what Pangloss had said about Morgan being somewhere in the city and his connection with the real estate agent.

"So, do you think we can trust Pangloss?"

"Trust him? No. But I believe him."

"So. What's all this happy crappy about the Real World and Pretenders?"

"I think you already have some idea as to that."

"Yeah, well, sure—but I'm new to this. I don't know the rules, or even if there are any."

Sonja sighed and looked into the far corner, as if watching something. She was still staring absently at the shadows when she spoke. "Humans think they know what reality is, what life's about. They think they know because they can think. 'I think therefore I know.' Their attitude is 'I'm at the top of the food chain, so I get to decide what's real and what's not.'

"What they don't want to be simply doesn't exist. Except, perhaps, in their dreams. Or nightmares. So they end up watching the shadows on the wall of the cave, thinking that's how the world *really* is. They never look at the things throwing the shadows. Or, if they do look, they don't *see* them. Most humans are both separated from and yet a part of the Real

World. Pretenders are, well, they're the ultimate predators. It's a generic term, really. It just means they're capable of passing for human. Like vampires, ogres, succubi, incubi and *vargr* . . ."

"The what?"

"Werewolves," she explained. "And then there are the seraphim, like the old man on the curb."

Palmer remembered the way the homeless person's eyes had seemed to burn like newly minted gold coins. "Are these Sara Lees, or what have you, dangerous?"

"Hard to say exactly *what* they are. One saved my life once. Take that for what you will."

There was a lull in the conversation and Palmer was suddenly, uncomfortably aware he was sitting in a hotel room with a good-looking, half-naked woman.

"Look, it's late and I'm not really used to staying up all night and sleeping all day." He moved to leave, but Sonja reached out and took his hand in hers.

"You don't have to leave."

Palmer wanted to go. He wanted to slam the door between his room and hers and barricade it with furniture. But part of him also wanted to stay. He looked down at her and saw his worried, embarrassed face reflected in her shades.

Jesus, do I really look that fucking neurotic? No wonder Loli nailed me as a sucker.

"I'm sorry if I frighten you. I don't mean to. But sometimes it's so hard to control . . ." She smiled then; it was as sad and delicate a gesture as he'd ever seen. "It's just that I get so lonely. And sometimes I need to be reminded what it's like . . ." She looked away and dropped his hand. She didn't have to finish the sentence because Palmer could hear it in his head. He wasn't sure if it was telepathy or simple empathy.

And sometimes I need to be reminded what it's like to be human.

"Look, Sonja, it's not that I don't—"

"Go." She refused to look at him. "Just go."

Palmer obeyed, uncertain as to what he wanted. Within ten minutes he was in his bed and sound asleep. He didn't hear her leave.

Sonja Blue left the hotel dressed in her faded jeans and leather jacket. She struck out toward Chinatown, scaling the steep hill with strong, purposeful strides. It would be another hour or so before dawn; still plenty of time for hunting.

She passed the dragon gate that marked the district's entrance; the shaggy-browed creatures with their trailing moustaches reminded her of the dragon decorating the hilt of her switchblade.

Grant Avenue was deserted, although she knew that by five o'clock the local merchants would start arriving to prepare their shops for another business day. Soon the narrow sidewalks would be crowded with wooden bins filled with exotic oriental vegetables, golden-skinned ducks dangling in the storefronts. The businesses hawking cheap electronic gadgets and knick-knacks from the Far East would not open their doors until well after dawn, but Sonja would have finished her hunt long before then.

You should have made him do it. After all, he owes it to you. You saved his life.

She grimaced and tried to ignore the Other's words. She knew all too well what would happen if she weakened and let it have its way. She paused, sniffing the chill morning air. She could hear the distant thrumming of the cable car track and, fainter still, the ringing of church bells.

Every doorway she passed sheltered a lumpy form, wrapped in discarded clothing and old trash. One housed a family of four; the weary parents squatting on the lower steps while their children slept on a pallet of folded cardboard. The woman watched her pass with tired, fearful eyes.

She paused and sniffed again. The scent was strong. She was close. Very close. She ducked into a narrow alley. The walkway was littered with aluminum trash cans filled with garbage. Apparently the Soon Luck restaurant didn't believe in separating their bottles and cans. The odor was nearly overpowering enough to mask the scent she'd been following. But not quite.

The *vargr* rose from its hiding place amongst the jumbled garbage containers, growling a warning at the intruder who had dared to interrupt its meal. The werewolf stood almost six feet tall, although its curved spine and crooked legs made it seem even taller. The pointed, vulpine snout curled into a menacing snarl, exposing sharp teeth stained with fresh blood and flecked with flesh and gristle. Sonja spied the savaged remains of a bag lady—a real one this time—at its taloned feet. The beast's russet pelt bristled, raising hackles along its back. The *vargr*'s thin, pointed penis slid from its furred pouch in ritual challenge.

Sonja Blue hissed, unsheathing her fangs. The werewolf looked confused.

"C'mon, Rin-Tin-Tin! Whassamatter, furball? You too lapdog to take on someone your own size?" She knew she was being foolhardy. She'd only tangled with one or two *vargr* before. They were as dangerous as the more advanced vampires, although they lacked psychic powers. Physically, though, they were incredibly powerful and close to immortal. She wondered what the hell she was trying to prove to herself.

The werewolf stepped forward, tossing aside the fifty-gallon garbage cans as if they were nine-pins. The beast reeked like a wet dog. Sonja palmed the switchblade and pressed the ruby stud in the dragon's eye. The *vargr* halted at the sight of the silver knife.

Sonja launched herself at the hesitant werewolf, knocking it to the ground. The *vargr* gave a yelp of surprise. The two opponents wrestled on the filthy bricks, knocking over even more garbage cans. Startled rats scurried for cover, their meals interrupted, while the werewolf and the vampire battled.

Sonja, already bleeding from a score of cuts from the beast-man's talons, cried out as the *vargr* sank its teeth into her shoulder, worrying her like a dog's chew toy. She stabbed blindly at her attacker and was rewarded by a yowl of pain and the smell of bile. She pulled herself free and staggered away from the wounded *vargr*. The bite on her shoulder had weakened her more than she realized.

Just before she fainted she saw the *vargr* hurrying down the alleyway. He was on the verge of reverting to his human persona, and the way he was hunched over told her he was trying to keep his intestines from spilling out.

When she opened her eyes again it was to find a strange man kneeling over her. She'd passed out propped against the alley wall. Her glasses were still on and the man could not see she was awake.

He reached into her jacket and removed her wallet. The man seemed pleased by the amount of money in the bill folder. He chuckled to himself. It was obvious he thought she was dead. He leaned forward again, in search of more loot.

She'd lost a lot of blood. She needed blood to heal.

The man looked genuinely surprised when the dead woman grabbed his shirt front, pulling him closer. Then there was only fear.

8

Russell Howard was a self-satisfied man. He was only thirty-seven, but already well on his way to becoming a multi-millionaire. Seven years ago he was a struggling real estate agent, handling third- and fourth-rate rental properties on the wrong side of Army.

Now he had a Lamborghinni with its very own phone and fax machine. His office took up half of the fifteenth floor of a spanking-new high rise in the Embarcadero; his clients were some of the wealthiest in the Bay Area, if not the state; and his name and face often graced the *Chronicle*'s society pages. Yes, Russell Howard was on his way to big things.

Thanks to his oh-so-silent partner.

Howard didn't like to think too much about his partner. It tended to make his palms sweat and his brain itch. Sometimes it even gave him nightmares. But if there was anything he'd learned from life, it was that money solved everything; and even if his problems didn't exactly disappear, at least they left him alone.

Howard sat in his wing-backed swivel chair and watched the shadows lengthen as the sun set. He'd just finished a late afternoon conference with a client and was contemplating calling his wife and telling her he'd be home late. He did not know the elevator was on its way to the fifteenth floor, carrying two visitors. And even if he had been aware of it, he would not have cared.

He occasionally read Dr. Seuss books to his three-year-old, Kristin, before she went to bed. Right now her favorite was *Yertle the Turtle*. The symbolism was lost on him.

The secretary looked up from her word processor to see two strangers, a man and a woman, enter the reception area. She frowned and glanced down at the calendar on her desk. It showed no more appointments scheduled for that day.

"May I help you?"

The man spoke first. "We're here to see Mr. Howard."

"Do you have an appointment?" she asked, her voice dripping icicles as she eyed his outlandish haircut.

"No. But he'll see us anyway." This from the woman in the leather jacket and mirrored glasses.

"I'm afraid that's not possible. Mr. Howard is a very busy man and—"

"It's time to go home."

The secretary stared dumbly at the woman in sunglasses for a heartbeat, then got up and switched off the word processor, snugged a plastic cover over the electric typewriter, retrieved her purse from its place in the filing cabinet, and marched out the door.

The sound of the outer door slamming shut brought Russell Howard from his office. He stared in surprise at the two strangers for a second before looking for his secretary.

"Where's Patricia?"

"She had to go home. Something came up all of a sudden. Besides, it's late. You work her too hard."

Howard was uncertain whether to be frightened or offended by the strange man and woman. They looked like they belonged on MTV or the back of an album cover instead of his reception area. The man seemed to be in his late thirties, dressed in faded jeans, a dark bulky sweater, and a black raincoat. His hair, while relatively short, was wiry and stood straight up from his head like he'd received a jolt of electricity. A profusion of gray frosted his temples and his chin was bisected by a narrow width of beard that made him look like a punk pharaoh.

The woman was much younger, wearing reflective sunglasses, tight-fitting jeans, steel-tipped boots, and a battered leather jacket over a Dead Kennedys t-shirt. Her dark, unruly hair made her look like an exotic bird.

"Who are you people? What do you want?"

The woman stepped forward. There was something familiar in the way she moved, but he couldn't place it. "My name is Sonja Blue, Mr. Howard. My . . . associate is Mr. Palmer. As to what we want—all we want is information, Mr. Howard. Information I have reason to believe you can provide." She motioned to the filing cabinets lining the wall. "Check 'em out."

Palmer nodded and began rifling Howard's files as if he worked there.

Howard's face had gone to the color of a ripe tomato. "You can't do that! I'm calling the police!"

Sonja Blue clucked her tongue reproachfully. "Now, that's not a very nice thing to do, is it?" She took another step closer to the realtor. He could see his own outraged features, twisted and twinned, reflected in her glasses. Menace oozed from her like an expensive French perfume. "Why don't you tell me where Morgan is, Mr. Howard?"

Howard's heart iced over. Now he knew why

she'd seemed so familiar; it was the way she handled herself, the way she talked, her mannerisms those of a creature impervious to threats and accustomed to power. Just like his partner.

He made a strange gargling noise that sounded like a deaf-mute's attempt at speech. He tried to slam the door on her, but she moved too fast for him. He stumbled backward into his spacious office with its muted pastel color schemes and trendy halogen light fixtures, his eyes riveted on the woman as she advanced on him. He could not look away from her. He remembered stories he'd heard as a child of snakes hypnotizing birds into their open jaws. When she grabbed him, it was with the speed and precision of a cobra striking.

She jerked him forward by his yellow silk power-tie and thrust her pale, ice-maiden's face into his own. He saw himself in her glasses again; this time his skin oozed beads of sweat like tiny pearls of mercury. She smiled, revealing canines as white as new bone and sharper than hypodermics. Howard moaned.

"I see Pangloss wasn't lying about your connection with Morgan. Most encouraging." Sonja Blue yanked harder on Howard's tie. He was suddenly aware that his feet had nearly cleared the floor and that he could no longer breathe.

Sonja dragged the strangling realtor around the desk and dumped him unceremoniously in his chair. Howard gasped and coughed and tried to free his neck of the power-tie cum garrotte. The windsor knot he'd done that morning was now the size of a small pea and could not be budged. The realization that he would have to destroy the eighty-dollar tie in order to get it off was enough to make him forget his predicament.

Sonja Blue walked back around the desk—an impressive walnut job the size of a pool table—and came to rest in one of the chairs he reserved for clients. This apparent resumption of the power structure Howard was familiar with triggered something instinctual in him: he automatically sat upright, attempted to straighten his ruined tie, and put on his best angry tycoon face.

"Now see here, whoever you are! I won't stand for this! How dare you come into my office and threaten me in such a manner!" He reached for the multi-line telephone on his right. "I'm calling security right this minute!"

"Touch that phone, and I will tear your fingers, one by one, from your hands. Is that understood?"

Howard blanched and let the receiver drop back into its cradle. "What do you want?"

"I've already *told* you. I want Morgan's address and the name he's using." When Howard remained silent, she sighed and crossed her legs. "Mr. Howard, you know what I am. You know what I am capable of. I *could* pop your memory open like a raw cauliflower and get my information *that* way. However, such measures are drastic and not necessarily effective. It would also lower your I.Q. by more than a hundred points, and I have serious doubts as to you escaping unimpaired."

"I can't tell you anything."

"You mean you *won't*."

Howard pulled a monogrammed linen handkerchief from his breast pocket and mopped his forehead, his hands shaking. "He'll kill me."

"So will I, Mr. Howard, if you don't tell me what I want to know."

"Look, I haven't done anything—"

"You traffick with monsters, Mr. Howard. Four hundred years ago you would have ended up in the hands of the Inquisition, your feet stuffed into iron boots full of molten lead. I am far more reasonable than Torquemada. If not as patient. Tell me what your connection is to Morgan."

"It's nothing important."

Sonja sighed again. "Mr. Howard, Lord Morgan would not bother to become involved with a dreary little human such as yourself unless you serve some purpose useful to him."

Howard shifted his weight on his buttocks, unhappy with his situation. "Look, he gives me money, okay? He's what's called a silent partner. He gives me money, I buy and manage properties for him. Nothing illegal about that."

"Indeed."

"I also find places for him to stay. He moves around a lot, okay? Never stays anywhere more than six months. There's nothing wrong with that, is there?"

"No. Nothing at all." It was obvious from her voice that she was thinking. Howard didn't want to know about what.

"Sonja?"

Palmer stood in the doorway, holding aloft a fat manila file folder. When Howard saw it he felt his guts knot into a sheepshank. Sonja took the file and began flipping through the documents inside, occasionally lifting her head to study Howard with her impassive mirrored gaze. It did not take more than the most cursory of glances to realize that the properties in question were in the worst sectors of Oakland. Howard patted his forehead with the damp handkerchief.

"Well." Sonja closed the folder and handed it back to Palmer, returning her full attention to Howard. "Things are starting to make sense. Those are the 'properties' you purchased and manage for your partner?"

Howard nodded weakly. "Look, I can explain—"

"I'm sure you can. But you needn't bother. I

understand all too well. Not all vampires are blood-suckers. Only the more primitive species feed in that manner. Vampires as old and as powerful as Lord Morgan require far more refined sustenance. They feed on human despair, hate, fear, anger, frustration, greed, cruelty, madness . . . And what better breeding ground than some festering hell-hole of a slum; where rats bite babies, old women are murdered for their social security checks, pregnant women smoke crack, children are abused, women are raped and beaten by both strangers and the men they love?" She smacked her lips and patted her belly in a broad parody of hunger. "That's good eating!"

Palmer snorted in disgust. "Fuckin' traitor!"

Sonja nodded in agreement and leaned forward, fixing Howard with her unseen stare. "Do you know what humans such as yourself are called? By the Pretending races, I mean, not your own species. No? You, Mr. Howard, are a bellwether. Some would prefer the term judas goat. Bellwethers willingly lead their fellow humans onto the killing floor, in exchange for a reward from the butchers. Bellwethers like to think themselves immune. But all that means is that, once their usefulness is at an end, they are the last of the sheep to die."

"He—he's staying in a place near the Marina. Where they're rebuilding from the quake."

It did not surprise her that Morgan would make his nest close to a scene of destruction and suffering. The psychic after-effects of a catastrophe would be as invigorating as sea air for such a creature.

"And his name?"

"I'm getting to that. He goes by the name of Caron. Dr. Joad Caron."

Palmer and Sonja exchanged glances. "*Doctor?*"

"Yeah, he's a shrink."

"Jesus H. Christ!" Palmer turned around and

walked out of the room. He had enough of Russell Howard to last him several lifetimes.

Howard decided it was time for him to make his move. The woman was preoccupied, staring off into space. He slowly reached for the drawer where he kept his gun. If he was lucky, he could get the drop both on her and the middle-aged punk in the front office. He'd learned enough about what the bitch called Pretenders to know that a bullet in the brain killed them as dead as humans.

It would look funny to the cops, but he could claim they were hopped-up crack addicts he'd surprised in the act of ransacking his office. Yeah, that would wash. If there was too much of a fuss, Morgan could pull a few strings—or whatever the hell it was he pulled—and quiet things down. Like he had during the Harvey Milk fiasco.

He felt the cool metal grip of the chrome-plated pistol as his fingers wrapped around it. Yeah, it would be easy. Easy as shooting clay pigeons.

Sonja Blue leapt onto the desk, snarling like a leopard freed from its cage. It happened so fast it seemed as if she'd materialized out of thin air; one second she was sitting in a chair three feet away, the next she was squatting in front of him like a desktop gargoyle. She crouched on her haunches, her arms bent and hands splayed across the expensive walnut finish. Her head was thrust forward, reminding Howard of an attack dog straining on its leash. The cockatoo crest on her head bristled like a wolf's hackle. Howard wet himself.

She jerked the gun out of his unresisting hand, studying it with mild distaste. A .22 automatic. She barked a humorless laugh as she turned the toy-like weapon over in her hands. "You'd have to do better than that, buddy. I've metabolized more .22 slugs than Carter's has Little Liver Pills!" She hopped off the desk, leaving deep scratches in the six layers of lacquered finish. After a moment's contemplation, she tossed the gun back to its owner.

Howard was too surprised to do more than ham-handedly catch it. He stared at the gun, then back at her. He set the weapon aside. He realized there was no way, even at such close range, he would be able to shoot her and still live.

"You're holding out on me, Howard."

The realtor shook his head vigorously in denial. "I swear I've told you everything I know about Morgan. What else do you want?"

"The truth."

"I *told* you the truth!"

"Not all of it. You told me what identity Morgan is operating under, yes, and where I can find him. But not where his lair is."

"*Lair?*"

"Yes, lair. Lion's have them. Bank robber's have them. Every king vampire has one. It is a place where they can retreat to, without fear of attack."

"Look, I told you he lives in the Marina area, somewhere off Fillmore . . ."

Sonja shook her head. "He moves every six months or so—you said so yourself. This place you mentioned is a nest, nothing more. I want to know where he can be found when he goes to ground."

"I told you everything—"

"Pick up the gun, Mr. Howard."

The crisp, surgical steel civility was back in her voice. Without wanting to, Howard picked up the discarded .22 by its muzzle.

"Place your left hand on top of the desk, Mr. Howard. That's right. Now spread your fingers. Yes, like that. Now wider."

Howard stared in horrified silence as his left hand did as it was told.

"Now, hit your left hand with the butt of the gun. Hard."

Howard emitted a strangled cry of pain and terror as the butt of the automatic smashed into the middle of his hand. His fingers writhed, but he still could not move his left hand no matter how hard he tried.

"Again."

Another powerful, hammer-like blow. Howard felt something like a green twig break in the middle of his palm. He tasted blood and realized he'd bitten through his lower lip.

"Where is Morgan's lair?"

Howard whimpered.

This time the pistol smashed the knuckle of his index finger. Howard wondered if he would pass out before every finger on his left hand splintered. He was afraid he wouldn't.

"If you do not tell me what I want to know, Mr. Howard, I will make you pistol-whip your right hand with what remains of your left one. Then, if you're still being uncooperative, I will have you start on your left hand all over again."

"Ghost Trap."

"Beg pardon?"

"Ghost Trap!"

The vampire looked genuinely puzzled.

"It's the name of a house, somewhere out in the Sonoma Valley. Supposed to be haunted or something. Some crazy millionaire built it back before the Depression." Howard's face was the same shade of yellow as his tie. Sweat dripped from the end of his nose in greasy drops. "That's all I know about it. I swear." Tears leaked from the corners of the realtor's eyes. "Jesus, isn't that enough? Please go away. Go away and leave me alone."

"Very well. I see no reason to prolong our visit. But remember, Mr. Howard—you cannot shake hands with the Devil and not get sulphur on your sleeve." With that, she turned and disappeared into the reception area. A second later he heard the door to the outer office shut.

Howard slumped forward, cradling his head in his good hand. He was shivering and sweating and stank of fear and urine. Part of him wanted to leap up and chase after the intruders, pistol blazing. But then he remembered the hissing, needle-toothed face thrust into his own slack, well-fed one, and his heart beat so fast it seemed to stand still.

He found himself glancing at his Rolex. Only fifteen minutes had elapsed since the moment he first saw the strangers in his reception room. Fifteen minutes. One quarter of an hour. That was all it had taken to ruin the last seven years of his life. Howard picked up the automatic by the grip this time, although it was sticky with his blood.

Morgan would find out. He had no doubt about that. Although Howard was without religion or faith, he knew there was a Devil. He knew it was a certainty rare amongst even the most devout ecclesiastes. And no matter how fearsome and cruel the creature that called itself Sonja Blue had been, he knew Morgan would be a thousand times worse.

"Don't you think we were a little hard on that guy?" Palmer asked as they waited for the elevator.

Sonja angled her head in his direction, but because of the glasses, Palmer was uncertain as to whether she was looking at him or down the hall.

She shrugged. "He is a bellwether. A traitor to the species."

"Yeah, but maybe he didn't really know what Morgan was."

"Oh, he knew. He knew all too well. Just as the president knows what's held in check within the walls of the Pentagon. He simply found it advantageous to pretend otherwise. He does not even have a renfield's excuse of having been twisted against his will."

The elevator arrived empty. As Palmer stepped into the car he heard a muffled report from the direction of Russell Howard's office. He looked at Sonja, who shrugged yet again.

"No matter how far up a sheep climbs, it will never get beyond the killing floor."

9

"Are you sure this is the right address?"

Sonja nodded. "It's the only 'Dr. J. Caron' listed in the phone book. What's the matter? You weren't expecting a gothic castle with gargoyles and a moat, were you?"

"No, but I thought it'd look, you know, *different* somehow."

Sonja gazed at the building across the street from the rental car. She didn't want to admit it, but she'd been expecting something different, too. The surrounding houses reflected the Mediterranean revival architecture popular in the 1920s; the low, pastel-colored single family dwellings lining the curving streets hardly looked like the kind of neighborhood to shelter a lord of the undead.

In the gathering dusk healthy-looking men and women, outfitted in expensive jogging clothes with Walkman earphones clamped to their heads, shared the streets with people walking their dogs. A few blocks over newer, no doubt even more expensive, buildings were being erected on the site of property damaged by the '89 quake. She had a hard time picturing Morgan strolling down to the corner grocery for a six-pack of Calistoga Water and a package of squid-ink pasta.

"Wait a minute! Someone's coming out. Is that him?"

Sonja stared at the middle-aged man standing silhouetted on the front porch. He was dressed in a charcoal gray suit cinched by old-fashioned leather suspenders. The suit jacket hung over one forearm. His hair was graying at the temples and pulled into a brief ponytail, his eyes shaded by lightly tinted aviator glasses.

She closed her eyes and pictured him as he'd appeared twenty years ago; a debonair jet-set English playboy bent on a wild weekend in Swinging London. His strong, Cary Grant-like features rippled, revealing glowing eyes and sharp fangs. She could hear the sound of his laughter as he forced her to take his cold member into her mouth. She pulled herself free of the memory before she relived the agony of simultaneous penetration.

She was shivering and her breathing had grown ragged. Palmer stared at her.

"You all right?"

"It's him." She was surprised how hard it was for her to even speak. She felt strangely feverish. She'd spent the better part of two decades looking for this creature, and all she could do was stare at him. Now was her chance. She could leap out of the car and nail him before he had time to reach the Ferarri parked in the drive. But all she did was shiver and gasp like a malaria victim. It felt as if her marrow had been replaced with lead.

Morgan got into his sportscar and pulled out into traffic. If he glanced in their direction, neither Sonja nor Palmer noticed it. The minute the Ferarri disappeared around the corner, the lassitude gripping Sonja loosened.

"Do you need to go to the hospital? You looked like you were going into shock."

She shook her head angrily, more to clear herself of the paralysis than to deny she needed help. "I'm okay now . . . I was afraid something like that would happen."

"What do you mean?"

"Morgan created me. Part of me—the vampiric self—was made in his image. I'm a member of his brood. The minute I saw him, I wanted to kill him. And I couldn't *move*! It was like someone had thrown a switch, shutting off my nervous system."

"You mean you were hypnotized?"

"It was more like my self-preservation instinct had been triggered. Some part of my brain considered killing Morgan the same as killing myself."

"Are you saying you can't lift a hand against this guy?"

"No!" Her denial was harsher and louder than it needed to be. She winced and fought to regain control of her temper. "It's a matter of will. That's how Morgan broke free of his own creator, Pangloss. He proved himself to have the stronger will."

"What about you?"

She shrugged. "I'll find that one out the hard way. Okay, since we're here and we know the monster of the house is out, what do you say to a little visit?"

Palmer sighed and pulled a leather wallet from his raincoat pocket. He flipped it open, displaying his collection of lock twirls.

Sonja grinned. "I like a man who's prepared."

It only took a few seconds for Palmer to pick the lock on the front door. He hesitated before opening it, gesturing to the sticker affixed to one of the windowpanes set into the door face.

Warning! This house protected by Phelegethon Home Security Systems!

"We'll just have to chance it. I'm betting Morgan wouldn't want the police showing up to check out a call."

"Whatever you say, boss."

Palmer crossed the threshold, wincing in anticipation. Silence.

Sonja moved cautiously into the vampire's nest, her head swiveling like a radar dish.

"He's not much on interior decorating, is he?" Palmer whispered.

The living room was devoid of furniture. The floor was covered by an off-white wall-to-wall carpet. To his left, Palmer glimpsed an equally barren dining nook.

"This isn't where he lives; it's just a nest. It's convenient for maintaining his identity. Kind of the vampiric equivalent of a 'place in the city.' Most nobles have nests scattered all over the world, mostly in major metropolitan areas; places were the neighbors wouldn't consider an absentee owner unusual."

"Jesus, this place gives me the creeps."

Sonja held up her hand for silence. She sniffed the air and frowned. "Do you smell something?"

"Now that you mention it, smells like one of the neighbors is having a barbecue." His stomach rumbled in response to the aroma.

She moved down the hall and stopped in front of a closed bedroom door. The smell of cooking meat was stronger than before. She turned the knob and stepped inside.

The gloom was illuminated by a small color television set atop a plastic milk crate. Opposite the flickering television was an easy chair. Sitting in the chair was a middle-aged man dressed in a rumpled suit. The reek of roast pork filled the otherwise empty room.

The man watching the TV slowly turned his head toward the visitors. Palmer was aghast at the lobster-red color of the man's skin. He looked as if he'd been boiled alive. The man opened his blackened lips and let his jaw drop.

Sonja was suddenly back pedalling, trying to escape into the hallway. Palmer stared in horror at the smoke and steam leaking from the boiled man's ears and nostrils. He almost looked funny; like one of those old Tex Avery cartoons.

A gout of flame leapt from the boiled man's throat, striking the wall a foot from Palmer's head, some of it splashing onto his shoulder. Palmer was too surprised to cry out, although he could smell his hair crisping.

Sonja grabbed him by the arm and jerked him out of the room. The pyrotic was getting to its feet, preparing to vomit another ball of fire. She slammed the door and hurriedly doffed her leather jacket, tossing it over Palmer's shoulder and forearm, smothering the flames. Satisfied the fire was out, she dragged Palmer in the direction of the front door.

Palmer looked back in time to see the boiled man lumber into the hall after them. He moved as if unused to arms and legs. He also seemed to be sweating bullets. Then Palmer realized that the man was dripping fat like a hot candle. The odor of bacon frying was omnipresent.

"We're *leaving*! Okay? We're leaving!" Sonja shouted at the melting man.

The pyrotic halted its clumsy advance and stared at them with the opaque eyes of a baked fish. It was still staring when they closed the door.

"I *said* I'm sorry, okay? How was I to know he had a fuckin' pyrotic as a home security system?"

They were back at their hotel, Sonja applying the last of the salve to Palmer's burns.

"I knew I shouldn't have let you talk me into this shit! I *knew* it! But do I listen to myself? Now I nearly get myself flash-fried by an escapee from a carnival sideshow!" Palmer winced as Sonja wrapped the gauze bandage around his upper arm. His right shoulder blade throbbed in time to his pulse.

"C'mon, it's not *that* bad. You've suffered worse." She nodded to the scar crossing his heart.

"You could have gotten us killed!"

"I could have gotten *you* killed. And for that I deserve the rebuke. I guess I was trying to prove something to myself; that I wasn't scared of the bastard. I was careless and stupid and you got hurt. I didn't want that to happen."

"You and me both."

Sonja finished dressing his wounds in silence. Palmer tried to find the strength to ignore the touch of her hands. At first the pain and fear had been enough to fuel his anger, but now it was fading. He wanted to stay mad at her. Being mad at her was a lot safer than liking her. He suddenly realized she'd said something to him. She was seated cross-legged on the floor, looking up at him as he perched on the corner of the bed.

"What was that? I didn't quite catch it."

"I said I keep forgetting you can't regenerate. I have to keep reminding myself how *frail* humans are."

Palmer allowed himself a smile. "I've been called a lot of things in my time, but 'frail' wasn't one of them. You keep saying 'human' like it's a brand name. Don't you still consider yourself, at least some part of you, to be like us? You're not like Pangloss. There's still something *alive* in you."

"Are you trying to flatter me? Don't answer that!"

She smiled and leaned her chin into her palm. "You know, most vampires would consider being favorably compared to humans a gross insult. Humans are no more than *milch cows*—reliable producers of the two things vampires need to survive: blood and negative energy."

"What about you? Are *you* insulted?"

She smiled again. "No. Because I'm not a vampire."

"Huh?"

"Oh, I've got all the traditional vampiric qualities: fangs, a taste for the 'forbidden vintage,' nocturnal habits, the powers of hypnosis, and all that jazz. But I'm not a *true* vampire. I never died, you see. I'm a freak—a species of one."

Palmer didn't know what to make of this confession. He'd assumed Sonja's shunning of the daylight was because she would burst into flames and turn into a charred mummy. It hadn't occurred to him that she might sleep all day because she'd been up all night.

"You must be lonely."

She tilted her head, studying him from behind unreadable mirrored lenses. "Do you like me?"

His cheeks colored and he became interested in counting the dots in the acoustical tile. "Well, uh . . . it's just that I . . ."

"I understand." Her smile disappeared and Palmer heard his own words echoing inside his head. *You must be lonely*. Right on. Way to go, Mr. Milch Cow.

"What I *meant* to say is: *of course* I like you." He was surprised to hear himself speak those words. He was even more surprised when he realized he was telling the truth. "You saved my life."

"Only because you were in danger on account of me. If it wasn't for me, you wouldn't be involved in this mess. You might not even have had your psychic powers activated. You'd be—"

"Stuck in the State Pen, getting my teeth knocked out and my asshole stretched, with no hope of parole until the next millennia. Believe me, as weird and as dangerous as this shit is, I could be a lot worse off." Palmer leaned over and touched her chin, tilting it upward. He didn't know *why* he did it; it just seemed like the thing to do. Just like it seemed natural to pull her into his arms. He felt himself growing hard and that, too, seemed natural. It had been months since he'd last had sex. With Loli.

He tried to shut the thought from his mind, but it wouldn't go away. Everything had seemed right and natural *then*, too. It had all seemed like some kind of beautiful, happy accident. He'd become so cynical it had made him naive. And Loli played him for the fool. From the very beginning, she'd been in charge, manipulating him like a puppet on a string, until he was no longer his own man. It had been a trap from the beginning, baited with honey and hot meat. And he'd never once suspected it until he'd faced the butcher on the killing floor. And the butcher had Loli's face.

Palmer made a strangling noise and pushed Sonja away from him. He pressed himself against the headboard, staring at her with wide, horror-stricken eyes. His penis went limper than cold pasta. "*You're* doing this! *You're* making this happen! It's not me, it's *you*!"

Sonja's face crumpled, and for a moment it looked as if she was going to cry. Then her features hardened and the left corner of her mouth curled into a humorless sneer. Her voice sounded ragged, as if her lungs were full of ice and razor blades.

"You fuckin' idiot! You're so damn neurotic, you don't even know what you really want, do you? You think I'm *making* you do this? Okay, I'll *make* you!"

Palmer tried to cry out as her will poured into him, seizing his brain in an invisible vise. All he could manage was a groan. His whole body felt numb, as if he'd been given a massive dose of novocaine. Although he could not feel any discomfort, the lack of sensation was worse than actual pain.

"Are you scared stiff yet? No? Then I'll have to see about that."

Palmer whimpered as his penis stirred. The numbness made it feel like it was a hundred miles away. He was vaguely aware of movement, but nothing else. The next stage was familiar. The last time he'd known such pain had been in New Orleans, when he'd narrowly escaped the "charms" of the succubus. His penis felt like an overinflated balloon on the verge of bursting. He gasped and struggled to keep his eyes from bugging out of their orbits.

"I could keep you like this for hours. Days, if I so choose. Of course, your bladder and testicles would rupture long before then. And even if you escaped being killed by your own sperm and piss, the blood vessels in your penis would be ruined for good. Assuming gangrene didn't set in and the doctors aren't forced to amputate, you'll be impotent for life." Sonja shook her head. "I don't understand what she sees in you. She must have a real weakness for fucked-up wimps; jerks with a taste for destructive relationships. *You* know what I mean, don't you?" She leaned forward, thrusting her face into Palmer's own. "Or do you need reminding?"

Her hair stood on end, waving like strands of seaweed. Palmer stared as Sonja's hair grew before his eyes; doubling, then tripling its length. As he watched, the hair turned from dark to light, becoming a raw honey blonde. Then her face rearranged itself; her flesh rippling, like a reflection in a disturbed pool. Then he heard a wet, squelching sound as the bones restructured. Her lips swelled, her chin becoming baby-doll round, her cheekbones sliding into place with a grinding sound.

Loli smiled down at him, her eyes screened by twin reflective mirrors.

"Hi, baby. Did you miss me?"

Palmer screamed.

He was free of the paralysis, his erection was gone, and he shivered like a half-drowned cat. Sonja stood in the far corner, her back to the wall, staring at the bed. Her face was her own again. She wrapped her arms around her stomach, as if she was struggling to keep from vomiting—or keep something from escaping.

"Get out!" She sounded as if she was in pain.

The sight of Sonja hugging herself, rapping the back of her head against the wall as if keeping time to unheard music, was almost enough to make Palmer forget what had just happened. Almost.

"Get *out* of here before I hurt you, damn it!"

Palmer couldn't tell if she was pleading or threatening him. He hurried into his room, slamming and locking the door behind him. He couldn't be sure, but he thought he could hear her talking to someone—or *thing*—and that she was being answered. Then he heard furniture being trashed.

Palmer retreated to the bathroom. He needed to take a shower. He wanted the hot water to turn his flesh the same boiled-lobster red as that of the pyrotic. Maybe if he could scrub off a layer or two of skin he'd feel clean again.

He sat on the toilet, smoking a Shermans with shaking hands, and watched the steam turn the mirror opaque. It almost obscured the tobacco demon squatting on his shoulder.

He closed his eyes, the roar of the water in his

ears, and heard Chaz's ghost whispering its warning again.

Yer in love with 'er already! You don't even know it yet, but I can see it in th' folds of yer brain.

And the horrible thing was it was true.

GHOST TRAP

A savage place! As holy and enchanted
As e'er beneath a waning moon was
haunted.

—Coleridge, *Kubla Khan*

10

She found him drinking espresso in a dark, smoky coffee bar across the street from the hotel. The sun was going down and she had her shades on. He glanced up from his drink, shrugged, and motioned for her to take a seat.

He expected her to say she was sorry or try to explain herself in some way. He'd played the scene before, but from the other side. He'd expected hesitant, incoherent emotional histrionics. Instead, she touched the top of his right hand with the index finger of her left hand.

Palmer gasped as her mind flowed into his. It was as unlike the brutal intrusion of the night before as a lover's caress from a molester's groping. There were no words, only sensations. The intimacy was both thrilling and intimidating. The temptation to let go, to lose himself in telepathic rapport, was strong. But so was his sense of self.

She recognized his fear of being subsumed and respected it, breaking the contact voluntarily.

He couldn't tell if she was looking at him or not, so he coughed into his fist and sipped his espresso before speaking. "No harm done."

She nodded and motioned to the paperback book at his elbow. "What's that?"

Palmer flipped the book over so that the cover was visible. "I found out what—and where—Ghost Trap is."

Sonja picked up the book and read the title aloud. "*The Architect's Guide to Haunted Houses?*"

"I found it at a B. Dalton's, of all places. Check out page 113."

Sonja opened the book and began to read:

Northern California has long demonstrated an allure for the eccentric, the artistic, and the wealthy. One of the strangest transplanted Californians to combine these elements was the architect-millionaire Creighton Seward (1870-1930). Seward, heir to an industrialist fortune, has been lost amongst the shadows cast by Frank Lloyd Wright. That all but a handful of his buildings have been destroyed in the sixty years since his death has helped to condemn him to obscurity. Yet, none can deny that Seward's genius was very real. As was the tragedy that consumed him.

After spending the better part of a decade designing competent but uninspired skyscrapers and palaces-away-from-palace for America's upper class in the Great Lakes area, in 1907 Seward took a sabbatical to Europe, taking his family with him. What truly happened on that tiny Mediterranean island will never be known. That Seward was found roaming its shores, delirious and naked except for his wife's blood, is certain.

The official report was that a disgruntled servant had murdered the entire household, including the children, while they slept. The only reason Seward survived was that he'd been awakened by the killer hacking his wife apart and overpowered him, smashing the fiend's skull open with the very ax used to dispatch his hapless family.

However, rumors persisted that the ax-murderer was none other than Seward himself, although no one could provide motivation for such a heinous act on his part. That Seward spent three years in a private asylum following his ordeal did not help the gossip. In 1910, Seward resumed his career. Whatever he might have seen—or done—that night in 1907 changed him forever, as is evident in his work.

Previously a mediocre architect, Seward's new designs foreshadowed the work of Gaudi and Salvador Dali. Seward only took on three commissions in the five years between his return to public life and his subsequent self-imposed seclusion, but each is a masterwork. Unfortunately, none of these structures remain standing, largely due to the so-called "Seward Curse."

While each of these buildings (two private homes in Minnesota and the old Zorn Publications skyscraper in New York) were incredible works of art and widely praised by the literati of the time, they proved to be uninhabitable. On the few occasions Seward would speak of his later work, he insisted that he had discovered, through the use of non-Euclidian geometry and quantum physics, a way of creating lines and angles that would pierce the space-time continuum. Whether this was so, or simply the ravings of a brilliant but sadly unhinged mind can never be verified. However, it was soon discovered that those who intended to live or work within these edifices were often stricken with vertigo and a nameless dread that lead them to flee the buildings. (It is believed that these incidents later provided the fantasy writer H.P. Lovecraft with the inspiration for his short story "Dreams in the Witch House.") In 1916, shortly before the Zorn Building, with its magnificent chromium gargoyles and eye-twisting zeppelin mooring spire, was scheduled for demolition, Creighton Seward disappeared from the public eye and would not resurface until his apparent suicide in 1930.

It was later discovered that Seward had "disappeared" into the hills of Northern California's Sonoma Valley, where he set about creating a personal testament to guilt and madness: the infamous Ghost Trap Manor. Using a previously existing three-story mansion as its core, Seward had carpenters constantly working on a twisting maze of weirdly shaped and cunningly designed rooms and corridors that would, by the time of the architect's death, cover acres of land and tower over six stories high. The mansion was completed in 1925 and the workmen departed, each paid handsomely to keep secret the location—and nature—of Creighton Seward's final masterpiece.

It is uncertain whether Seward spent the last five years of his life in complete isolation, or if he shared the house with servants. When his nephew and heir, Pierce Seward, had the rambling house searched for signs of his uncle in 1930, it took the searchers three days to locate the body.

The exact manner of Seward's demise is unknown, although he is believed to have starved to death. Many of those who originally searched the house later complained of experiencing attacks of vertigo and extreme nausea.

Notes found amongst Seward's personal effects hinted at the architect's intended use for his unconventional home. Seward apparently suffered from the delusion that the ghosts of his slain family were haunting him. Consumed by guilt and fear, he devised a house that would effectively "confuse" the pursuing spirits and keep them from finding him: thus explaining Ghost Trap's bewildering number of blind staircases, doorways that open onto brick walls, and windows set into ceilings.

Apparently Seward himself lived in the original "normal" rooms that served as the nucleus for the sprawling mansion. Why the architect would wander into the maze of "ghost rooms" without provisions or a map is not certain. For lack of a better verdict, the coroner listed his death as a suicide.

For over fifty years Ghost Trap remained shuttered and sealed against the elements as part of the Seward estate. Then, in 1982, it was sold to a San Francisco real estate agent and land developer, acting for an unnamed third party. Ghost Trap remains closed to the public, although whether anyone currently walks its halls is unknown.

*   *   *

On the page opposite the text was a partial schematic of the house's floor plan. Sonja stared at it for a moment before realizing what she was looking at.

"I'll be damned!"

"I don't doubt it. What's up?"

She pointed at the diagram. "Can't you see? Look at that!"

Palmer frowned at the jumble of lines and curves. "So? It looks like a kid went crazy with a spyrograph. Big deal."

"You're seeing it with human eyes. Look again. Look *harder*!"

Palmer shrugged and looked at the drawing again, this time focusing his attention on it. To his dismay the lines *writhed*, as if they had suddenly taken on three-dimensional life.

"Shit!"

"It's *Pretender* script! A form of—I don't know, call it a magic formula or glyph!"

"Are you saying this Seward guy was a werewolf or a vampire or something?"

"It's possible. Although I suspect he wasn't full-blooded, whatever he was. Probably wasn't even aware of his heritage. There are plenty of half-bloods and changelings out there, ignorant of their true nature and powers until something happens, later in life, to trigger it. They can be as dangerous as a pure-bred Pretender, given the right circumstances. Catherine Wheele, for example."

Palmer tried to keep his jaw from dropping. "I always wondered about her! Did you have anything to do with the fire?"

Sonja's manner stiffened. "That's old business."

Palmer let it drop.

"Like I was saying, Seward didn't design a trap

for unwanted ghosts—he created the physical equivalent of a psychic jamming station!"

"Come again?"

"This entire house is a protective charm! No wonder Morgan is using it as his lair! It's probably the only place on earth he can relax without fear of being attacked, at least on a psychic level. No wonder the networks don't have any information on him. He's practically invisible!"

"Is this a good thing or a bad thing?"

"Hard to say. Obviously it's worked to Morgan's advantage. From what little information there is to go by, I'd say we're going to need a counter-charm just to get inside the door."

"So how do we go about getting one of these 'counter-charms'? Open a box of breakfast cereal?"

"It won't be that easy, I'm afraid. Before we left New Orleans, I checked with Malfeis to see if there was a reliable alchemist in the San Francisco area . . ."

"You mean they're not listed in the Triple-A Guide?"

"Funny, Palmer. Remind me to laugh. You don't have to go if you don't want to."

"Did I say I wouldn't? Where do we have to go this time?"

"Chinatown."

He knew they were in for trouble the moment Sonja ducked into the alleyway. Since he had no choice, he followed her into the narrow, foul-smelling back street. It was dark and they had long left the caucasian tourists on Grant Avenue behind them. He realized his basic instincts had been correct when he heard the sound of boot leather on concrete.

There were three of them blocking the way. Palmer was pained by how young they were. The oldest of the group was barely nineteen. The Chinese youths wore their hair short and choppy, and Palmer sensed the aggression rolling off them in crackling waves.

The taller of the trio, stainless steel *shuriken* decorating the front of his leather jacket, stepped forward. His eyes were fixed on Palmer. "This is Black Dragon territory. No dogs or round-eyes allowed."

Sonja's fingers brushed against Palmer's bunched fist, touching his mind with her own. *Let me handle this.*

She moved to intercept the gang leader, speaking in Cantonese. "We're looking for Li Lijing. We meant no disrespect."

The youth scowled. His challenge had been aimed at Palmer; he had not expected the woman to know the tongue of his ancestors. "Li Lijing? The apothecary?"

"Yeah, Loo, maybe the geezer needs a fix of powdered rhino horn so he can get it up!" A slender boy with bristling, raven-back hair giggled.

"All we want is to speak with the *kitsune*."

"*Kitsune?* You're talking Japanese trash, white girl!" sneered the boy. "What's the matter, can't you tell the difference between Chinese and Japanese?"

"Round-eyes can't tell the difference between shit and tuna fish!" The third Black Dragon laughed, and yanked a pair of *nunchuks* from the waistband of his jeans. "Only way they learn the difference is if you *beat* it into them!"

Palmer couldn't tell what the trio were saying, but he didn't like the way they were laughing or the way the one with acne let his *nunchuks* drop to the length of their chain.

"Loo! Hong! Kenny! Is this how you greet people looking for my shop? No wonder my business has been so poor!"

The youths jumped at the sound of the old man's voice, looking more like children surprised at a naughty deed than dangerous street toughs. An ancient Chinese gentleman stood at the top of the stairs leading to a basement shop, leaning on an ornately carved cane.

"Go play hoodlum somewhere else! I will not have you harassing paying customers! Have I made myself clear?" The old man poked Loo in the ribs with the end of his cane. The boy looked embarrassed but did not protest the treatment.

"Yes, Uncle."

"Go now before I change my mind about paying you for the work you did for me!" The old man watched the leather-jacketed youths retreat and made a sour face. "Youth today! No respect! You must forgive Loo, my friends. He works for me, opening and sorting boxes of herbs from the old country. He is a good boy, but his brain is too often filled with foolish Western nonsense—no offense."

"None taken. I assume I am speaking to the honorable Li Lijing?"

The old man nodded, smiling cryptically. "And you are the one they call the Blue Woman. Malfeis told me I might expect a visit from you. That is why I was eavesdropping. Loo is a silly boy, but I have a fondness for him. It would pain me to dig a grave for one so young. Ah! It is rude of me to keep you chattering on my doorstep! Please, come inside and make yourself comfortable."

The apothecary's basement workshop was dark and close, the ceiling a foot over their heads. Various kinds of herbs and spices hung from the rafters, filling the space with an exotic aroma. Palmer noticed a stuffed Chinese crocodile suspended from the rafters and a bewildering collection of sub-human skulls in an open cupboard—one of which boasted a cyclopean eye socket and a large horn growing from its forehead.

"Permit me to light another lamp," Li Lijing said as he busied himself with an antique hurricane lamp. "You and I certainly do not need it, my dear, but your companion might benefit from some additional illumination." Li Lijing turned to face Palmer, a sharp smile on his long, black velvet snout. "Is that not so?"

Without meaning to, Palmer let out a startled yelp and stepped back from the humanoid fox.

"You're a werewolf!"

Li Lijing looked pained and shook his pointed ears in disgust. "Hardly! I am *kitsune* not *vargr*! Would you compare a panda to a grizzly bear? An Arabian stallion to a Clydesdale? A samurai to a priest?"

"Forgive my companion, Li Lijing. He is new to the Real World and has yet to meet a *kitsune*, much less a *vargr*. He meant no offense."

The *kitsune* snorted as he hobbled through the shop, the staff he carried helping to balance him on his crooked legs. "I have come to expect such ignorance from humans. Still, it is a sore spot with me. But I can not find it in myself to dislike their species. I have lived long amongst humankind. Why, I even took a couple as wives!" He made a barking sound that Palmer recognized as laughter. "I will tell you a secret! Loo is not my nephew, but actually my great-grandson! Not that he knows this. As far as he is concerned, I am merely a good friend of the family who arranged for his father to escape the mainland. He calls me uncle out of respect, but is ignorant of his blood. I favor the boy, as he reminds me of his grandfather—my son—who was lost to me during the invasion of Manchuria. Ah, but I must be old and foolish to succumb to such sentimentality, yes?"

Li Lijing sat down behind a low teak desk carved with scenes of *kei-lun*, the chinese unicorn, frolicking in the perfumed gardens of K'Un Lun, the City of

Heaven. "Now, what is it I can do for you, my dear?"

"I need a counter-charm."

"I see." The *kitsune* pushed aside a scroll of rice paper and his collection of bamboo calligraphy brushes and picked up an abacus. "What kind of spell are you interested in negating? Protection? Ensorcellment? Bedevilment? Containment? There is a difference in the prices, you know . . ."

Sonja motioned for Palmer to hand the alchemist the book. "You tell me. I'm sure I'm nowhere as adept at reading conjuration patterns as you are, Honorable One."

Li Lijing accepted the compliment by fluttering his pointed ears. "You do me great honor. Now, as to this particular charm . . ." He pondered the drawing for a long moment, scratching his muzzle in contemplation. "This is a protective ward of immense potency. You were wise to consult me. Anyone—Pretender or human—trying to violate these lines of power would be risking their sanity, if not their very lives!"

"Can you do it?"

"Of course I can do it! Did I say otherwise? It's just that the preparation of the proper counter-charm will not be without some expense . . . or danger."

"I'm willing to pay what it's worth."

The *kitsune* smiled as if he'd just been handed the key to the hen house. "Malfeis didn't lie, for once. You *are* a class act!" The alchemist barked another laugh and returned to his estimating, the abacus beads rattling like hailstones on a tin roof. "Let's see, I can have the appropriate counter-charm ready within the week—"

"Twenty-four hours."

Li Lijing looked down his long black nose at her. "That's extra, you know."

Sonja shrugged.

The abacus beads were flying now. "Very well. I'll have Loo deliver it to your hotel once it's ready. However, I would advise that you, not your companion, be the one to use it. Frankly, a charm of this magnitude has no business being handled by humans. No offense. Now, as to the settling of my bill . . ."

Sonja produced a small envelope from inside her jacket and tossed it onto the desk. Li Lijing lost no time in opening the packet and dumping its contents onto the blotter. Palmer stared at the handful of human teeth.

"I trust this will prove satisfactory. They once belonged to Hitler. I have papers that will verify it."

"That won't be necessary! Their power speaks for you. Yes, this is most satisfactory. It is always a pleasure doing business with a client of such refined sensibilities as yourself, Mistress Blue!"

11

"Sonja? You awake?"

Palmer glanced into the rearview mirror as she sat up in the back seat of the rental car. In the bright sunshine she looked pale and unhealthy, out of her element. She grimaced and smacked her lips as if trying to rid her palate of an offensive aftertaste.

"Daylight: phooey."

"I thought you said you weren't allergic to sunlight."

"I'm not. But I *am* nocturnal. Being awake during the day is . . . unnatural. Believe me, if I was allergic, you'd know it! Vampires exposed to direct sunlight develop a speedy case of skin cancer, bordering on leprosy: noses falling off every which way, ears dropping like leaves. Hardly a sight for the weak of heart—or stomach."

"Ugh. Sounds like it."

"What is it you wanted? Or did you disturb my beauty sleep just to see if I'd dissolve *à la* Christopher Lee in *Horror of Dracula*?"

Palmer blushed and returned his attention to the highway. "No, it's just—well, I wanted to see the charm Li Lijing gave you."

Sonja sighed. "You heard what he said about humans handling it."

"Look, I'm not interested in *using* the damn thing, I just want to look at it. Is that okay?"

"I can't see what harm it could do. Besides, it might do you good to realize what kind of explosive we're playing with here."

"It's that powerful?"

"You'll see. Why don't you pull over at the next rest station? The last thing I need is to have you plow the car into the back of a semi by mistake."

"I never slam into the back of trucks by *mistake*!"

A few minutes later, Palmer pulled the car into a roadside rest area, thoughtfully provided by the California Highway Commission. He killed the engine and turned around in the front seat, facing Sonja.

"Okay, let's see this powerful ju-ju."

Sonja pulled a package wrapped in blue tissue paper out from under the seat and handed it to the detective. "Remember, you asked for it!"

Palmer wrinkled his nose at the strong spices. The tissue paper crackled under his fingers. Frowning, he unwrapped the talisman.

When he saw what it was, he instinctively tossed the thing away from him as if it was a poisonous spider. He felt a bitter surge of vomit scald the back of his throat, but he could not look away from the withered severed hand nestled in the blue tissue paper like a perverse corsage.

"It's *horrible*!"

"It's a Hand of Glory. Lijing assures me that it is especially potent."

"It's got *six fingers*!"

"Yes, that's the secret of its power. It once belonged to one of the hereditary Mayan priest-kings. There was one particular royal family that was so inbred they all had six fingers and toes. They were known as *Chan Balam*, the Jaguar Lords. It was considered a sign of divinity."

Palmer swallowed the burning knot in his throat and watched an elderly man in tan slacks and a cream-colored windbraker lead a miniature schnauzer toward a grassy stretch marked "Pet Path." He suppressed the urge to get out of the car and sprint for the nearest parked car. Unfortunately, he knew he was more likely to get another hole in his chest from his fellow motorists than a free ride back to normalcy, so he remained seated.

"For crying out loud, are you going to leave it lying out where everyone can see it? Why don't you just mount it on the dashboard?"

The idea of touching the Hand of Glory was repugnant beyond belief, but she was right. If anyone got a good look at what was on the front seat, they'd have every CHIPS officer north of Los Angeles breathing down their necks. Grimacing in distaste, Palmer picked up the severed hand.

He was somewhere warmer, where the screeching of macaws and the screams of howler monkeys echoed from the lush green canopy outside his door. A naked brown child sat framed in the doorway, playing with a baby spider monkey on a leash. The child's forehead was oddly shaped, sloping backward. At first Palmer thought the boy was retarded, then the child smiled and turned his face toward him. The child's eyes were dark and sparkled with a natural wit. Confused, Palmer scanned the room he found himself in, frowning at the detailed charcoal renderings of Mayan dignitaries offering sacrifices to the gods decorating the white-washed stone walls. Above his head handwoven nets full of museum-quality Pre-Columbian pottery hung from brightly painted, ornate wooden rafters.

The naked child laughed at his pet's antics, lifting a six-fingered hand to his mouth. Palmer glanced down at his own nude body and saw he was seated, cross-legged, on a stone bench carved in the likeness of a jaguar. His breath was coming heavier now, but it had nothing to do with the oppresive humidity. Palmer stood up and walked to the doorway.

He was wobbly on his feet and had to steady himself by placing one hand against the wall. His hand had six fingers. He brought his other hand to his face and felt the stingray barb piercing his lower lip and the ritual scars on his cheeks. His gaze dropped to his borrowed body's exposed genitals. He knew he should be alarmed by the sight of a second stingray barb skewering his penis, but Palmer felt strangely disconnected from the mutilations done to his flesh.

The child looked up at Palmer from his place on the stoop and smiled. The baby spider monkey squatted on the boy's shoulder, chattering to itself as it searched its master's hair for vermin. Suddenly William Palmer, never married and an avowed enemy of small children, knew how it felt to be a husband and a father.

Somewhere, in the jungle, a jaguar screamed.

"Palmer! Palmer, are you all right? Answer me, damn it!" Sonja was in the front seat of the rental car, shaking him by the shoulders. She actually looked scared. Palmer wondered if he should feel honored or worried. "Damn it, Palmer! Say something! Don't make me come in there and get you!"

"Sonja?"

"You're back. Good. I don't like dream-walking under these circumstances. What happened?"

"I don't know—one minute I was here in the car with you, the next I was in a jungle in Central America. What's that awful taste in my mouth?"

"Blood." Sonja pulled a linen handkerchief from her pants pocket and offered it to the dazed detective. "You had some kind of seizure; blood started running out of your nose. You also probably bit the side of your mouth, if not your tongue. Now, what's this about you being in Central America?"

Palmer shook his head in disbelief as he dabbed at the corner of his mouth. "It was weird. It wasn't like a dream. It was more like being there. Or *remembering* being there. I was sitting in a stone house and I could hear the birds and monkeys outside, just like in the Tarzan movies. There was a boy . . ." Palmer frowned as he tried to recall more of his vision, but it was already fading.

"Palmer, do you believe in reincarnation?"

"I never really gave it much thought, to tell you the truth. Just like I never gave much thought to vampires and werewolves." His smile wavered and Sonja saw the fear in his eyes. "It's true, then?"

"To a point. There is such a thing as reincarnation. But not every human being is reincarnated. I don't know how it works—nobody does for sure, unless it's the seraphim, and they're not talking. But there are a number of humans who are pre-born. The Pretenders call them old souls. Most never know who—or what—they were before, and that's as it should be. But every now and again, they get a glimpse of their previous incarnations. Various random incidents can cue a buried memory. Or, as in your case, you can accidentally make contact with the physical remains of your previous self."

Palmer hunched forward, resting his forehead against the steering wheel. "Holy—!"

"You spoke while you were—away. Are you aware of that?"

"No. What did I say?"

"You said the word 'Tohil.' Does that mean anything to you?"

He closed his eyes and the sound of macaws calling to one another from jungle perches filled his ears. "Yes. Yes, it does. It was my son's name."

*　　　*　　　*

"So that's Ghost Trap. The guy who built it really *was* crazy!"

Palmer was perched atop a nearby hill overlooking the infamous manor house, squinting through binoculars at the valley below. Not that he needed them to see Creighton Seward's fevered brainchild; the rambling mansion filled the small dell to overflowing.

Sonja pointed to the center of the grandiose concoction of towers, turrets, and flying buttresses. "You can still make out the original house in the middle. It looks like a spider squatting in the middle of a web. See anything?"

Palmer shook his head and lowered the binoculars. "Sealed up like a fuckin' drum. All the shutters are closed. I spotted what looks like an old stable off to one side—Morgan's sports car's in it. Our boy's here. No doubt about it."

"I never thought he wasn't. I can *feel* him."

"Looking at that house is making my head hurt." Palmer massaged the bridge of his nose. "I can't imagine anyone actually *living* in that monstrosity!"

Sonja scowled down at Ghost Trap. Morgan could be anywhere inside its labyrinth-like belly. She glanced up at the afternoon sky, careful not to look directly at the sun. It had taken them three hours, following narrow asphalt roads that twisted through the hills surrounding the Sonoma Valley like black snakes, before they located the isolated area that separated Ghost Trap from the rest of the world. There were still several hours to go before it got dark and Morgan would stir from his daily coma.

Still, in a place like Ghost Trap, where daylight rarely pierced its heart, Morgan might possibly be up and about. She was loathe to mention it to Palmer, but she was in bad need of recharging. It kind of scared her. She used to be able to function perfectly well during the day, but right now she felt like she'd just come off a week-long drunk. The temptation to crawl in the trunk of the car and enjoy a quick nap was strong.

"Put a sock in it," she muttered to the Other, as it whined for the seven hundredth and fifty-second time that the sunlight was making it sick.

"Huh?" Palmer looked up from his binoculars.

"I wasn't talking to you."

"Uh . . . right. Whatever you say."

"I'm going down there."

"When?"

"Now."

Palmer sucked on his lower lip. "You figure it's safe?"

She barked a humorless laugh. "It's *never* going to be safe! Still, I think I stand a better chance during the day. Hopefully, he won't be expecting anything. And if Lijing's talisman does what it's supposed to"—she hefted the Hand of Glory before stuffing it into her leather jacket—"he won't know I've breached his defense before it's too late to do him any good. What about you? You packing?"

Palmer pulled a loaded .38 Special out of his waistband and held it up so she could see. "Figure this'll do the job?"

"Honey, you shoot *anything* in the brain, human or not, with that damn thing, you'll kill it!"

He nodded and returned her smile. Sonja gave him a thumbs up signal and began walking. Palmer watched as she moved into the trees and made her way down the rugged hillside. When he could no longer see her, he focused his binoculars back on Ghost Trap.

He quickly scanned the windows and turrets for signs of movement, having already learned that if he let his eyes linger too long on any particular architectural detail it made his eyes water and his head hurt.

His attention was caught by a fleeting glimpse of a pale, moon-like face glowering from a fifth-floor window. Swearing as he fiddled with the binocular's field of focus for a closer view, Palmer's heart thumped at 4/4 beat. But by the time he could refocus, the face was gone, the window once more shuttered. Or had it ever been open in the first place? Perhaps it had been an illusion created from staring too long at the weird house. And if not, whose face had he seen at the window? It sure wasn't Morgan's. He contemplated hurrying after Sonja and telling her what he'd seen.

Before he could get to his feet, he saw a shadow emerge from the treeline just beyond the east side of the mansion's ruined gardens and flit through the tangled rosebushes. He watched, awed by the woman's supernatural grace as she deftly avoided empty goldfish ponds and crumbling statuary and made her way to what had once been the coal cellar.

He smiled when he saw her yank the heavy-duty padlock off the cellar doors and whispered under his breath, "That's m'girl!"

Then she was gone, swallowed by Ghost Trap. Whatever dangers lay hidden within the mansion's sprawl, she would have to face them alone. And maybe, if he was lucky, she would never come out.

12

Sonja took a deep breath and paused to orient herself.
The moment she entered the confines of the mansion
she'd been hit with a surge of nausea. The empty
coal cellar tilted under her feet, as if the ground was
made of india rubber. Something in her jacket
twitched.

She removed the Hand of Glory Li Lijing had
given her. The six-fingered hand was now clenched
into a fist. Hoping that was a good sign, she returned
it to her pocket. She took a cautious step toward the
stairs leading to the rest of the house, then another.
The nausea was gone, although she was unable to
shake the feeling of disorientation.

The first floor was dark, the bare wooden boards
furry with dust. As she walked through the series of
oddly shaped interconnected rooms, it became obvious that they had never been furnished. Some had
never even been plastered and painted, the wooden
slats giving the smaller rooms an austere, almost
monkish flavor.

Sonja was impressed by the demented genius of
Ghost Trap's creator. Even to her mutated senses,
the building was disturbing. She found her eyes
drawn to lines that both originated and intersected
beyond the field of normal vision. She doubted an

unprepared human could withstand more than an hour's sustained exposure to Ghost Trap's peculiar brand of architectural design without losing consciousness or going mad. The weirdly angled doorways and out-of-kilter rooms reminded her of the starkly rendered Impressionistic scenery from *The Cabinet of Dr. Caligari*.

The second floor was much like the first, as was the third. The house was indeed as huge and mazelike as she'd feared. She could feel Morgan's presence, hidden somewhere within the massive sprawl of zig-zagging walls and staggered staircases; but whether the vampire lord was hiding in the attic, the basement, or the room next door was impossible for her to divine. All she could hope for was that if Morgan was conscious of her intrusion, he was equally helpless in pinpointing her exact location.

Judging from the thickness of the dust coating the floorboards and banisters, she doubted that the section of Ghost Trap she found herself in had seen any visitors—human or Pretender—since the day Creighton Seward's body was recovered, sixty years ago.

As she left a sitting room with faded, green patterned wallpaper and an upside-down fireplace made from Italian marble, she glimpsed something pale out of the corner of her eye. Turning to confront the apparition, she stared at a little girl no more than five or six.

Sonja knew the child to be dead because she could see through her. The ghost-child wore old-fashioned clothes and held a porcelain doll in her chubby arms. Both the girl and the doll had golden hair that fell to their shoulders in ringlets. The face of the china doll was marred by a hairline fracture that ran from its brow to the bridge of its nose.

"Hello, little girl."

The phantom child smiled and lifted a hand still chubby with baby fat and waved hello in return.

"Little girl, do you know how I can get to the middle of the house?"

The ghost shook her head "no." Sonja wished the tiny specter would speak, but knew that the dead often lost the ability to communicate coherently with the living after a few years. The use of dumb-show might be aggravating, but at least it was reliable.

"Is there anyone around who *does* know?"

The little girl smiled again, this time nodding "yes." She turned and signaled for Sonja to follow her. Sonja tried not to look at the brains spilling from the back of the child's smashed skull.

The ghostly child flickered from room to room like a pale but playful moth while Sonja followed. Finally the phantom entered a long, narrow room paneled in darkly stained walnut with bronze satyr faces studding the walls. On closer inspection, Sonja saw old-fashioned gas jets protruding from the grotesquely leering mouths. Suddenly there was an icy draft, as if someone had thrown open the door of a massive freezer, and the thirteen gas jets burst into flame, filling the room with the odor of blood, perfume, and butane.

The tiny ghost-child hurried over to where her mother stood revealed, dressed in a high-collared morning glory skirt, her hair—the same golden hue as her daughter's—puffed at the sides and pulled into a knot atop her head. Even with the left side of her face reduced to pulp, the eye hanging from its stalk onto the ruined cheek, it was obvious she had once been a stunningly beautiful woman.

The ghost-child tugged at her mother's skirts and pointed at Sonja. Her lips moved but all Sonja heard was a skewed, half-speed garble.

"Mrs. Seward . . ."

The dead woman looked up, surprised at being recognized. The undamaged side of her face frowned.

"Mrs. Seward, I need your help in finding my way to the center . . ." Sonja stepped forward, one hand outstretched.

Mrs. Seward looked down at her daughter then at Sonja. As she opened her mouth, the flames issuing from the gas jets intensified. The ghost-woman, now looking more terrified than terrible, motioned for her child to leave. The little girl obeyed, rolling herself into a ball of witch-fire and bouncing from the room.

There was a distant whistling sound, as that of air being sliced by an axe, followed by a hollow booming. Whatever was creating the noise was making its way toward the room Sonja occupied with the late Mrs. Seward.

The ghost gestured for Sonja to follow, and moved to one of the walnut panels set into the wall. Her long, bell-like skirt left the thick fur of dust on the floor undisturbed. Mrs. Seward pointed to the molding where the plaster met the paneling and passed through the wall. It took Sonja a few seconds to locate the hidden catch that opened the secret door. The booming sound had grown considerably closer as she closed the panel behind her.

Mrs. Seward was waiting for her, glowing in the gloom of the secret passage like a night-light. Sonja followed her spirit guide through the narrow passageway to a cramped circular staircase that pierced Ghost Trap's various levels. Mrs. Seward motioned for her to go downstairs.

"How many levels? One? Two?"

The dead woman held up two transparent fingers and mimicked opening a door. Sonja nodded to show that she understood and began her downward climb. After a couple of steps she paused and looked back at the ghost-woman.

"You *are* trapped in this place, aren't you? You and the children."

The ghost nodded, nearly dislodging her dangling eye.

"How can you be freed?"

The ghost hastily traced letters in mid-air. The ectoplasm hung suspended for a few seconds before wavering and losing shape, like a message left by a haphazard skywriter:

Diztroe Tarappe

The dead were notoriously bad spellers.

Before Sonja could ask anything else, Mrs. Seward disappeared. Sonja shrugged and resumed her descent into the bowels of Ghost Trap.

On the second level she found a narrow oak doorway at the base of the stairs. She could tell the door opened inward, but other than that had no idea where it might lead or what might be on the other side.

Taking a deep breath and hoping it didn't open onto a room full of hungry ogres, Sonja grasped the handle and yanked the portal open.

She found herself faced not by tigers, but with a lady.

The woman was seated in a tastily upholstered easy chair, reading a thick paperback romance novel, her slippered feet resting on an ottoman. The room seemed very cozy, in a Victorian kind of way. Somewhere nearby a grandfather clock measured out the afternoon. A small, cheery fire crackled away in the fireplace. The woman had yet to notice the intruder standing in her sitting room.

Sonja frowned and moved further into the room, allowing the secret door to silently close behind her. She was wondering if the petite negro woman was another ghost, albeitly a bit more opaque than the last, when the woman looked up from her book and smiled at her. Her eyes were the color of claret. Sonja's right hand closed on the switchblade in her pocket.

"Hello," said the woman, putting aside her romance novel. "I'm sorry, I didn't hear you come in. Are you one of our Father's servants?"

Sonja adjusted her vision, scanning the woman to see her true appearance and strength. To her surprise, the black woman did not reveal herself to be a wizened crone or rotting corpse. She remained exactly what she looked like: a young African-American woman in her early twenties. Sonja hesitated pressing the ruby eye on her switchblade.

Why are you hesitating? She's just another vamp. Just another filthy bloodsucker. What's your problem, woman?

"Is there something wrong?"

Sonja shook her head, the back of her hand pressed against trembling lips. It wasn't possible. It *couldn't* be. But she could clearly see the aura, crackling around the woman's neatly corn-rowed head like a halo of fire. The only time she'd previously seen such an aura was in the mirror.

He is plotting on revolutionizing Pretender society . . . Something about creating an army of silver-immune vampires.

The woman struggled to her feet with a deep grunt and Sonja noticed for the first time just how huge the other woman's belly was.

It was worse than even Pangloss could have imagined. A lot worse.

13

"Is something wrong? Should I call Dr. Howell?" The pregnant woman reached for a cellular phone resting on the table next to an array of medication vials.

Before she had a chance to touch the receiver, Sonja wrapped one hand in her dark, abundant braids, yanking the woman's head back, exposing her *cafe au lait* throat. The point of her switchblade pressed against the pregnant woman's pulse.

"Who are you?" Sonja's words hissed like live steam.

"I'm Anise." She spoke loudly and slowly, as if communicating with an emotionally disturbed child. She was trying not to sound frightened, but Sonja saw how her hands clutched at her swollen belly. "What are you doing? You're hurting me . . ."

"Where is Morgan?"

"Our Father?"

Sonja cranked another length of braid around her fist, yanking Anise onto her tiptoes. "He's not *my* father, bitch! Answer me, damn you, or I'll go in and *take* what I want to know! Who else is in this fuckin' spook-house?"

Anise's eyes flickered, tracking something behind Sonja's shoulder.

The thought that there might be two of them entered Sonja's head the same time the fireplace poker came down on her skull.

Of course there are two of them, you pathetic ninny! The Other shrieked delightedly as the pain and rage sparked and fed on one another. *There has to be two of them! And baby makes three. Vampires that breed together bleed together.*

The Other wanted out. It wanted out *bad*. The Other wanted to twist the head off the bloat-bellied bitch. The Other wanted to gouge the eyes out of the asshole with the poker. The Other wanted to yank the little unborn shit out of its mother's womb and snap its head between her teeth like a terrier worrying a rat.

"No. I'm not letting you out. Not yet. Save it. Save it for Morgan."

As Sonja struggled to keep the Other under control, another blow fell across her shoulders, knocking her to the floor. She felt ribs crack and blood fill her mouth.

"Fell, stop it! I said *stop!*"

Anise grappled with her mate for control of the poker. The male was tall and thin, his features pale and finely chiseled. His hair was the color of raw pine, hanging to his shoulders in long silken tresses. His rubescent eyes were dilated, like those of a panther scenting its prey. Sonja knew that wild, cruel look all too well.

"I told you they hated us! They're all crazy with jealousy, because our Father loves us more than them!"

"No, Fell! She's not a renfield. Look at her. *Look!*"

Fell grudgingly turned his gaze on Sonja. The poker in his hand wavered.

Sonja grinned crookedly, spitting out a mouthful of blood. "The little lady's right you know—I'm not a renfield." She was up and moving before Fell had a chance to react, kicking the weapon out of his hand and catching it in mid-air.

Anise screamed as Sonja slammed the fire tool's butt into Fell's abdomen, knocking him to the floor. Sonja pinned him to the floor by firmly planting her boot on his throat. She reversed the poker, gently pressing its point between his eyes.

"Anyone moves, I'll ram the damn thing through his brain."

"Anise! Go get help!" Fell hissed, trying not to move.

"I'm not leaving you!"

"Do what I say, Anise!"

Tears trickled down Anise's cheeks as she shook her head no.

"You can cry." Sonja moved the poker away from Fell's forehead, but kept a firm boot planted on his adam's apple. There was awe and envy in her voice.

"Of course I can cry!" Anise wiped at the tears with the flat of her palm. "Everyone can cry."

"No. Not everyone. Have you ever seen Morgan cry?"

Anise stared at her as if Sonja had started speaking in tongues. "What do you mean by that?"

"It doesn't matter. What matters is Morgan. I want to know where the bastard is holed up."

"Our Father?"

"Stop calling him that!"

Fell and Anise stared at her as if she'd told them not to call the sky blue or the grass green.

Sonja cursed and stepped away from Fell, motioning for him to join his mate. "Get up!"

Fell looked toward Anise, then back at his attacker, as if expecting a trick.

"I said *get up*!" Sonja snarled, kicking him in the rump. This time he did as he was told, hurrying to where Anise stood. Fell wrapped his arms protectively around his wife, glowering at Sonja with unalloyed hatred.

"Well, if this ain't a fine little family reunion, eh?" she chuckled and twisted the poker into a pretzel. "I guess Big Daddy never told you you had an older sister. Not surprising, though. I doubt he knows I even exist."

"Can my wife sit down?" Acid dripped from Fell's words.

Sonja shrugged. She watched Fell help his pregnant wife ease into her easy chair. Sonja noticed that their auras were nearly identical, although the female's seemed the more robust of the two. She idly wondered if that had something to do with the mutant lifeform inside her.

On closer inspection, she saw that while the energy sheaths surrounding the two were similar to hers, they were definitely weaker. She had learned a long time ago how to guess the relative ages of various Pretenders by their auras. Anise and Fell were still quite young, by Pretender standards.

That explained a lot of things. If her own early development was anything to go by, they were still "mute"—incapable of telepathic communication.

"I'll give the bastard credit—he doesn't plan small."

"I take it you're referring to our Father."

Sonja grimaced. "Why don't you come off that 'our Father' bit, blondie, before you piss me off so bad I forget I'm trying to be nice and rip out your fuckin' tongue?"

"Nice? You call brutalizing my wife and attacking me *nice*?"

"So I'm lacking in some social graces."

Anise reached up and took her husband's hand in hers, her eyes fixed on Sonja. Despite their reddish hue, they could still pass for those of a human. "You seem to know a lot about our Father—Morgan, as you call him. I have never seen a creature such as you—outisde of Fell and myself. Not even our Father, the few times He has favored us with His presence, is like us. You say you are our sister. How can that be so?"

"You talk about Morgan as if he's some kind of god."

"He is our Creator. He is our Father." Anise smiled up at her husband, who squeezed her hand in return. Sonja felt a sudden, sharp pain of envy. "From His Essence were we conceived, and in His Image were we shaped. We came into being within moments of one another and have been conscious of no other life, no other love."

Sonja fell silent, eyeing Anise speculatively. In 1970 she herself had emerged from a nine-month coma and discovered her long-term memory blank. She'd been desperate for an identity, any identity, to fill the void inside her. It wasn't long before she fell into the hands of a cruel, street-wise pimp named Joe Lent. Lent had been more than willing to shape her in his image and prescribe the limits of her world.

In the months between her initial awakening and the brutal beating that triggered the Other's emergence and resulted in the bloody murder of her erstwhile benefactor, Sonja had seen Lent in much the same light Anise and Fell viewed Morgan. And why not? Lent had given her life form and meaning. She had needed him the same way an empty pitcher needs water. But that innocence had ended with Lent's murder and the restoration of her memory. Her life had been a living hell ever since.

Sonja knelt before Anise and stared into the other woman's face. Fell tensed but Anise did not flinch or draw away when Sonja touched her chin.

"I'm sorry," she whispered to Anise, "but it's time for childhood to end."

Sonja's eyelids twitched as she downloaded into Anise's mind. The pregnant woman jumped as if she'd received a jolt of electricity, her eyes rolling back in their sockets. Her jaws snapped shut, an exposed fang slicing open her lower lip. The biggest problem with physically kick-starting another person's memory was the risk of triggering defensive shock. If Sonja wasn't careful, Anise might retreat into catatonia rather than deal with her memories.

"Anise! What did you *do* to her?"

Sonja was conscious of Fell's hands on her person, but she was too busy to shrug him off. All she needed was to give a little *push* . . .

You're no longer Sonja. Now you're Anise. Only you're not really Anise. You're Lakisha Washington. You grew up on Fourteenth Street in East Oakland; a part of the city so vile, dirty, violent, and hopeless that the police consider it an unofficial free-fire zone. Your mother is a junkie who sells herself for drugs. Your father is a nameless white man who happens to have the right amount of money and lust. Your mother leaves you alone in your crib, screaming and squalling in fear of the rats, while she goes to meet her dealer. The neighbors break in and rescue you after six hours.

You live with your grandmother after that. Your mother fades from your life, until her death from an overdose on your seventh birthday is meaningless—the death of a casual friend of your grandmother.

Despite the odds, you thrive in an environment as hostile to innocence as the surface of Venus. You do well in school, striving to prove yourself, better yourself. You want to escape so bad you can taste it. You manage to avoid the other pitfalls that ensnare many of your friends and classmates: drugs, teenage pregnancy, alcoholism, dropping out.

You want more of life than drudging for minimum wage at the corner Kentucky Fried Chicken outlet.

Your determination to succeed inspires respect and contempt amongst those trapped. You get a reputation for being a "nice" girl, one that's going places, but too smart and self-possessed to attract the opposite sex. You graduate valedictorian with an out-of-state scholarship. For the first time in your young life you escape the bone-grinding, soul-numbing poverty you were born in, but never succumbed to.

Your grandmother dies in a charity hospital during your sophomore year. Despite your grief you're relieved; it means you'll never have to go back to Fourteenth Street ever again. You work as hard in college as you did in high school, landing a degree in Business. To your delight you're recruited by a prestigious financial firm stationed in San Francisco. You return to California, but this time you're on the right side of the Bay. You have a nice apartment in the Twin Peaks district, overlooking the city. From your balcony you can glimpse the place of your birth, on those rare occasions you look in its direction.

Separated from you by time and a large body of water, it looks deceptively serene. But never inviting. You are happy. Everything you've set out to accomplish, to prove to yourself and others, has been attained beyond your wildest dreams. You're respected at work, you're making more money than most Americans your age, white or black, male or female, and everything is looking up.

No one knows you're the bastard daughter of a whore who died with a syringe dangling from her arm, stuffed between a couple of garbage cans like a broken doll left for the trash collectors to find. There's no reason for them to know, and no way they ever will.

That's when the dreams start. The bad ones. About the things in the dark with the red glowing eyes and the razor-sharp teeth, watching you as you lie helpless in your bed. The dreams get so bad they intrude on your work. So you do what any other self-respecting young urban professional would do: you get yourself a shrink.

Dr. Joad Caron comes very highly recommended; many of his clients number amongst San Francisco's political and financial elite. He is handsome, sympathetic, understanding. The kind of psychiatrist a young woman can open her soul to without fear. Dr. Caron tells you there is nothing wrong with turning your back on the squalor and unhappiness of your past; that you need not feel guilty because you are now a part of the system that exploits your friends in the old neighborhood. You owe nothing to anyone, except yourself. Soon the dreams go away. But your dependence on Dr. Caron grows. Your will seems to dissolve when you are in his presence. But this does not frighten or worry you. Instead, you feel at peace.

One day Dr. Caron invites you to a weekend retreat hosted at his "place in the Valley." You are one of ten patients, five women and five men, who find themselves in Caron's strange, rambling mansion. All of you are single and live alone. All of you are either orphaned or estranged from your parents. All of you are people no one will miss. But you don't know that until the experiments begin.

Dr. Joad introduces a form of drug therapy, created by himself and a quiet, moon-faced man known as Dr. Howell. Each participant is given various dosages, injected intravenously. Dr. Caron mutters something about finding a "worthy vessel." Then all hell breaks loose.

Three subjects die of convulsions within minutes of injection. Two suffer massive coronaries. Another two blind themselves by plunging their thumbs into their eyes. One patient, screaming like a wounded animal, leaps onto the blinded subjects and tears at them with his bare teeth. You do none of these things—you go to sleep. A long, long sleep filled with dreams of a sterile environment full of hypodermic syringes and intravenous drips.

And when you awake, you are no longer Lakisha Washington. You are Anise, because your Father tells you that

*is your name. That is as it should be. And your Father,
knowing you are lonely and need companionship, gives you
a mate: Fell. He is beautiful and you love him, as your
Father commands. Which is as it should be.*

"Damn you, get your hands off her!"

Fell's fist smashed into Sonja's face, knocking her
away from Anise and sending her glasses flying
across the room. Sonja lay dazed on the floor, blood
seeping from her broken nose, as Lakisha/Anise's
persona receded and her own identity reasserted
itself.

Anise sat staring at her hands as if she'd never
seen them before. She trembled like a malaria victim
and would not look at Fell.

"What did you do to her?" Fell delivered a vicious
kick to Sonja's side. She took the blow without com-
plaint. She deserved the pain. "Answer me! What
did you *do*?" He cocked his leg for another kick.

"Leave her alone, Fell."

"My glasses—"

Anise nodded. "Help her find her glasses, Fell."

"Anise, what's gotten into you?"

"Do as I *say*, Fell!" The acid in her voice caused
him to flinch. He did as he was told, retrieving
Sonja's mirrored sunglasses.

Sonja sat huddled on the floor, her upper lip
smeared with blood. As Fell neared, she lifted her
head and glowered at him. Fell's stomach knotted at
the sight of her raw eyes and over-large pupils.

"Get used to it, kid," she hissed, snatching the
glasses out of his hand. Fell wondered what she
meant.

"I don't know if I should thank you for what you
did, but I remember now." Anise sat with her hands
resting on the swell of her stomach, her gaze fixed
on Sonja. "I remember it *all*."

"Self-knowledge is the hardest. I know what you must be feeling . . . thinking."

Anise nodded slowly. "It wasn't all one way. I picked up some of your memories as well."

"What are you two talking about, Anise?"

The pregnant woman leaned forward, ignoring her mate as if he was not there. "What does he want from us?"

Sonja pointed at the other woman's midsection.

"The baby?"

"That's more than just a baby you're carrying around, honey. It's his ticket to godhood."

Anise frowned. "I don't understand . . ."

"Whenever vampires attack humans, they infect them with a kind of virus. The virus generates drastic mutations in the human's biochemistry and physical structure. It reshapes half of the host's chromosomes so they resemble the vampire's. It's not unlike human conception, except that the fetus is an adult corpse. Because part of the new vampire is the same as its Maker, there is a certain . . . biological fealty. Obedience to the Maker is in the blood."

Anise slumped back in the chair. "Then it's hopeless to try and fight him."

"No, it's *not*! Morgan can only dominate you if you don't fight him! How do you think Morgan came into being? He was Made, just like I described. But he had the force of will to break away from his Maker, to assert his personality over that of his creator. You can do it, too, Anise. For the sake of your child, you've *got* to!" Sonja was not a hundred percent certain what she'd just said was true, but she was unwilling to accept biochemical predestination, whether natural or supernatural.

"It all keeps coming back to my baby. Why?"

"Vampires like Morgan are incapable of live birth. They can't breed true. Most vampires are severely flawed because . . . well, because they have to use dead meat. Their brains are screwed to the max. Only a handful are resurrected without some form of brain damage. It takes a new vampire a *long* time to develop into something as powerful as Morgan; decades, possibly centuries. Think what it would mean to Morgan to have a *living* vampire, one capable of perfectly replicating itself, bearing *his* chromosomal structure.

"Within the time it takes for a *single* king vampire to germinate, he'd have an entire *army* of obedient myrmidons, each immune to silver and capable of movement during the day! And not a single one of them possessing bothersome memories of having once been human. No wonder the renfields hate you. You're threatening to make them redundant! Morgan's out to make himself a god-emperor, Anise! And you're providing him with his first high priest."

"Anise, that's bullshit and you know it! Our Father would never do anything like—"

"Shut up, Fell! Just *shut up!*" hissed Anise, baring her fangs. Rebuffed, Fell bit his lower lip and looked away. Anise returned her attention to Sonja. "What do you want me to do?"

Sonja surprised herself by saying, "Come with me."

"Leave? You want me to leave?"

"Not leave. Escape!"

"Where could we go?"

"There's a *world* out there, Anise! I could find somewhere safe for you to have the baby. If not here, then in Central or South America."

"But Morgan . . ."

"Let *me* worry about Morgan, okay? So, what's the verdict? Are you with me?"

"I—yes. I'm with you." With a grunt Anise hoisted herself out of the chair.

"*Anise*! Darling, what's gotten into you? You've never acted toward me this way before! What did that crazy woman *do* to you?"

"She woke me up, Fell! I'm not a sleepwalker anymore. I'm finally doing something for myself that's *my* idea!"

"You're *not* going through with this!" He grabbed her upper arm. "I positively forbid it!"

Anise jerked her arm free of her husband's grasp. "Back off, asshole!"

Fell looked like a pole-axed young animal; left alive but forever altered. Sonja almost expected to see him stagger and fall.

"Come on, if we're going to leave, it better be now." Sonja motioned to the secret doorway she'd entered through.

"No, there's another way out. One that leads directly to the outside. I'm not supposed to know about it."

"Good. If we leave now, we should still have another hour or two of sunlight in our favor." Sonja shot a sharp look at Fell. "How about you? Are you coming with us?"

Fell opened his mouth as if to speak, then shook his head.

"I should kill you, you know."

He lifted his chin and squared his shoulders. "So why don't you?"

She didn't answer him. She was still puzzling over his question when Anise lead her out of the parlor and into the hallway.

The heart of Ghost Trap, compared to its protective outer layers, was a large, comfortable late-Victorian mansion, decorated with antiques. As far as Sonja could tell, they were on the ground floor. It hardly looked like a vampire lord's *sanctum sanctorum*.

Anise motioned to a small, narrow door set into the side of a staircase.

"This leads to an underground tunnel that connects the main house with what used to be the stables. It's how Morgan and the renfields get in and out."

"What are you doing out of your room?"

Anise gasped and Sonja melted into the shadows. A stern-faced woman with the characteristic wan complexion and pinched face of a renfield glowered disapprovingly at Anise from the foot of the stairs.

"I was bored. I wanted to take a walk."

The renfield stepped forward. "You know you're not allowed to roam the house unsupervised! Did Dr. Howell tell you to do this?" There was an edge in her voice suggesting she would like nothing better than to accuse the good doctor of malpractice.

"No one told me to do anything! I decided to go for a walk on my own."

The renfield blinked and frowned as if Anise had suddenly started speaking in Swahili. "No one decides things for themselves. Who were you talking to?"

"I wasn't talking to anyone, just myself."

"You're a lying little shit." The renfield's lips peeled back, displaying a set of tobacco-stained teeth.

Anise struck the renfield with her open hand. The blow knocked the woman to the floor. The human supported herself on one forearm; the right side of her face already swelling. She fixed hate-filled eyes on Anise and spat a mouthful of blood and loose teeth.

"I don't care if you *are* his prize broodmare. I'll burn your brain for that!"

"I don't think so."

The renfield jerked her head in the direction of Sonja's voice just in time to catch a steel-tipped boot under the chin. She fell back against the worn oriental carpet, her neck broken.

Anise stared at the dead woman. "You killed her!"

"Had to be done. Couldn't risk her raising the alarm."

Anise stared at her own hand, still smeared with the dead renfield's blood, then at Sonja.

"C'mon. We're wasting time!" Sonja shouldered the renfield's body and opened the door leading to the tunnel.

"You're taking her with us?" Anise looked genuinely repulsed.

"I've got to stash this stiff *somewhere*, don't I? We can't leave Little Miss Sunshine here lying around for the housekeeper to stumble over."

Anise followed Sonja into the space under the stairs. They wedged the renfield's corpse into a corner then descended a short, wooden stairway leading to a dark, brick-lined tunnel. The place smelled of damp earth, spiders, and rat piss. Neither woman was bothered by the lack of light as they hurried along. At the end of the tunnel were a series of iron rungs leading to an overhead trapdoor. Sunlight filtered around the cracks, illuminating fungus spores dancing lazily in the air.

"Okay, up you go, young mother."

Anise placed one hand on the bottom rung, looked up at the dim sunlight, then back at Sonja. "What about Fell?"

"He had his chance."

"He doesn't understand, Sonja! It all happened so fast. He's still unaware of what's really going on. He's scared of you. Maybe if I tried talking to him . . . maybe then he'd listen."

"Anise . . ."

"I didn't ask for this!" Her voice was both angry and frightened. She sounded like a child trying to control her sense of grief and betrayal. "All I wanted was to be free of the nightmares! To get rid of the red-eyed things in the dark! Now I wake up from the dream and find myself still in the nightmare. Everything is upside down and crazy. I'm pregnant and I don't . . . I don't like men, Sonja."

"I know." Her voice was soft, conciliatory.

"But, still, Fell's the father of my child. I owe him something!"

"Anise, if you go back there, your chances of escape range from slim to none. How are you going to get away? You're not going to get very far on foot."

"Honey, you can't grow up in East Oakland without learning how to boost a car."

Sonja contemplated knocking the pregnant woman unconscious and dragging her back to the car, but cast it aside. "Okay. Go back and get him. We'll arrange to rendezvous later this evening. There's a town nearby called El Pajaro. I'll be checked into the motel there. Look for a rented Ford Escort. But I promise, Anise, if you fall back under Morgan's control, I'll have no alternative than to kill both you *and* your baby. Is that clear?"

Anise nodded. "It's been over one hundred and twenty-five years since the Emancipation Proclamation. I have no intention to bring a child of mine into the world as a slave."

"I better be going, then." Sonja paused, then flung her arms around Anise's shoulders, dragging her into a hasty embrace.

Anise returned the hug and whispered, "God's speed, sister."

Anise watched Sonja climb into the sunlight then turned back into the darkness. She wanted to cry, but her eyes remained frustratingly dry.

THE PINK MOTEL

No woman can call herself free who does not own or control her body. No woman can call herself free until she can choose consciously whether she will or will not be a mother.

—Margaret Sanger

14

Palmer was well into his second pack of Shermans when Sonja re-emerged from the undergrowth. He was surprised to find himself glad to see her.

He got up from where he'd been squatting in the shade, the binoculars' eyepieces capped. He had stopped studying Ghost Trap shortly after Sonja entered the building; he didn't like the reverberations the house kicked up in his hind-brain. He grinned a welcome to his partner.

"It's about time you got back! I was starting to get worried. There's only an hour or two before it gets dark. So, did you score? Did you off the bastard?"

"Get in the car."

"You *did* kill him, didn't you? I mean, we're not going to have to worry about some heavy-weight bogeyman coming down on our asses, are we?"

"We'll talk about it later, Palmer."

His smile faltered. "You didn't do it."

"I *said* we'll talk about it later!"

Palmer ground out his smoldering cigarette with a sharp twist of his heel. "I should have known," he muttered as he crawled behind the wheel. "I should have fuckin' *known*."

The Pink Motel provided the only lodging in El Parajo, a tiny hamlet of three thousand souls. Palmer scowled at the sign fronting the parking lot—a Tinkerbell clone hovered over the garish tubing spelling out the motel's name. The glowing end of the neon fairy's magic wand dotted the *i* in the word *pink*.

He looked up as Sonja returned from the registration desk, sliding into the passenger seat next to him. She held up a piece of pink plastic with a key dangling from its end.

"Room Twenty. I told him we were a honeymooning couple and didn't want to bother the other guests."

"No problem there," Palmer commented drily, scanning the empty gravel parking lot. He put the car into gear and drove to the end of the twenty-unit motor court. The exterior of the long, L-shaped building was an aged pink stucco the color of well-chewed bubble gum.

The inside of the room was no better. The walls were a pale bisque, while the carpet looked, and felt, like dirty cotton candy.

"It's like I'm in the belly of a huge snake." Palmer groaned, eyeing the worn chenille spread covering the queen-sized mattress.

Sonja grunted and stared at the picture hanging over the bed; it was a cheap flea market print of a Sam Keane waif with over-huge eyes and a tiny mouth set into a simpering pout. Snorting in disgust, Sonja yanked the offending artwork off the wall and sailed it into a corner. She flopped heavily onto the bed. The box springs squealed in protest.

Palmer was surprised by how tired she looked. In the week since their lives had merged, Palmer had come to think of her as preternaturally energetic. She was definitely the most intense woman he'd ever known. The sight of her sprawled across the bed sparked a vague lust in him.

"I feel so old sometimes." Sonja lifted a hand to

her brow, slowly rubbing her forehead. "So horribly, horribly old. And I'm not even forty yet." Her laugh was dry. "I wonder how the truly ancient ones feel? Vampires like Pangloss. They must be so very tired. I've heard that when they grow weary of continuing, they simply go to sleep. A hibernation that lasts for years, decades. Sleep: the stepchild of Death." Her voice had a smoky, far-away fell to it. Palmer wondered if she was aware she was speaking aloud.

He sat next to her on the bed and stared at the worn carpet between his shoes. "Sonja—what happened in that house?"

"I discovered I'm not alone."

"What?"

In a soft, weary voice she told him about Anise and Fell and Morgan's plan to breed his own race of designer-gene vampires.

"And you left them there? *Alive?*"

"You don't understand, Palmer . . ."

"You're damn right I don't understand! Why didn't you kill them?"

"I couldn't."

"Wouldn't, you mean!"

"No. *Couldn't.*" Sonja removed her sunglasses, exposing her eyes to him for the first time. "I don't fully understand it, myself. I used to think I could reclaim what I once was by killing what I'd become. It didn't work. Maybe it's time for me to build instead of destroy. I've been lonely, Palmer. So terribly lonely."

Palmer forced himself to look into her eyes. She silently stiffened, squaring her shoulders in preparation for rejection. The pupils were huge, dilated to maximize even the feeblest light source. They were the eyes of a hybrid, neither human or vampire. At first he was repulsed by how raw and inhuman they'd looked; but now, he could see a perverse beauty in them. Even without touching her mind, he knew how much of herself she'd exposed to him simply by removing her glasses.

He kissed her without really knowing why, yet confident the action was genuinely his. His hands slipped under her shirt, his fingers tracing old wounds. She arched her back and moaned in pleasure. The way she stretched her lithe, tight body reminded him of the panthers at the zoo—so beautiful and so deadly with their predator's grace.

Her flesh was pale, marked by numerous scars. He closed his eyes and ran his hands over her naked torso. He had expected to be repulsed by the sensation, but found himself fascinated by the complex designs. It was like reading braille; each scar a story bonded forever to her flesh.

She helped him out of his clothes, her fingers tracing the scar over his heart. Palmer felt a tremor of apprehension in the back of his mind, as memories of Loli's betrayal surfaced then disappeared.

She closed about him like a velvet fist. Her arms and legs wrapped about his, holding him fast. He knew he could not break free of her embrace, but he felt no urge to escape. If she had wanted to force this upon him, she could have done it long ago.

Her mind reached out and touched his, teasing it from its cage of bone. She laughed, a telepathic birdsong echoing inside his head, as she urged him to surrender both body and mind to passion.

As he shucked his skin, the jungle surged behind his eyelids. He saw a beautiful woman with intricate ritual designs scratched into her cheeks and brow smiling at him. The smell of burning copal filled his nostrils. Then he was free of his flesh, their minds twining together like mating snakes.

He could not see her, but he knew Sonja was there, both within and outside him. It was a delicious feeling, one that transcended the human physical vocabulary. It went beyond any sensations he'd ever derived from sex or drugs or any other form of carnal gratification. He experienced the raw essence of orgasm, cut free of biological imperative—the promised reward of the faithful of Islam: the thousand-year climax. Or at least ten minutes worth.

Suddenly he was back in his body, rutting like a bull in heat. Sonja convulsed under him, thrusting her pelvis against his with bruising urgency. His shoulders stung and something warm trickled over his bare skin. The sight and smell of his blood dripping from her fingernails stoked his lust even higher. Sonja arched her back, her muscles as taut as bow-strings, and yowled like a cat; her lips pulled back in a rictus grin as she bared her fangs. Palmer groaned as her contractions milked him dry.

He lay atop her, sweat and blood drying on his back, and smoothed the hair away from her face. There were no words. None were needed. He studied the tilt of her cheekbones and the shape of her nose in the failing daylight filtering through the rose-colored curtains. As he drifted into sleep, it occurred to him that this was the first time he hadn't needed a smoke after sex.

The room was in deep shadow and someone was banging on the door. Sonja moved with the speed and agility of an animal, untangling herself from their lover's embrace. She moved so fast he didn't even see her slip her glasses back on.

Palmer yanked on his pants and moved to answer the door, minus his shirt and shoes. He glimpsed Sonja out of the corner of his eye, moving along the baseboard like a tiger preparing to pounce. The sight of her muscles coiling and uncoiling underneath her moon-pale skin inspired a brief rush of lust in him.

He opened the door the width of the safety chain and peered out at a small-boned African-American woman shivering in the dark. Now that the sun was down, the air had a bite to it.

"Whattayawant?"

The woman tossed back her braids and looked him directly in the face. Her pupils were inhumanly large. The eyes of a hybrid. "I need to see Sonja."

"It's okay, Palmer. Let her in." Sonja was standing at his elbow. She'd moved so quietly he wasn't aware she was behind him until she spoke.

Palmer opened the door and Anise hurried in. She wore the same loose cotton dress she'd had on earlier that afternoon, only now there were dark, tulip-shaped stains on its front.

Sonja motioned for Palmer to keep watch at the window before pulling on her Circle Jerks t-shirt. "Where's Fell?"

Anise shook her head, causing her braids to sway. "It went bad. Real bad! Worse than I thought it would. I'm lucky I got away at all." She started pacing back and forth; the way she waddled and wrung her hands while she spoke made Sonja think of a worried penguin.

"What happened?"

"I went back and tried to talk to him, like I said I would. It was impossible! It was like his ears were sealed with wax. I told him that I didn't love him—that it was impossible for me to care for him. I wasn't going to be Morgan's brood bitch anymore! He tried to keep me from leaving. I ended up hitting him with one of the fire-tools. There was a lot of blood. I tied him up and stuffed him in one of the closets. While I was busy doing that, I was surprised by one of Morgan's renfields. I . . ." She grimaced in distaste. "I killed him with my bare hands."

"How do you feel about that?"

Anise stopped her pacing and took a deep breath. "It was easy. Too easy."

"And?"

"It felt good." She shuddered. "Sweet Jesus, what am I turning into? What did that bastard *do* to me?"

Sonja did not answer. She looked at Anise's face and wondered what she could possibly say to make the fear go away, yet also curious as to how long it would be before Anise's version of the Other would make itself known. Or was it already active, ready for more murder and mayhem?

It had been so long since Sonja had last imagined herself truly human. Sometimes her life as Denise Thorne seemed little more than a pleasant, if vivid, dream. She imagined how must it be for Anise to wake up and find herself not only married to a man she didn't love and pregnant against her will, but no longer human, and was humbled by her sister's underlying strength.

"Think you're up to a three-hour drive to San Francisco?"

"What choice do I have? We sure as hell can't stay here! Morgan no doubt already has his dogs out looking for me. I'm ready when you—uh-oh."

"What do you mean 'uh-oh'?"

Anise grimaced. "I think I spoke too soon."

Palmer turned away from the window. He looked like he'd just swallowed a lemon. "Does she mean what I *think* she means?"

Anise emitted a groan as her water broke.

"I'm afraid so," sighed Sonja.

15

The first contraction doubled Palmer over.

He was coming from the bathroom with an arm-
load of towels when it hit, crashing against him
like a wave. The phantom pain radiating from his
pelvis caused him to stagger and nearly drop what
he was carrying.

"Screen yourself! She's broadcasting!" hissed Sonja,
snatching the towels from his numb fingers.

"Now you tell me." Palmer groaned as he tried to
force the pain back long enough to erect a mental
barrier.

Anise gave a strangled cry and dug her fingers
deep into the mattress, shredding the bedclothes like
rotten silk. Palmer felt her pain press against his
shield like a heavy, insistent hand, but, remarkably,
the barricade held.

"This is not good. Not good at all." Sonja brushed
a stray lock of hair from her face, leaving a smear of
Anise's blood on her brow. "She's broadcasting like
a damn communications satellite! Of all the times for
her psychic powers to decide to kick in! Morgan's
renfields will be able to zero in on our location soon,
if they haven't done so already."

"Is there any way we could get her in the car and
back to San Francisco?"

Sonja sighed and jerked a thumb over her shoulder. "What do *you* think?"

Anise lay on her back, gripping the metal bedstead with bloodless hands. A lamp situated on the dresser, its light muted by a towel thrown over the shade, provided the room's only illumination.

There was something primeval in the way Anise lay, sweating and grunting, with her dress pushed up and her legs spread open. All they needed was a shaman shaking a medicine rattle and dancing around the room in a ceremonial headdress to complete the scene.

"How long until the baby comes?"

"I don't know. Minutes. Hours. It's hard enough to tell with a normal pregnancy, much less something like this."

"Great."

"You got the gun?"

Palmer nodded to the .38, still in its holster, hanging from the back of a chair.

"Better put it back on."

"Sonja? Sonja, where are you?"

"I'm here, babe. I'm not going anywhere." Sonja moved back to the bed, mopping the sweat from Anise's face with a damp washcloth. "How you doing, kid?" Sonja took Anise's hand and clasped it in her own.

"It hurts, Sonja. A lot."

"So the Bible tells me so. That's only natural, Anise."

"No, that's not it—not all of it, anyway. There's something else." She grimaced as another spasm racked her body. "It's like passing a broken bottle. I—" She gave a brief cry and slammed her head against the pillows, squeezing her eyes shut. "Sweet Mother of Christ, what did I ever do to be punished like this? What?"

It was as if an invisible fist was squeezing her stomach. Just as she thought the pain would continue into infinity, the baby's head emerged from between her thighs.

Sonja moved to help the infant free itself, then stopped. The baby's head was bulbous, its eyes as black and flat as those of an insect. It had a flat nose with slits instead of nostrils and a tube-like mouth made of gristle, lined with tiny, lamprey-like teeth. It whipped its tiny, powerful shoulders back and forth until it finally freed one arm.

Five tiny fingers, complete with curved talons, hooked into the gore-stained bedclothes, giving it the leverage to drag the rest of it free of the birth canal. The newborn vampire child lay exhausted on the filthy sheet like a large maggot, glistening with birth fluids.

Palmer stared at the thing on the bed and wiped his mouth with the back of his hand. Sonja moved to cut the umbilical with her switchblade. The creature lifted its oversized head on a surprisingly steady neck, regarding her warily with its flat black eyes.

"Easy . . . easy, now . . ." she muttered under her breath, as if addressing a skittish, potentially dangerous animal.

"Sonja? Sonja? What's wrong with the baby? Why can't I hear it crying? Why isn't it crying, Sonja?"

Swallowing her reluctance at touching the thing, Sonja severed the umbilical, quickly tying off the end. As she worked, she noticed that the infant was completely smooth between the legs, lacking even an anus.

"Sonja? Why don't you answer me?" Anise struggled into a sitting position. Sonja maneuvered herself between mother and child.

"You don't want to see it, Anise! Please, believe me!"

"What's wrong? Is it dead?"

"No, it's not dead. It's—well, it's not a baby."

"What do you *mean* it's not a baby?"

"Anise—"

"Woman, let me see my child!"

Sonja sighed and turned to pick up the creature and hand it over to its mother. But it wasn't there anymore.

"Shit, Palmer! I thought you were watching it!"

"You didn't tell me to! Hell, the thing just got born! How was I to know it'd go walk about?"

"Where'd the little bastard go?" Sonja stepped away from the bed, scanning the shadows along the baseboard.

There was a blur of motion at the corner of Palmer's eye. He contemplated taking his gun out of its holster but quickly discarded the idea.

It's just a baby, for chrissakes! A really seriously ugly, mutant vampire baby, yeah. But it still wouldn't be cool to blow it away. It's just a baby.

Something small darted out from under the bureau and latched onto Palmer's right calf. He screeched as its ring of lamprey teeth began chewing its way to the meat beneath his pants leg.

Swearing and hopping on his free leg to keep his balance, Palmer tried to shake the hell-baby loose. On his second kick, he sent the creature sailing halfway across the room. The infant landed on its back and squealed like a suckling pig pulled from its mother's nipple.

Palmer risked a glance at his calf—his pants leg was shredded and blood oozed from dozens of tiny punctures in his skin. He looked like he'd been attacked with a needle-studded ping-pong paddle, but was otherwise unharmed.

The hell-baby flailed the air with its chubby arms and legs like a tipped turtle desperate to right itself.

"That's quite enough of that!" Sonja said sternly, snatching the shrieking infant off the dirty floor. She frowned at Palmer's leg. "You better see to that before infection sets in."

"What about *that*?" he retorted, jabbing a finger at the baby.

"Don't worry. I'll handle it." She held the tiny struggling mutant like a live rattlesnake, her fingers clamped behind the holes where its ears should have been, and presented it to its mother.

"I can take care of it, if it's what you want." Sonja's voice was flat and without emotion. She could have been offering to take out the garbage.

"No. It's my child. It's my responsibility."

Anise stretched out her arms to accept the wriggling infant. She fought to keep the repugnance she felt toward her own flesh and blood from showing on her face, but it was difficult. The mutant stopped its angry thrashing the moment Anise touched it, regarding its mother with unreadable, bottomless eyes. The gristle that formed its mouth puckered and unpuckered rapidly. It wanted to nurse.

"It's not its fault," she said sadly. "This was how it was born. It can't be anything else." She laughed. It was a hollow sound. "You know, I actually was considering having a child before all this happened. Not anytime soon—but sometime, when I could afford it. Maybe make a trip to the friendly neighborhood artificial inseminator." Her lips twisted themselves into a bitter parody of a smile. "I never thought I'd end up with . . . with . . ." She swallowed and took a deep breath. "Like I said—it's my responsibility."

She snapped the baby's neck like a green twig. It didn't even have time to cry. Anise stared at its tiny, motionless body and ran a trembling hand over its bulging brow.

"Poor little thing. It didn't ask for any of this."
She suddenly grimaced and the mutant baby's corpse
slipped from her arms and landed on the floor with
a dull thud.

"Anise, what's wrong?"

"The contractions. They've started again. I—Oh
Lord, not again! I can't go through this again!" Anise
grabbed Sonja's shoulder as she pushed, digging her
fingernails deep into the other woman's skin. "Ah!
Oh, Jesus! Make it stop!" She drew a shaky breath
through her teeth. "Whatever the first one did trying
to get out—it screwed me up real bad, Sonja! I mean
it! I don't know if I can—" A third contraction
turned her words into a swallowed scream.

"Don't worry, Anise. Everything will be all right.
I'm not going to let anything happen to you, understand?" Sonja untangled herself from Anise's grip
and resumed her place at the foot of the bed.

Anise's second child came into the world wrapped
in a caul. Sonja split the thick membrane shrouding
the infant, relieved to see what looked to be a normal, human baby face underneath. She gave its tiny
flanks a small pinch and was rewarded with a
healthy, indignant wail. She swiftly severed the
umbilical cord and wrapped the newborn in a clean
towel. She smiled and held it out to its mother.

Anise turned her head away, pressing her face into
the pillow. "I don't want to see it."

"It's all right—you can look."

Anise hesitated for a second, then cautiously lifted
her head. Sonja was frightened by how drawn and
sick she looked. She peered cautiously at the child
wrapped inside the impromptu swaddling.

It was still as red as a piece of raw meat, but she
could tell the child shared her coloration. It squalled
like a siamese cat in heat and had the face of a minia-
turized prize-fighter.

"She's *beautiful!*"

"Yes, she is, isn't she?" Sonja whispered, placing the tiny bundle in her mother's arms.

While Anise was preoccupied with the baby, Sonja scooped its dead twin off the floor and wrapped it in one of the discarded, blood-caked towels. It would have to be burned later on. It wouldn't do to leave something like that for the housekeeping staff to find the next day.

She stared absently at the blood smearing her hands, then licked her fingers. She knew she was pushing her own tolerance dangerously far. She needed to feed, and her surroundings weren't helping much. The room reeked of blood.

Palmer limped out of the bathroom. He'd ripped open his right pants leg from the knee down and wrapped his calf with strips torn from his undershirt.

"How's the leg?"

"It's been better."

Sonja found herself staring at the crimson seeping through the makeshift bandage and quickly looked away.

What was I thinking? This is a man I think I might actually love! And I was imagining what his blood would taste like! I was actually picturing slicing open the artery in his leg and drinking from it! Sick! Sick! Sick! Can't you let me have any happiness?

The Other laughed, but no one else heard.

"Sonja?" Anise was looking at her funny.

"Uh, sorry. I guess I was busy—thinking."

"I said, how do you like Lethe?"

"Lethe?"

"I think that's what I'll name her. I like the way it sounds, don't you? It's from Baudelaire. A name is the least I can give her before I die."

"Anise, listen to me. I know you've experienced massive internal damage, but you're not going to die.

I know this, because I've suffered a hell of a lot worse in the past. You'll regenerate, but you're gonna need blood. If you don't feed soon, your body will start cannibalizing itself. Do you know what that means?"

"You're saying I'm going to have to kill someone if I want to stay alive."

"Basically."

"I can't do that, Sonja! I don't care what that bastard did to me—I refuse to be a monster."

"Look, you won't have to do anything. I'll hunt for you. There are plenty of transients, people no one will ever miss. Drunks, hitchhikers, bums . . ."

"My God, Sonja! You sound just like him!"

"I'm not going to let you die!" Sonja was surprised she was shouting. "I won't *let* you!"

Lethe started at the noise and began to cry again. Anise did not look at Sonja as she spoke, but instead addressed her words to the newborn baby at her side, smoothing the few wispy strands of hair on her daughter's brow.

"I can't do it, Sonja. I can't take the step beyond. I don't have your . . . courage. I had enough to break free of Morgan, but not enough to deal with continuing my life by killing others. Not that I'm condemning you for it. But I can't live knowing I'm responsible for another human's death, no matter how worthless that person may be."

"That's what you're saying now! I felt the same way, myself, years ago. But later, once you get used to it, you'll see things differently."

"I know. That's what I'm afraid of! Please, Sonja. Don't try to talk me out of this. I know what I'm doing."

"But what about Lethe? What about her?"

Anise smiled sadly and kissed her daughter on the forehead. "I hope she can forgive me for not being there while she grows up. But if there's one thing she needs more than anything else right now, it's protection. I promised myself no child of mine would be born a slave, and I mean to keep that promise! That's why I'm trusting you to protect her, Sonja. You and poor Mr. Palmer over there."

"Anise, I'm the last person on earth you should put your faith in. I'm a murderer—and worse—a hundred times over. Every day I fight to keep the demon inside me from taking over, and a lot of times I *can't*! You might as well hire Typhoid Mary as a babysitter!"

"You judge yourself too harshly, sister. Here, take the child. Leave now. Morgan will be here soon. I can feel him calling to me."

Sonja cocked her head as if listening to distant music. Yes, she could feel him too, now. She could take him. She was sure of it. But she was equally sure Morgan had at least two renfields with him. What about Palmer? He could handle himself in a fire-fight, but what about his ability to handle a combined psychic assault? And should either one of them fall to Morgan's forces, where would that leave Anise's baby? She couldn't protect them both at the same time.

Sonja bent and kissed her on the cheek. "Goodbye, Anise."

"My name is Lakisha. Anise was just a dream. And not even mine."

"You better give me the baby now."

Anise hesitated for a long moment, staring at her daughter as if committing to memory every detail of her face. She suddenly closed her eyes and thrust the infant away from her. "Here! Take her! Take her before I change my mind!"

"Is there anything you want before we go?"

"Leave me the gun."

Palmer looked sharply at Sonja.

"Give it to her."

Lakisha smiled weakly as she accepted the .38. It wasn't much of a trade-off, her child for the gun, but it'd do.

Sonja paused on the threshold, cradling Lethe against her worn leather jacket.

"Look after my baby, Sonja."

"Like she was my own."

16

"There's the car, milord. She must be inside the motel room," observed the chauffeur.

"A brilliant deduction, as usual, Renfield," Morgan sighed from the back seat of the Rolls.

He peered over the top of his tinted aviator glasses at the Ferrari parked outside Room 20 of the Pink Motel. The automobile was his, although the paperwork and owner's registration in the glove compartment claimed that the legal owner was one Dr. Joad Caron. The vanity plates agreed. But since Morgan was also the good doctor, whatever belonged to Joad Caron belonged to him. Including his patients.

Morgan glanced at the human seated beside him. The renfield was an ethnic Chinese whose ancestors had served as the imperial court's seers for six generations. They had deliberately interbred, cultivating some of the finest human psionic talents Morgan had run across in his travels. What was equally impressive was the line's reputation for relative sanity and stability, something rare amongst the more powerful wild talents. Morgan acknowledged his servant's special status by addressing him as something beside the generic renfield.

"Wretched Fly: scan."

The sensitive nodded silently, tilting his head to one side, like a robin listening for worms.

"She's there. Alone."

Morgan scowled. "Are you sure? Not that I do not doubt your abilities, my friend. I don't like to be caught unawares, that's all. Something our mischievous Ms. Blue seems to be quite adept at."

"She is alone. And in pain."

Morgan weighed the information carefully. It was possible Anise's would-be savior had abandoned her after all, although Morgan was curious as to why his enemy would leave the breeder alive.

Fell had informed him of how Anise had babbled on about "free will" and "the right to choose" before beaning him with the ash shovel. The speed and ardor of Anise's conversion bothered Morgan. He'd picked her as a breeder because of her keen psychological need to be assimilated by the dominant class structure. His programming should have held. That this rogue could have penetrated his defenses and undone so much work in so short a period of time troubled him. That his enemy had claimed to be one of his own by-blows disturbed Morgan even more.

Over the years there had been rumors circulating amongst the Combine of a strange creature stalking various revenants, vampires, and their attendant renfields. A predator that preyed on predators. The stories amongst the brood masters credited the maverick Pretender with immense strength, the ability to walk in daylight, and an unheard-of immunity to silver.

Some thought their antagonist the product of human technology, created to destroy the Pretender race. Morgan imagined the stories to be the result of a group of pathetic, senile ancients made paranoid by centuries of intrigue and counter-plots. Morgan had been amused by their need to create a bogeyman.

Still, it had given him the idea to create his own race of hybrid vampires. With his specially-bred *homo desmodus* under his control, he would soon have the likes of Baron Luxor and Marchessa Nuit kowtowing before him, pledging fealty for all eternity. Or however long Morgan saw fit for them to continue.

But now his dreams of glory were collapsing, undermined by a creature he'd imagined mythical. Morgan savored irony, but not at his own expense.

"Signal the others," he said, straightening the cuffs of his Saville Row silk suit.

Wretched Fly nodded, silently relaying his master's commands to the occupants of the second car.

The doors of the accompanying Mercedes popped open, and two figures climbed out. One was a renfield. The other had once been a particularly obnoxious insurance salesman who had tried to pressure what he thought was Dr. Caron into buying a policy. Now his body housed a fire elemental. The renfield gave the pyrotic a wide berth, wary of the fierce heat it radiated.

Morgan climbed out of the Rolls, followed closely by Wretched Fly. The gravel crunched under his handmade Italian shoes as he crossed the parking lot to Room 20. The door was unlocked. Not that it mattered.

Anise lay curled atop sheets befouled with blood and the fluids of childbirth. Her pallor was grayish and her eyes sunken in their orbits. She clutched a bloodstained bundle to her breast. She cringed at the sight of Morgan standing in the doorway, flanked by his most trusted—and powerful—renfields.

"You disappoint me, my child."

She closed her eyes, trying to subvert the conditioned responses his physical presence triggered in her. But simply shutting off the visual cues wasn't enough. He was all over her: in her mind, in her nostrils, in her tastebuds. He was everywhere and everything. He was unavoidable and undeniable.

"I'm not your child!" She tried to make her voice hard, but the words came out sounding more petulant than angry.

Morgan's lips pulled into a thin, cruel smile. "If I am not your father, who is? God? Satan? A honky from Watsonville out for cheap pussy? Is this how you show your gratitude? By running away and killing my servants? Is this how a daughter repays her father for all the things he's done for her?"

"Done *to* her, you mean!" Her lower lip was trembling, but the hate in her eyes remained undimmed.

"Come now, my child! This isn't the way I want things between us! You're mixed-up, confused . . . you don't know *what* to believe, do you? Your friend abandoned you, didn't she? Left you alone and helpless. She talked about freedom and free will, didn't she? Those are nice, pretty-sounding words, aren't they? But they're just words; simple-minded phrases deluded humans use to coerce themselves into believing themselves masters of their destiny. They are meaningless!" He opened his arms wide. "Come home with me, Anise, and all things will be forgiven."

Anise felt her defenses start to melt. She still hated Morgan, but part of her wanted to rush into his strong, protective arms. Thinking on her own and deciding for herself was exhausting, even frightening. Things would be so much better if she refuted the pretense of free will and let Morgan take control. It would be so easy to say yes and surrender, to become like him . . .

No! That's what he wants! That's what he's betting on! Stay angry! Stay angry! Don't let him win! Be strong, woman! If not for yourself, for Lethe!

"You can't fool me anymore, Morgan. I can see you for what you really are. I'm not going back!"

The pyrotic, its skin the color of barbecued meat, wandered over to the corner of the room where an old black-and-white Zenith television sat bolted atop a pedestal. The pyrotic's eyes resembled hard-boiled eggs, but this did not seem to impinge on its ability to navigate. It punched the television's "on" button and stepped back. *The Beverly Hillbillies* theme song blared from the TV's speakers at full volume.

*"Come and listen to my story 'bout a man named Jed,
A poor mountaineer barely kept his fam'ly fed . . ."*

Morgan spun around, his face livid. "Turn that shit off! Renfield! Get that damned elemental away from that accursed idiot box!"

The pyrotic showed its displeasure by making a noise like live steam escaping a radiator. The renfield grunted and moved to turn off the television. There was a loud crack and the side of the renfield's head disappeared.

Morgan spun to face Anise, his ears ringing from the gunshot. The muzzle of a .38 was leveled directly between his eyes.

"Put the gun down, Anise."

"My name's Lakisha!"

Morgan pretended not to hear her. "I said put down the gun, *Anise*."

She fired the gun a second time, but her hand was shaking too hard; the slug struck Morgan in the shoulder instead of the head.

"Nice try, Anise. But no cigar."

"I told you my name's Lakisha, asshole!" she hissed, and shoved the gun in her mouth and pulled the trigger. Her head opened like a cracked pinata, spraying the wall with the raw material of memory. Morgan stared for a long moment at the mess dripping from the walls as if divining omens.

Wretched Fly removed the bloodstained bundle from the bed and held it out to his master for inspection. Morgan grimaced at the sight of the mutant baby's hideous puckered mouth and skeleton-like nose and snatched the offending corpse from Wretched Fly, shaking it like a rag doll.

"This is Howell's doing! He promised that the child would be able to pass for human! The bastard lied to me! Lied! I'll make that junkie *pay* for this!" He hurled the dead baby back at its mother, turning his back on the tableau in disgust. "Torch it!"

The pyrotic stepped forward. Its mouth dropped open and a gout of liquid flame leapt free, consuming the bed and its lifeless occupants. The smell of burning mattress and roasting meat filled the room.

Morgan stepped outside Room 20, scowling at the night sky without seeing it. His mouth tasted of ash. There was only one thing that could wash away the bitterness of failure—the blood of his enemy.

"Hey, you! Keep your hands where I can see 'em!"

An elderly man armed with a double-barreled shotgun hurried across the parking lot from the motel's office. His bathrobe flapped open, exposing faded pajama bottoms and a stained T-shirt.

"What in hell's going on here? I heard gun shots! Where's the Smiths?"

"Smiths?" Morgan raised an eyebrow in amusement.

"You know who I'm talking about—the young couple that rented Number 20. You better answer me, fellah, or I'm liable to blow a hole in you! I ain't one to be fucked with!"

"Indeed."

Wretched Fly and the pyrotic stepped out of the motel room to stand beside Morgan. The motel manager frowned and took an automatic step backward. His eyes widened as he caught sight of the flames reflected in the windows.

"You crazy bastards set fire to my motel!"

Morgan, bored with the confrontation, turned his back on the man. "Take care of him," he yawned, waving a languid hand at his servants.

"Where you think you're going, asshole?" The manager's voice wavered as he fought to control his anger. He stepped forward, shouldering the shotgun. "You're staying put until the state police get here!"

The pyrotic belched and a fireball the size of a ripe cabbage struck the old man in the chest. He dropped his weapon and clawed at the flames eating his clothes and skin, spreading it to his hands and upper arms.

Screaming like an angry bluejay, the old man threw himself to the ground and rolled in the dirt and gravel, spreading the fire to his pajama pants and hair. During his final, conscious moments, he tried to drag himself back the way he came, his ears filled with the sound of his own flesh hissing and crackling like bacon fat in a frying pan.

He succeeded in crawling nearly six feet before he was completely consumed.

The pyrotic squatted next to the smouldering remains and inhaled the blue-white flames back into his nose and open mouth. The intense heat had reduced the old man's skull to the size of an orange. Wretched Fly signalled impatiently for the elemental to get back in the Mercedes.

Morgan slid behind the wheel of the Ferarri, sneering at Anise's crude hot-wiring job. Within seconds he was speeding down the highway, the Rolls and Mercedes following in his wake. The night was young and there was much to done.

THE SHADOW BOX

Shape without form, shade without colour,
Paralysed force, gesture without motion.
                    —T.S. Eliot, _The Hollow Man_

17

"What the hell are we gonna do with a *baby*, for crying out loud? I don't know the first thing about what they eat or nothing!"

Lethe, nestled in an impromptu bassinet made from clean towels and an open bureau drawer, waved her arms and kicked her legs as if semaphoring her agreement with Palmer's statement.

"Well, here's where you're gonna *learn*. I went down to the all-night drug store on the next street and picked up this crap," Sonja explained, tossing a box of disposable Pampers at him like a medicine ball.

"You think I'm taking care of *that*, you're crazy!"

"You can't stick the kid in a tube-sock and hose her off once a week! I bought enough canned formula to last her a few days, plus a couple of bottles and a pacifier. You can cook her formula on this hot plate . . ."

"The hotel rules say no cooking in the rooms!"

"The old gent behind the desk didn't bat an eye when we came back from our 'winery tour' with a newborn baby. What makes you think the management is going to notice a lousy hot plate? Look, we promised Anise we'd take care of her . . ."

Palmer held his hands up, palms outward, and

shook his head from side to side. "*You* promised, not me! I'll fight fuckin' ugly monsters for you, babe. I'll even allow myself to be involved in breaking and entering and murder charges. But I am *not* changing diapers!"

"Palmer!"

"Just because I fucked you doesn't mean I want to start a family, especially like this. Besides, how do you know she won't turn into something like the first one?"

"She's just a *baby*!"

"If she's just a baby, what is it with her eyes?"

Lethe gurgled and kicked and waved her arms even more. Sonja plucked at her ward's makeshift blankets. She'd had little experience with children, especially ones so young, but she was certain Lethe was unusually active for a baby not even a day old. She'd be damned if she was going to mention that to Palmer. He was spooked enough as it was. Lethe peeked out of her swaddling with golden, pupil-less eyes and gave Sonja a toothless grin.

"So, okay, her eyes are screwed up! Is that a fuckin' crime?"

"No, but you weren't the one her evil twin tried to turn into Gerber's strained beef!"

"I'm not asking you to take her to raise, damn it! I'm just asking you to baby-sit. If we're going to be on a jet to Yucatan within the next twelve hours, I've got to check with a few of my . . . connections. And I sure as hell can't do it dragging around a papoose!"

"Okay, I'll do it. But just this once!"

"Great! I'll try to be quick about it. Everything you need for fixing her bottle should be in the bags. Just read the labels on the cans—they're pretty self-explanatory."

Palmer grimaced at Sonja's back, then turned his disapproving gaze onto Lethe.

"Sure, you're cute *now*. But if you try anything funny, you're going out the fuckin' window. You got that, munchkin?"

Lethe cooed and yawned, exposing soft pink gums.

"Yeah, well, don't you forget it."

The pay phone stood on the corner of Guerrero and Twenty-First Street, opposite a television repair shop with dusty windows full of half-assembled or partially demolished Philcos and Zeniths. The black-and-chrome face of the phone was covered with graffiti, the coin box had been forced, and a yellow adhesive strip bearing the legend "Out of Order" was plastered over the coin slot.

Sonja scanned the corner: across the street a couple of young men dressed in bomber jackets and tight-fitting leather pants strolled arm in arm, walking their Pomeranian, while an intense-looking middle-aged man with heavy eyebrows ducked into an espresso bar. Somewhere a police siren wailed, throwing echoes against the hills.

Satisfied the area was clean, she sauntered from her watching place inside a doorway and picked up the dead receiver. The plastic was cold and hard in her hand. Sonja placed the earpiece to her head and casually stabbed the pay phone's push buttons. There was stone silence, then the sound of a receiver half a country away being lifted off its hook.

"Yeah?" A heavy, almost liquid voice.

"I want to talk to Malfeis."

The voice on the other end slurped. "Yeah. Sure. Who should I say is calling?"

"The Blue Woman."

"Sonja! Chicky-baby! Sorry 'bout the slug. Breakin'

in a nephew—what can I say? So, what can I do for you, sweet thing?"

"Got tired of being a skatepunk already, Mal?"

"Hey, what can I say? I like innovation as much as the next guy, but a classic's a classic!"

"Mal, I need help . . ."

"Help?"

"Mal, I'm between your cousin and the deep blue sea! I've put my foot in it big time! I need magic, man!"

"What about Li Lijing?"

"He's just an alchemist, Mal. I'm talking *serious* mojo!"

"Uh, look, sweetie, I wish I could help you out, but—"

"But *what*?!"

"I don't know *what* you did out there, cupcake, but Morgan's stock's falling like a lead turd in the Marinaras Trench! And a lot of the big boys in the First Hierarchy aren't exactly overjoyed, if you catch my drift. I'm in deep with the family over this, Sonja. I'm not supposed to give you the time of day, much less tell you where to score."

"Mal! Damn you, you know I'm good for it! I can get you Ed Gein's brain—pureed. How about Mengele's jawbone? The *real* one, not that fake they dug up in South America. C'mon, man! I'm not shitting you—I *gotta* score!"

"Okay. Tell you what—since you've been such a good customer in the past, I'm gonna help you out. But just this once, *capiche*? I don't want it getting around I'm a soft touch."

"Thanks, Mal! I owe you!"

"More than you realize. Awright, here's what I want you to do. There's this bar south of Market called the Shadow Box. Go there and wait for my operative. He should be there in the hour."

"What's he look like?"

"Don't worry—you'll know him when you see him."

It was after midnight and things were just getting heated up at the Shadow Box.

A disc jockey in a neon-encrusted sound booth generated a thundering, synth-heavy mixture of euro-pop, retro-disco, and acidhouse. Klieg lights hanging from the rafters threw elongated shadows of the dancers onto the stark white walls. Sonja noted the dancers' stylized movements, striking high fashion poses, and how they centered their attention more on their own shadows than on their partners. It was times like these she was embarrassed at ever having been human.

"Talk about dancing with yourself," she muttered in disgust.

A gaggle of stylishly coiffed and painted future executives squeezed their way past, jostling her in their hurry to reach the dance floor. Sonja briefly contemplated hamstringing one of them, but pushed the thought aside. She couldn't risk calling attention to herself.

Bars and nightclubs always brought out the worst in her. She suspected it had something to do with the volatile emotions generated in such places that stimulated the Other, exciting it to mayhem. Even now she could feel the Other's silent, ominous presence just under the surface of her ego, like a shark patroling its territory. She reflected on how Mal *could* have picked a rendezvous site a little less crowded, but beggars don't exactly get a choice in such matters.

The music got faster and louder, the shadows on the walls jerking and prancing like Burmese puppets.

Sonja consulted her wristwatch. Mal had said her contact would arrive within the hour.

She felt it then: a spiky, adrenalin-charged surge of anger and excitement, as cold and bracing as vodka straight from the freezer. The hairs on the back of her neck bristled.

The emotion wasn't hers, however. It was being broadcast—unintentionally—by someone in the bar.

Someone *really* pissed off.

Sonja turned to scan the interior of the club. Within the last few minutes the number of people entering the bar had doubled. The Shadow Box was a solid wall of young men and women; dancing, drinking, and talking over the music blaring from the speakers.

She shifted spectrums, searching for telltale Pretender aureole. All she came up with was the comparatively weak flickering of human consciousness, augmented by drugs or hormones.

The second jolt of hate struck her, and she gasped as if caught in the grip of an intense orgasm. The Other moaned in pleasure and Sonja bit her lip, hoping the pain and blood would sidetrack it long enough for her to regain control.

Emotions as dark and powerful as hate provided vampires with as much nourishment as a seven-course dinner and a high that made crack look like baby aspirin. Her hair crackled with static electricity as she metabolized the charge.

She had to get out of here. Fuck Mal's mojo-worker. She had to get away from this place, crammed full of empty-eyed foodtubes. She hadn't fed since she'd taken down the pickpocket in Chinatown, and it was making her weak, susceptible to the Other's inner voice. She had to leave or something really *bad* was going to happen.

Sonja pushed away from the bar and began shouldering her way to the exit. She bumped against a tall man with half his head shaved and a diamond stud in his left nostril, sloshing beer on his leather pants.

"Hey, bitch! Watch it!" The man with the pierced nose grabbed her elbow. She went rigid and snarled, the sound rumbling from her ribcage like the growl of a big cat. He let go.

That was close. Too close.

She took a deep, shuddery breath and resumed pushing her way through the massed bodies. Before she'd gone ten feet, a second hand clamped her shoulder. The hate that flowed into her was so strong it was as if she'd been stuck with a syringe full of one hundred percent pure China White.

She didn't resist as her attacker spun her around to face him.

She smiled crookedly. "The bastard set me up, didn't he? I'm gonna cut his stash with the bones of martyrs next time! I'd damn him to hell if it wasn't redundant."

Fell bared his fangs in ritual challenge. "I don't know what you're babbling about, whore, and I don't care! You killed Anise and my baby and I mean to even the score!"

"You always talk like a fucking cliche, Fell?"

He moved fast, even by her standards, slamming his fist into her jaw. Sonja's head snapped back, blood filling her mouth. The crowd surrounding them was too densely packed for her to be able to stagger back more than two or three steps.

Sonja spat out a few broken teeth and wiped her chin with the back of her hand. "Okay. Okay. I deserved that and I took it. But I *didn't* kill Anise, Fell! You've got to believe me, no matter what that bastard told you—"

Fell threw a second punch, but this time she was

ready for it and caught his fist and held it. Fell grimaced and tried to pull free.

"I'm *trying* to be nice here, but you're not making it easy for me. I don't want to hurt you, kid—"

Fell swore and moved to strike her with his other fist, but she was ready for that, too. Fell tried to jerk free, but she tightened her grip even further.

"Let me go, murderer!"

"Why should I?"

The hate churning in Fell flowed into her like smoke into a bottle. The charge was so powerful that the hair on her head lifted like the crest of a cockatoo. She laughed, and blue-white sparks flew from the tip of her tongue. Her voice sounded like she'd swallowed ground glass. It was the voice of the Other.

"You don't get it, do you? You don't even have a fuckin' clue! How Morgan thought he was going to create a super-race using a lap dog like you for stud is beyond me! Go ahead, lover boy! Keep hating! Hate me as hard as you can! It only makes me *stronger*!"

Her grin disappeared as she let go of his hands and grabbed Fell by his shirt front, yanking him toward her so their noses touched. The hate he'd been radiating turned to fear. Delicious.

"You wanna play with *me*, you gotta play hardball, sucker! You got that?"

A clutch of secretaries out for a night on the town screamed as Fell crashlanded onto their table, sending broken glass and spilled beer flying. Fell, blood streaming from his nose, shook his head, trying to clear it of the ringing.

Sonja grabbed Fell by his long yellow hair and yanked him to his feet. He tried to pull away, but she refused to let go.

"I'm gonna make you a man if it *kills* you!" she hissed. She pointed at the dancers on the dance floor, entranced by deafening rhythms and their own shadows. "See that? You're no better than they are! You're fighting your own shadow, not your real enemy!"

"Liar!" Fell yanked free, leaving her holding a handful of hair. "You do nothing but lie and destroy things! You turned Anise against me! You ruined everything I cared about!" He delivered a karate kick to her gut, sending her flying backward into the bar.

She grabbed a chrome-plated bar stool and hurled it at Fell. The people closest to the two combatants tried to move back, but those near the door, deafened by the music and unaware of what was transpiring, would not let them escape.

Snarling his defiance, Fell snatched a nearby human, lifted him over his head, and threw him at his opponent. Sonja ducked as the screaming man crashed into the mirror behind the bar.

The bartender yelled something and disappeared behind the counter. Sonja vaulted the bar just as he resurfaced with a shotgun. She snatched the gun from him before he had time to close the breach.

"I'd suggest you get your ass home," she growled, snapping the shotgun closed with a flip of her wrist. The bartender turned and fled into the stockroom.

Sonja swung the weapon at Fell as he began to climb over the bar. He froze at the sight of the double-ought pointed at his chest.

"Even a full-fledged vampire would have problems surviving a blast from this distance, much less a pantywaist like yourself! Whattaya think, pretty boy? Wanna chance it?"

Fell eased back, his eyes never leaving the shotgun.

"Yeah. That's what I thought." Sonja hopped onto the counter. "But before we take care of business, I think I ought to clear the field of interference!"

She could see them now, standing near the exit.

Two renfields—one negro, the other oriental. They were the ones responsible for crowding the bar and cloaking Fell from her scans. Fell was nowhere near self-aware enough for such psionic sleight-of-hand. They were also creating a veil, blinding the crowds nearest the door to the fact there was a brawl going on. They were setting up a killing box, all right. But for who?

She caught the negro renfield with the first round, spraying his brains across some slumming yuppies. The second round missed the oriental and struck an investment banker from Pacific Heights standing next to him. The renfield shrieked and clamped his hands over his eyes as the dead man's skull fragments flew like shrapnel.

The veil lifted. Suddenly people were screaming and shouting and knocking over tables and trampling each other in a wild scramble for the exit. Their panic made her giddy, as if she'd inhaled nitrous oxide. She only had a moment to enjoy the rush before Fell was on her.

His face was contorted into a mask of animal rage. He was not advanced enough to tap into the emotions that swirled about them, but he definitely had a contact high. He pounced like a young lion bringing down its first kill, bearing her to the floor. His strong young hands locked around her throat.

He was going to squeeze until the lies and evil spurted from her ears like dirty water. He was going to rip off her head and shit down her neck. He was going to snap her arms off at the shoulders and beat her with them. He was going to make her pay.

Sonja snarled and shoved her knee into Fell's groin. He gasped and let go of her throat, toppling onto his side, clutching himself. Sonja staggered to her feet and grabbed him by the scruff of the neck, holding him aloft like a kitten. She slammed him against the wall, pushing his head back by pinning his throat with her left forearm.

She took a second to assess his wounds. He looked bad. His eyes were nearly obscured by flesh the color of eggplant, his nose was broken, and his swollen, drooping lower lip made him look like a mule. No doubt his cellular regeneration was slower than her own.

"Just—just wait until our Father comes!" he gasped through bleeding lips.

"You dumb bastard! You stupid, mindless meat-puppet! You don't understand, do you? He set us *both* up! You don't stand a snowball's chance against me, and he *knows* it! He sent you here to die, Fell! You were supposed to distract me until the renfields could work up a serious enough whammy to take me out."

"You're lying!"

"Look, jerkwad, I don't have the time or the patience to do this right. I *ought* to kill you, but since you're Lethe's father—"

"Lethe?" Fell blinked in confusion.

She reached into a pocket and withdrew her switchblade. "What's your name?"

Fell looked at her as if she had asked him who was buried in Grant's tomb. "Fell."

"Wrong." She flicked the knife and neatly cut off his left ear. Fell screamed and tried to escape, but it was hopeless; her grip was unbreakable. "Okay, I'm asking you *again*. What's your name?"

"It's *Fell*, damn it! You know that! What's the matter with—" His protest dissolved into another scream as the switchblade sliced open his left nostril.

"No, no! You're not *listening*! I said what's *your* name?"

"What do you *want* me to say? It's Fell! It's *always* been Fell!"

"I'm only gonna ask you one more time, pretty boy, then it's for real, understand?" she sighed, cutting away his right eyebrow. "What is your *name*?"

"I *told* you it's—" His eyes widened and his mouth slackened, as if he'd just remembered something important. "Oh. Oh, my God. It's Tim. My name is Tim."

Sonja sighed and allowed him to slump to the floor, hiding his mutilated face behind bloodstained hands. His shoulders shook as he tried to cry. She could hear sirens coming closer.

"C'mon, kid." Her voice softened as she patted the top of his head. "C'mon, we can't stay. The cops will be here soon."

Fell shrank from her touch, regarding her fearfully. "Aren't you going to kill me?"

"No. Look, I'm sorry about hurting you like that, but it was the only way I could get you to come out. Now, let's go! There's someone you need to meet."

"Who?"

"Your daughter."

18

Palmer leaned against the headboard of the bed, cradling Lethe in the corner of his left arm while holding her bottle in his right. He was amazed something so tiny could possess such an appetite. He didn't look up at the sound of the hotel room door being unlocked.

"That you, Sonja?"

"Yeah, it's me."

"You know, you were right about her, Sonja. She's not like the other one! She's got such tiny fingers! And each one has a perfect little fingernail . . ."

"Uh, Palmer? We got company."

Palmer stared at the young man standing next to Sonja. One side of his face looked like someone had used a tenderizer on it. There was blood crusted on his nose and right brow. He shifted uneasily, like a schoolboy brought before the principal.

"Palmer, this is Fell. Lethe's father."

"Is—is that her?" Fell's voice was almost a whisper. Sonja nodded. "Sure is."

Fell took a hesitant step forward. "Can I hold her?"

"I don't see why not," Sonja said. "After all, she's your daughter."

Fell moved to take the baby. Palmer frowned and

221

tightened his hold on Lethe, pressing her tightly against his chest.

"It's okay, Palmer. Fell's his own man now."

Grudgingly, Palmer surrendered Lethe to her father's embrace. Fell's bruised lips pulled into a smile at the sight of his daughter's face.

"She's beautiful! She looks so very much like Anise." Fell's voice began to shake. He sat on the end of the bed, the baby in his lap gurgling and cooing contentedly. "This is happening too fast. There's too much to think, too much I'm remembering!"

Sonja knelt beside Fell, placing a hand on his shoulder. "Start from the beginning. Who are you *really?*"

"My name is—was?—Timothy Sorrell. I was a sophomore at Berkeley. English Major. I'm from Indiana, originally. My parents and older sister were killed in a car crash when I was ten.

"I got passed around a lot by my relatives. They were good people, but they didn't know what to make of me, so they left me to my own devices. I was a morbid child. Fascinated and terrified by death at the same time. I really got into stuff like vampires, ghouls—the undead. By the time I went to college, I dressed in black all the time and spent most of my money on occult literature.

"My first few months at Berkeley were okay. I even met people who didn't think I was all that weird! But during my sophomore year I started having these . . . dreams."

"What kind of dreams?"

"Bad ones. Full of blood and walking dead things. When I was younger I used to dream I was a vampire, but these were different. In the old dreams, I played Christopher Lee or Frank Langella, seducing nubile young women. But these newer dreams . . . They were different.

"Sometimes I'd see myself and I looked like a rotting corpse. My victims weren't beautiful women but old bag ladies and scuzzy-looking whores—they screamed and tried to get away instead of surrendering, so I hurt them even more for trying to escape. It wasn't at all like in the movies!

"But what scared me the most was the feeling of *pleasure* I got from watching them scream and die. I'd always been considered eccentric, but this was the first time I was honestly worried about my own sanity. That's when I decided to seek professional help.

"Dr. Caron was highly recommended." Fell laughed, the sound dry and brittle. "He seemed to understand what I was going through. Soon after I began seeing him the nightmares returned to the old familiar erotic dreams. He told me I should not feel ashamed for being . . . well, dissatisfied with my station in life. After a few sessions, he invited me to partake in a special experimental therapy session at his estate in the Sonoma Valley. I think you know the rest."

Sonja nodded. "He picked people who wouldn't be readily missed and displayed certain . . . tendencies he could work to his advantage. Of the ten he handpicked, you and Anise were the only ones to survive, am I right?"

Fell nodded, looking down at his daughter, who was innocently playing with one of his blood-smeared fingers. "It was horrible—I can still hear the screams, even now. But, in a weird way, it wasn't all bad.

"I remember thinking how beautiful Anise was back . . . back when we were human. I knew I didn't stand a chance with a woman like that. I was kind of surprised she was even in the group. She seemed so *together*. I was happy for the first time in my life—or after it. I know now that Anise never really cared for me—that, unconsciously, she was only doing Morgan's bidding. But Morgan didn't have to *make* me love her! That's why losing her hurt so much. It was *real* love, not pretend!

"When Morgan told me that you'd killed both her and the baby, I went mad. I wanted to avenge myself and prove to Morgan that I was worthy to be his son." His laugh was bitter. "So what do I do now?"

"You come with us to Yucatan. Raise your child in peace."

"How can I? *Look* at me! I'm not human!"

"Neither am I. Nor is your child. Fell, you don't *have* to go through this alone. I know what you're feeling! I can teach you how to master your powers! That's a luxury I never had. I learned things on the streets, the hard way. There's still plenty of things I don't know or understand, but maybe, together, that'll change. But I *can* tell you that the next stage of your development will be dangerous, and if you're not careful, it will cost you your soul."

"You mean I still *have* one?"

"You're not truly undead, Fell. You never died. Just like I never did. Usually it takes years for a vampire to reclaim the intellect and memory he had before his resurrection. Some never do. The only difference between the two of us was that I was a fluke, while you were deliberately created.

"I'm not sure how, but Morgan succeeded in altering your genetic structure into that of a vampire's without killing you. Right now you're still more human than vampire—that's why you were able to impregnate Anise—but soon the vampiric side of your personality is going to emerge. And, believe me, you're going to need advice on learning how to control it. There's no going back to what you were, Fell. Adapt or die, those are your only choices."

"What about Morgan? He's not going to simply let us go."

"I'm well aware of that. I promised Anise I'd protect her baby from Morgan. There's only one way I can do that, and that's kill him."

There was still enough of the old programming clinging to Fell's synapses to make her words sound blasphemous. "Do you think you can really do that?"

"There's no way around it, Fell! As long as Morgan continues, we'll be constantly looking over our shoulders. We'll never know a moment of peace without wondering when he'll make his next move. We won't be safe and, more to the point, neither will Lethe. It's got to be done."

"When?"

"How about tonight?"

Palmer jumped up, making "time-out" gestures with his hands. "Now wait a minute! What happens if *you* end up getting killed instead of Morgan? What then?"

"If I'm not back at dawn, take Fell and Lethe to the airport. There are one-way tickets to Merida waiting for you at the Taca International desk. Once you've arrived in Yucatan, check into the Smoking Gods Hotel. The manager there is holding an envelope that, essentially, transfers Indigo Imports—and all its assets—over to you. It's the best I could do on such short notice."

Palmer frowned. "You had this already planned, didn't you?"

She shrugged. "I told you I'd take care of things, didn't I? You were planning on retiring from the private detective racket, anyway. Now you can relax and sell stuffed toad mariachi bands and Day of the Dead tableaux to trendy Manhattan boutiques, just like you always dreamed."

"I'm going with you."

Sonja glanced down at Fell, still holding his newborn daughter in his arms. "Are you sure about
that?"

"The bastard *used* me! He preyed on my weaknesses and exploited me! If I don't deserve to help
kill him, who does?"

Sonja nodded. "We'll take the car. I'm betting he
won't expect us to move against him so quickly. In
fact, it's likely he thinks I've killed you by now."

"What about me?" asked Palmer.

"I need you to look after Lethe and make sure our
luggage is ready. If you don't hear from us come
dawn, take a cab to the airport and do what I told
you."

"But—"

Sonja took Palmer's hands into her own and squeezed
them gently. He felt her voice inside him, whispering in his brain.

*I have to do this, Palmer. You can't stop me from going.
We both know that. But please try to understand why.*

Palmer struggled to answer her on the same plane
and was surprised to "hear" his own disembodied
voice echoing inside his head.

*I understand. At least in part. I need you. Please come
back.*

*You're going to do just fine, whether I'm with you or
not.*

That's not what I meant.

Oh.

She smiled, and it was as if she was sixteen and
human again. Palmer turned to retrieve Lethe from
her father. The poor bastard looked like a mile of
bad road.

"Don't worry. I'll take good care of your baby."
Palmer smiled, doing his best to reassure Fell. "I
used to have a kid, myself, a long time ago."

*   *   *

Palmer didn't like what was happening at all, but there wasn't much he could do about it. When it came down to battling powerful six-hundred-year-old vampire lords, twenty-five years of street-smarts weren't much help.

Still, a part of him chafed at being ordered to mind the baby and pack the bags. Not that he resented looking after Lethe. If anything, he was astonished by how easily the golden-eyed infant had managed to override his ambivalence toward children.

He put Lethe back in her makeshift cradle and tossed an open suitcase on the bed. He didn't envy Sonja and Fell their task, but part of him wished he could be with them. After all, he'd been in on the case since the beginning, and it was only natural for him to want to be there when it ended—no matter what the outcome.

Sonja was right, though. Lethe was their biggest concern. Since she was unable to protect herself, it was up to him to make sure she didn't fall into Morgan's hands. The very thought of the bastard turning the child into one of his drones made Palmer so mad he felt giddy.

There was a knock on his room's door, interrupting his train of thought. Palmer paused at the threshold connecting his and Sonja's rooms. It couldn't be maid service, not at one in the morning. There was second knock, this one heavy enough to rattle the doorframe.

Palmer pulled his backup gun, a Luger, free of its case on the bed. Checking the breech, he stepped into the other room, closing the connecting door behind him.

"Who is it?" he barked.

The hinges on the door bulged inward as the doorknob turned sharply left then right. There was the sound of metal and wood grinding together, and the door flew open, its lock snapped. It hung from its hinges like a broken bird's wing.

The ogre had to duck his head under the lintel to enter the room. Dressed in a trench coat over a black turtleneck sweater and corduroy jeans, Keif looked like a young, upwardly mobile linebacker on the go. He emitted a rank odor of bull-ape aggression that made Palmer's testes crawl.

"Pangloss say you come now."

"He promised to leave me alone! I—I'm Sonja's renfield now!"

The ogre chuckled, exposing a mouthful of yellow, serrated teeth. "She leave. Gone play with Morgan. She not coming back. Pangloss say he got dibs."

Palmer pointed the Luger at the ogre. "Back off, Kong! I don't care if the Pope himself wants an audience! I'm not going anywhere with you!"

Keif growled and advanced. Palmer fired. The bullet struck the thick ridge of the ogre's brow and slid across his bald pate like a pad of butter on a hot skillet. Except for a thin red line bisecting his skull, Keif showed no ill effect from being shot in the head at close to point-blank range.

"That stung," the ogre grunted, cuffing Palmer with the back of his hand.

It was like meeting the business end of a weighted Louisville Slugger. Palmer sailed across the double bed, landing on a small table in the corner that collapsed under his weight.

Palmer struggled to sit up, his vision swimming from the blow. He cringed at the sight of the ogre lumbering closer, displaying his fearsome shark's grin. Then, to his amazement, the giant halted.

Keif tilted his head and sniffed the air with wide, gorilla-like nostrils. He beamed an idiotic smile, a rope of thick saliva dangling from his lower jaw. The ogre's behavior was gruesomely familiar.

"Baby. Keif smell *baby*." A gray, forked tongue snapped out of the ogre's gaping mouth, licking cracked lips. His eyes narrowed as he regarded Palmer. "You got baby round here?"

"No! I mean, of course not. What would I be doing with a baby? You must be smelling the Joneses down the hall. They've got plenty of babies—at least three or four! Nice big, fat, juicy babies. There are no babies here though! No, sir!"

The ogre didn't seem convinced. "Baby smell *strong*." He snuffled again, casting for scent like a blood hound. "*Real* strong!"

Lethe began to cry.

The ogre grinned in triumph. "Keif right! You got baby!"

"Leave her alone, damn you!"

But it was too late. Keif was already heading toward the connecting door, following the infant's thin, kitten-like wail. Palmer pulled himself to his feet and staggered after the ogre, trying to ignore the pain in his head. The door connecting his and Sonja's rooms now stood wide open, yanked off its hinges.

Gasping for breath, Palmer stared in horror at the sight of the ogre holding the crying baby upside-down by her ankles like a live chicken.

"I said leave her *alone*! I'll go peacefully if you just leave her alone!"

The ogre didn't seem to hear him. "Yum-yum! Babies good eatin'!" Keif tilted his head back and dropped his jaw, lifting the frightened infant at arm's length, lowering her into his gaping maw.

Suddenly Palmer smells copal burning and he is back in the jungle. He is walking along the narrow path that runs from his people's village to the natural spring that provides them with their drinking and cooking water. His young son, Tohil, is several lengths ahead of him. Tohil laughs and tosses rocks and sticks at the monkeys and birds in the nearby trees. He turns to wave at Palmer with his small six-fingered hand. Palmer envies the boy his spirit and energy. He has no doubt that Tohil will grow up to be a fine ballplayer. Before he finishes the thought, the green parts and a jaguar leaps from its hiding place and grabs the startled boy. Palmer sees the jaguar's sharp fangs sink into his son's shoulder, sees the blood leap from his son's skin. Palmer hurls his spear at the great cat, but it is deflected by a branch. Tohil screams his father's name as he is pulled from the path into the jungle. Palmer runs to where the jaguar ambushed his only son, but all he finds are bloodstains, bright as rubies, splashed across the broad leaves. The men from the village search for Tohil the rest of the day, but the boy is never seen again.

"NO!"

Grief and rage pulsed through Palmer. He seized the anger coursing through him and channeled it outward, and it was as if he'd suddenly discovered a third arm, invisible to him until that moment. Palmer *squeezed* the ogre's skull just as it was about to drop Lethe, headfirst, into its razor-toothed mouth.

The ogre grunted as if stricken by a gastric attack. It staggered drunkenly, thick black blood trickling from its nostrils and ears. Keif gave a bullfrog-like croak and let go of the squalling baby, pointed a trembling finger at Palmer, and took an unsteady step in the detective's direction.

"You . . ."

A pink fluid seeped from around the ogre's eyes. A froth of blood and mucus dripped from the corners of his mouth. Palmer took a step away from the advancing child-eater.

"Did . . . this . . ."

Jesus, what does it take to kill one of these bastards? A direct nuclear strike?

Kief collapsed onto the floor, his brains reduced to a jellied consomme seeping from his eyes and ears.

Lethe was still crying. Palmer stepped over the fallen giant and checked on the child. Luckily, when Keif dropped her he'd been standing over the bed. The minute Palmer picked her up, Lethe's wails died down to whimpers.

"There, there, sweetheart. Bad monster's gone now."

Or was it? If Pangloss was still hot for his bod, he was sure to send other operatives once Keif didn't show up with the goods. He couldn't stay here, that was certain. Even if the management had overlooked the hot plate in the room, Palmer doubted they were willing to ignore gun shots, a screaming baby, and an undeniably dead motherfucker.

Palmer reclaimed his Luger, wrapped Lethe as warmly as he could, and put on his coat. It looked like his only option was to take a cab out to the airport, sans baggage, and wait things out there.

With Lethe was tucked inside the front of his raincoat, Palmer felt like a pistol-packing kangaroo. He could just imagine what some of his old cronies would have to say about *this*. He hurried to the stairway exit just as the elevator down the hall pinged open. He didn't look to see who—or what—got out.

Four flights later Palmer strolled through the lobby, trying his best to look nonchalant while gasping for breath like a landed trout. The wizened oriental seated behind the registration glanced up from a Cantonese newspaper, shrugged, and resumed his reading.

Once outside, the panic Palmer had been suppressing since the ogre had appeared in his room finally kicked in. He hurried through the shadowy streets, no longer sure of what he thought he was doing or where he was going. The plans he'd made back in the hotel seemed far away and to belong to someone else.

He'd become so distraught, he didn't realize he'd gotten lost until he turned a corner and found himself at the end of a blind alley.

Palmer stared at the peeling movie posters and graffiti scrawls for a long moment before seeing them. His heart was beating way too fast and his breathing sounded ragged. He wanted a smoke real bad, but he'd left his Shermans back at the hotel room.

Lethe, curled inside his coat, was a ball of warmth pressed against his belly. Feeling her there reassured him and helped him swallow the fear rising inside him. Behind him, a bottle skittered across pavement and broke.

There were several of them blocking the entrance to the alley, huddled together like mounds of ambulatory garbage. Palmer felt the tension drain as he realized he was looking at street-people and not Pangloss's hirelings. Lethe stirred against him and gave out a kittenish mew.

One of the street-persons, a man dressed in filthy castoffs with newspapers swaddling his feet, shuffled forward. To Palmer's surprise, the vagrant responded to Lethe's call with his own, slightly deeper version. The others grouped behind him grew excited and muttered amongst themselves.

Palmer took a tentative step forward. "Uh, look, I know this sounds weird, but can anyone here tell me where I am?"

An old woman, her hair the color and consistency of a dirty string mop, sidled closer to him. She wore several layers of sweaters over a dingy, printed house dress. She smiled, displaying bare gums and golden pupil-less eyes that glowed in the dark.

"Shit!" Palmer jumped back from the old woman,

his skin tingling as if he'd just received a mild electric shock. Although he'd never really seen them, he knew these were what Sonja had referred to as "seraphim."

The seraphim with its feet wrapped in newspapers made a reassuring hand gesture, then it spoke. From cracked, filth-caked lips rushed a mixture of crystal chimes, birdsong, silver bells, and crashing tide. The beauty of the seraphim's language brought tears to Palmer's eyes. And even though he could not make out a single word, he understood perfectly.

Nodding his assent, Palmer unbuttoned his coat and held Lethe so the assembled seraphim could see her. They grew agitated and crowded in closer so that they could touch her dusky baby flesh with their calloused, dirty hands. Lethe did not seem to mind and responded to their strange, ethereal language with her own, babyish version.

The sweater woman made a sound like a dolphin and began spinning in place, like a bedraggled whirling dervish. Soon the others joined in her dance. Palmer watched in dumb fascination as blue-white sparks leapt from the twirling seraphim's outstretched hands and hair. Within seconds the ragged street-people had been transformed into pure light, spinning around him like luminous dust devils.

Palmer was so dazzled by the beauty of what was happening, he was caught off guard when one of the light-beings danced forward and plucked Lethe from his hands.

"Hey! What do you think you're doing!? Give me back my baby!"

Lethe giggled and clapped her hands as she was lifted high into the air on a pillow of colored lights. The other seraphim joined in, transforming themselves from electric-blue tornadoes to rainbow-colored clouds.

One of the seraphim twined about Palmer's shoulders, whispering to him in its strange not-language.

He need not fear for the child. She would be returned to him when it was safe. Palmer tried to snare the bright intelligence with his own mind, but it was like trying to trap quicksilver in his bare hands. The seraphim eeled its way free of his grasp, more amused than insulted by such a clumsy attempt at interrogation.

Lethe bobbed in the night air, smiling down at Palmer like an infant saint taken up by angels. Within moments she had drifted away from view, like a balloon caught in a jet stream.

Palmer knew he had nothing to fear from the seraphim. If anything, Lethe was safer with them than with him. Now he was free to follow Sonja. Provided he could find ready transportation.

As he left the alley he scooped up a loose brick, hefting it experimentally. It'd been a long time since he'd boosted a car without his tools. Not since the Sex Pistols' American Tour, at least.

THE TIGER'S CAGE

Thou who, abruptly as a knife,
Didst come into my heart; thou who,
A demon horde into my life
Didst enter, wildly dancing, through
The doorways of my sense unlatched
To make my spirit thy domain.
                    —Baudelaire, *The Vampire*

19

Fell sat beside Sonja while she drove, his posture rigid. In his faded denims and loose-fitting cotton shirt, he could almost pass for a college boy. Provided you ignored the bruises and dried blood on his face.

"I'm sorry I did those things to you, kid."

Fell started, blinking rapidly. "Huh? Oh. Don't worry about it. I understand what you were trying to do." His hand strayed to where his ear had been. "Besides, it'll all grow back, won't it?"

"In time. Your regenerative powers at this stage aren't so advanced that you'll recover overnight, though."

"How long, then?"

"I'd give it a couple of days. Maybe a week."

Fell grunted and glanced at his warped reflection in the windshield. "What about my eyes? When will my eyes be like yours?"

Sonja shrugged, trying to pretend it didn't matter. "Hard to say. It took mine several years to mutate. Maybe yours never will. Maybe it's different with different people. Who knows?" Sonja cleared her throat. "Uh, there's a few things I need to know about Morgan's setup at the house, if you don't mind talking about it."

"Sure. Go ahead."

"Anise mentioned someone called 'Dr. Howell.' Who is he? Another vampire?"

Fell looked back down at his hands. Without his realizing it, they had become fists. "No. He's not a vampire. He's human."

"A renfield?"

"I've never given it much thought before, really. But, no, he's not a renfield. I guess he's just a normal human. If you could call Doc Howell normal." Fell snorted. "He's Morgan's pet mad scientist, although they don't get along too well—and Howell openly *loathes* the renfields."

"Interesting. If that's the case, what hold does Morgan have on him?"

Fell smirked and held up his left arm and panto-mimed sinking a hypodermic needle into his bent elbow with his right hand. "The Doc's a stone junkie. Morgan provides him with all the heroin, morphine, and opium he can handle. And then some."

"And this guy's a scientist?"

"That's what he keeps saying. He's some kind of hot-shot geneticist. Occasionally he'd get hopped up and start ranting about how *he* was our true father, not Morgan! I always thought it was just crazy talk. We got a lot of that from the renfields, whenever they'd bother to talk to us at all."

"How many servants does Morgan have at Ghost Trap?"

Fell frowned. "I'm not sure. I never saw them together at one time. They avoided us as much as possible. There might be as many as six. Plus Wretched Fly."

"Wretched Fly?"

"Yeah, Morgan's top renfield. He was at the disco."

"The oriental?"

"Yeah, that's him."

"Well, I took out one at Ghost Trap this afternoon and one at the bar, and Anise said she'd killed one while escaping. That depletes his backup by half," mused Sonja, ticking off the kills on the fingers of her right hand. "Does he have any mercs?"

"What?"

"Muscle-for-hire. Various species of Pretender make their way by hiring themselves out to vampires as powerful and well connected as Morgan. I know he's got a pyrotic on the payroll. Did you see any ogres? *Vargr*? Skindancers?"

"Whozits?"

"Boy, he sure did his best to keep you ignorant, didn't he?"

Fell flushed. "Anise and I were restricted to a suite of rooms on the ground floor for most of our . . . lives. The first few months we were kept in a sterile environment, and only Morgan and Doc Howell were allowed in. Most of the time we stayed in our rooms, except for when we were escorted to and from Doc's laboratory on the second floor.

"We were only allowed outside once—it was during the day, and we were under heavy supervision by the renfields. Dr. Howell was there, too—taking notes. I guess they wanted to see if we'd turn into crispy critters when exposed to the sun."

"Weren't you even a little bit curious as to what was really going on?"

Fell's face reddened even deeper. "No, not really. At least I wasn't. I know that's a horrible thing to admit to, but it's the truth. Anise was a *little* more inquisitive than I was, and that didn't become part of her behavior until after she became pregnant. Until yesterday afternoon, it had never occurred to me that the life I was living was in any way . . . unusual.

After all, I didn't have anything to compare it to, did I?" Fell shook his head, amazed at his own naivete.

"But what *really* makes me sick is that a part of me, deep down, *liked* Morgan running my life for me. And what's worse, I *enjoyed* what I had become! I was never any good at sports back when I was Tim Sorrell, Super-Geek. I never did real well with the girls. I was a gold-plated wimp, if ever there was one. Although I didn't consciously remember any of that stuff, it was still buried inside me.

"There's a fully outfitted gymnasium on the second floor we were allowed to use. I can bench-press eight hundred pounds. *Me!* Scrawny little 'Dracula Weirdo' Sorrell!" He flexed his biceps, parodying a Charles Atlas-style bodybuilder.

For a fleeting moment he was what he had once been: a bright, sensitive nineteen-year-old boy, standing on the threshold of manhood. Then the smile disappeared and he was staring at his hands again.

"Morgan used to talk about 'the cattle' and how easy it is to control them. Sometimes he'd bring in humans from outside . . . I don't know who they were. Transients, I guess. And he'd let me . . ." He closed his eyes, trying to blot the image from his memory. "I'd *play* with them." His voice shook, the words burning his tongue. "Sometimes there was sex. Man. Woman. It didn't matter. And then after . . ."

"Fell, you don't have to tell me this."

"But I *have* to! I *have* to tell someone!" His voice was high and tight, like a frightened girl's. "My god, Sonja, if I can't tell *you*, who *can* I tell it to?"

She pursed her mouth into a thin line and nodded. "Go on."

Fell took a shuddering breath, anxiously knotting and unknotting his fingers in his lap. "After the sex was over, I'd bite them on their arms and legs and groin . . . Like I was kissing them, only they were screaming and bleeding instead of moaning with pleasure. And it wasn't because I was hungry, either! Morgan provided us with all the bottled blood we could ever need. I did it because . . . because it felt *good*! It was better than sex or drugs or anything else. It made me feel *alive*! It was like my nightmares, only I wasn't scared of the things I was doing anymore.

"Morgan would stay in the room and watch me do these things. I pray to God he was controlling me, making me do those horrible things. Because if he wasn't, *I* did them!"

"What happened was in the past. You've regained your conscience, and with it self-autonomy. Whatever you may have done while under Morgan's influence, it's over and done with. It's up to you to realize that and accept it, Tim."

"Don't call me that. I'm not Tim anymore, not where it really counts. I don't know who—or what—I am. Part of me remembers what it was like to be Tim Sorrell. I can still recall all the times the bigger, more popular kids made fun of him, called him names. I can remember the hatred he felt for them. I can remember his parents, and how he felt about them, but it's not the same as when I *was* Tim. But I'm not what Morgan wanted me to be, either. When I think of things I did before I regained my sense of self, it makes me want to puke. I guess I'm Fell more than I am anything—or anyone—else. Just like you're more Sonja Blue than Denise Thorne."

"How did—?"

"The skull-peeping works both ways. When you were working me over at the disco I kept getting, I dunno, *flashes*. Of you and Morgan. What he did to make you . . . what you are."

A muscle twitched in Sonja's cheek as she tightened her grip on the steering wheel. "I see. But you're right, I don't really think of myself as Denise anymore. She's more someone I used to know."

"Do you like her?"

She reflected on that for a moment before answering. "Yeah, I guess I do."

"I like Tim, too. Now that it's too late to do him any good."

"What do you *mean* you can't find him?" Morgan bellowed, hurling an antique ivory music box at the cowering renfield.

The renfield dodged at the last moment, wincing as the music box smashed against the teak paneling next to his head.

"J-just that, milord. The doctor is not in his laboratory, nor is he in his room."

"Are you saying he's managed to escape?"

"No. Not exactly. He's . . . he's somewhere in the house."

"How astute! Then if he's still in the house, *why* haven't you brought him before me?"

"He's not in the *nucleus*, milord. He's . . . somewhere in the *outer* house. He's in the Ghost Trap." Having delivered this news, the renfield pulled his neck in between his shoulders like a turtle.

"*Damn* him! Damn his junkie soul to a thousand drug-free hells!" Morgan shrieked, knocking books and rare antiques from a nearby bookshelf with an angry sweep of his arm. "*He* did this to me! He *deliberately* set out to ruin my plans!" The vampire spun back around to face the trembling renfield, pointing a finger at the whey-faced psychic. "You! I want the outer house searched, is that clear? Take the others with you!"

"But—but, milord!"

"Do it!"

The renfield fled the library, leaving Morgan to fume in silence.

He should never have trusted Howell. Never! The scientist had been unstable long before the drugs became a factor. But Howell's erratic behavior was what had allowed Morgan access to him to begin with. As much as it galled the vampire lord to admit it, the mistake was his own. He'd been intimidated by the scientist's facility with technology, allowing him far more autonomy than was prudent. And now Morgan was paying the price for not keeping his pet bio-geneticist on a tighter leash.

If news of his humiliation at the hands of a mere *human* ever got out, he'd be the laughing stock of the Combine! Worse, he would be perceived as weak, and *that* would endanger his alliances and encourage another round of brood wars against him. He might even be forced to surrender his title of Lord! It would no doubt please snapping jackals like Pangloss and Verite to see him brought low.

This was what his reliance on technology and science, humankind's sorcery, had brought him to. He should never have relied so heavily on something of human manufacture! These things were always confusing and somewhat frightening to Pretenders, and Morgan was no different. Yet, its inherent power had been too lucrative to leave to mere humans to exploit.

While Howell might be a necromancer of unparalleled power in his post-nuclear wizard's workshop, it would do him little good once he was strapped to a chair. Morgan had all kinds of interesting things planned for the good Dr. Howell. Depriving him of his precious white powder was only the first of many cruelties to be inflicted on the thankless swine. Perhaps a few judiciously applied medical probes would make him more appreciative of his betters. Of course, the good doctor would be forced to personally oversee his own flaying and subsequent vivisection. Morgan had long since evolved beyond the need to soil his hands with the blood of his victims.

But first the conniving bastard had to be caught. Morgan struck his desk with a balled fist, cracking its imported Italian marble. While Brainard Howell might be devious, vainglorious, and ungrateful, one thing he definitely was *not* was stupid.

The bastard knew that the outer layer surrounding Ghost Trap's nucleus was dangerous, especially to Pretenders and humans with psychic abilities. While this had worked in Morgan's favor in the past, Howell's escape had turned that advantage against him.

There were *things* roaming Ghost Trap that did not like outsiders, and Morgan was in no hurry to meet them face-to-face.

"Milord?"

Morgan glanced up from his reverie and glowered at Wretched Fly. The renfield stood in the doorway to the library, the right side of his head wrapped in sterile gauze.

"Are they dead?"

"Milord—there were *difficulties*."

"Explain yourself."

"The woman, the one called Blue, uncovered our presence. My companion was killed outright. I was momentarily . . . incapacitated." He touched the bandage shrouding his right eye gingerly.

"Then what of Fell?"

"I don't know, milord. The rogue had the upper hand the last I saw her. Milord, she was *tapping* him!"

Morgan frowned. "Are you sure?"

"I'm *positive*, milord! The nimbus configuration

was quite distinct. She was absorbing and metabolizing the negative energy generated by the breeder."

Morgan fell silent. He hadn't been expecting that. Perhaps it was better that his plans had collapsed, after all. His schemes had revolved around a race of vampires incapable of living on anything but blood. Feeding on emotions was something only the more advanced species were capable of. Fell had shown no signs of battening onto his terror-stricken prey for anything but plasma during the little "tests" Morgan had arranged.

"Are you certain this rogue isn't a true vampire?" he hissed.

"I am sure of it, milord. Her aural configurations were identical to those of the breeders, although much stronger."

Morgan cursed under his breath. This was *not* turning out the way he'd hoped.

"Milord—"

"What is it, Wretched Fly?"

The renfield cleared his throat. "Milord, I have failed you. And since I have done so, I offer now my life to you, for you to destroy as you see fit."

Morgan suppressed a smile. "I can do that *anytime* I want, Wretched Fly. But I appreciate the offer. No, you are too valuable to me, my friend. The eye—it is gone?"

"Yes, milord."

"Then that is payment enough for your failure."

"As you wish, milord."

Morgan watched as his maimed lieutenant left the room. It had been centuries since Morgan had last known the treachery of mortal flesh. The mere thought that he had once been restrained by the limits of bone and muscle, fearful of disease and pestilence, was enough to make his skin tighten.

*   *   *

"Christ, I never realized how big this house was before! I mean, I knew it was *large*, but I never truly comprehended its *scale* . . ." Fell whispered in awe, tilting his head to ogle one of the ninety-nine lightning rods decorating the spires and turrets of Ghost Trap.

"Look, once we're in there I want you to stick with me, understand? The inside of this place is designed to confuse and trap the dead. It also does a good job scrambling the synapses of anything more complicated than a worm. If regular humans have a hard time dealing with it, you can imagine what it'll do to Pretenders! I still have the protective charm I used from the first time I entered the house, but I can't guarantee it'll extend itself to include you. Have I made myself clear?"

Fell swallowed hard and nodded. Sonja surprised herself by giving the boy a brief hug. Shit, the kid was brave. Fell's cheeks reddened.

"Uh, Sonja . . ."

"Later, kid. We'll talk about it later." With that she turned and put her fist through one of the downstairs windows, reaching inside to open the lock.

"No wonder Morgan wouldn't let us wander loose around here." Ever since they'd entered Ghost Trap's rambling confines, Fell had spoken in a low, reverential whisper, as if in church. "You could get lost and never find your way out again!"

"That's not all you have to worry about. There are *things* that walk these halls. Most people would call them ghosts. Spirits of the dead."

"But ghosts can't hurt you, can they?"

"Normally, no. But Ghost Trap is hardly what I'd call normal. Just keep an eye out for anything that looks like a little girl or a woman dressed in old-timey clothes."

"Are they ghosts?"

"No, they're fuckin' *tour hostesses*! Of course they're ghosts! What did you expect? I think I can find my way back to the fire room . . ."

"The what?"

"Never mind. Just keep your mouth shut and your eyes open, okay? I—" She halted and tilted her head at an angle. She shot Fell a look from the corner of her eye. "You hear that?"

"What? I don't—" He stopped, his jaw dropping open. It was faint, but he could just make out the sound of someone whimpering. "Is—is it a ghost?"

"It doesn't sound like one. The dead tend to be mute." She motioned for him to follow her, moving stealthily through the shadows and dust of the empty rooms.

They found the source of the whimpering in a room lined with wallpaper that sparkled faintly in the illumination provided by a flashlight dropped on the floor. Fell touched the wall nearest him and felt the gold and crushed crystal wallpaper underneath his fingertips. It had the texture of sandpaper. Sonja picked up the flashlight and turned the feeble beam on its owner.

A middle-aged man dressed in a rumpled dark suit sat huddled in the far corner of the room, his face pressed tightly against the wall. His suit and hair were smeared with dust and cobwebs. One side of his face was bloody from where he'd been rubbing it against the wallpaper. He'd recently wet himself and the astringent ammonia smell clung to him. He twitched and whimpered like a kicked puppy.

"I recognize him," Fell whispered. "He's one of Morgan's renfields. But what's he doing here?"

"Whatever his reasons for entering this place might have been, I doubt he was looking for us," Sonja muttered. She took another step toward the man crouched in the corner. He stopped shivering and bared his teeth, foam flecking the corners of his mouth.

"Renfields aren't terribly stable to begin with. And being somewhere like this, I'm not surprised the bastard lost it totally," Sonja muttered as she moved closer. "Still, he might be of *some* use—"

The renfield shrieked and launched himself at her, his fingers clawing at her glasses. Sonja cursed and smashed the butt of the flashlight against her attacker's skull. The renfield collapsed to the floor, his head caved in. Sonja tossed the broken flashlight over her shoulder and bent down, lifting the dead renfield by his suit lapels.

"Waste not, want not," she growled, sinking her canines into his still-warm throat. After a minute or two, she withdrew, handing the corpse to Fell. "Here. Drink."

Fell's eyes widened and he took a step back. "No. I can't."

"You're no virgin! You said so yourself! Now, drink! You're gonna need it!"

"I . . ." Fell meant to protest further, but he'd already caught the scent of blood on her breath. His mouth began to water. He quickly battened onto the dead man. The blood was already below body temperature, but it was enough. He let the drained corpse drop.

"Feel better?"

"Yeah. I know this sounds horrible, but I feel like I've got my second wind now."

"Good boy!" She grinned, clapping him on the shoulder. "Now, all we have to do is—"

A loud scream broke the silence, bouncing through the rooms like a rubber ball, before being cut off in mid-note. Sonja and Fell exchanged looks and headed in the direction of the noise.

They found the second renfield in the hall Sonja had called the "fire room." The gas jets were still blazing as they entered. The renfield lay sprawled in the middle of the room, his skull smashed like an overripe pumpkin dropped from the top of a ladder.

Fell glanced about nervously while Sonja tried to find the secret panel the late Mrs. Seward had shown her. "This little girl and lady you mentioned—are they, uh, good ghosts or bad ghosts?"

"They're—ambivalent. Like most dead. But if you mean are they friend or foe—I think they're friendly. No, they're not responsible for this."

"Then who—?"

"Found it!" Sonja stood back, allowing the secret door to pivot open. "C'mon!"

Fell gave the mutilated remains a final glance over his shoulder before following Sonja into the secret passage.

The rental car was parked on the south side of the house, its hood still warm.

They're here, all right. Now all I have to do is catch up with them, Palmer mused sourly, nervously eyeing Ghost Trap's sprawl.

His own transport, a BMW he'd "borrowed" back in San Francisco, was in no shape for a return journey. Steam seeped from under its hood, while something dark and viscous dripped from the undercarriage. Probably ripped the oilpan off a mile or so back. Obviously, the car had not been designed to navigate Sonoma County backroads at high speeds.

Spying an open groundfloor window, Palmer checked to make sure his Luger was securely holstered before climbing over the sill in pursuit of his partner.

Three steps into the Ghost Trap, he realized he'd

made a *big* mistake. If he'd found the exterior of Ghost Trap disorienting, it was nothing compared to the interior.

He remembered how, as a child, he'd pestered his parents into allowing him to enter the House of Horrors at the state fair. He'd promised them that it wouldn't give him nightmares—he was too old to be scared; he was a big boy now, not a little kid. Finally, they'd weakened and allowed him to go in. His self-assurance in his proclaimed maturity vanished the minute the wooden double doors swung shut behind him, cutting off all contact with the world where light, parents, and rational thought ruled.

Surrounded by dry-ice mist, black lights, and prerecorded screams and rattling chains, he'd shrieked at the sight of a department store mannequin dressed to look like Frankenstein. He'd been so scared he wet himself and was escorted outside by one of the employees, a pimply-faced teenager dressed in a hunchback costume. His father had called him a sissy, and they'd been forced to leave the fair early because of his "accident."

Now, thirty years later, the same paralyzing terror he'd experienced in the House of Horror was close to claiming him again. His scalp prickled and his bladder ached as if full of ground glass.

He trudged through the oddly designed rooms, barely noticing such oddities as doorways set three feet off the ground, windows that opened onto blank walls, and fireplaces that served as staircases.

With every room, he found it harder and harder to think straight. Why was he here? Why had he entered this horrible place? He knew he must have had a good reason. Or at least *some* kind of reason. Right? Now if he could only remember what it was . . .

Palmer staggered as the floor dropped out from under him. The walls bowed inward, as if made from rubber. He retched while leaning against a sharply canted doorway, the acid burning his throat. His dad was really going to yell at him now. He shouldn't have eaten all those corndogs before riding the Tilt-A-Whirl. Now they were going to have to leave the fair. But that didn't sound like such a bad idea. He'd already been too long at the fair. Now if he could only remember where the car was parked . . .

Palmer collapsed onto his hands and knees as dry heaves shook his body. His forebrain throbbed fiercely, keeping time like a jazz drummer.

I'm gonna die in here. I'm gonna wander around lost inside this hell hole until it kills me. Just like Seward. Sonja . . .

He lifted his head and found himself staring at a small boy.

The child looked to be no more than three years old, dressed in a sailor's suit. The boy held a teddy bear close to his chest with his left arm because he was missing his right one. A knob of bone and bloodless flesh protruded from his mangled shoulder. Although the child's face was still round with baby-fat, his eyes were solemn. Palmer dimly noticed that the child was transparent.

"Little boy . . ."

The child did not waver or disappear.

"Little boy . . . I need . . . help . . ."

A young girl clutching a china doll joined the boy, both of them watching Palmer with interest. The girl leaned toward her brother and muttered something that Palmer could not make out. Moving together, the children grasped Palmer by his shoulders and pulled him back onto his feet. He gasped and felt a strong chill run through his body at the touch of their tiny fingers on his flesh.

The children were in front of him now, motioning for him to follow. Shaken and weak, Palmer lurched after them. He had no way of knowing if these creatures were friend or foe, but anything was better than crawling around in circles in his own filth.

The children froze like fawns scenting the approach of a hunter. First the boy then his sister disincorporated, transforming themselves into fist-sized globs of light. The change was so abrupt it looked to Palmer as if the children had rolled up like windowshades.

Palmer pressed his hands to his eyes, even more disoriented than before. What had happened to his tiny spirit guides? Or had he imagined the whole thing? And if not, what was it that had frightened them away?

The scream ripped through him like a bullet. As he listened, it ended abruptly, cut off in mid-shriek. The echo was so distorted it was impossible to tell if it had been a male or female voice.

"Sonja!"

Palmer weaved in the general direction the scream had come from. His brain churned and stretched inside his head, pressing against the plates of his skull. Sonja. He had to find Sonja. That's why he'd come into the House of Horrors. Now he remembered. Once he found Sonja she'd make the pounding in his head go away.

Palmer stared at the thing with the ax for several seconds before realizing he'd discovered the source of the scream.

The creature was shaped like a man, only taller. It carried a large, cruel-looking ax, which it was using to dismember what was left of a man in a dark suit. The ax-murderer made weird tittering noises while it hacked away at its prey. The victim's head had been cracked open from the top of his skull to his upper palate.

The thing halted in mid-swing and turned to look at the new intruder, and Palmer's bladder let go, just as it had in the House of Horrors back in 1961. Only this time he knew there was no way he would be escorted to safety by a sympathetic teenager tricked out in monster drag.

The ax-murderer had two heads. The head on the left was the larger of the pair, boasting a bat-like snout, a mouthful of jagged teeth, and pupil-less eyes the color of fresh blood. The head on the right was that of a man in his mid-thirties, the eyes brimming with a grief that extended beyond anything Palmer had ever known. With a start, he recognized the face of Creighton Seward, Ghost Trap's architect.

The two-headed monster stepped forward, hoisting the ax that grew out of its left wrist in place of a hand. Palmer wanted to turn and flee the abomination before him, but he remained frozen, unable to move.

Seward's lips were moving, whether praying or arguing with its grotesque twin, Palmer couldn't tell. As if in reply, the ax-murderer's head sneered and emitted more high-pitched titters. Suddenly Seward's head turned and bit its neighbor on the cheek, ripping free a wad of flesh. The ax-murderer's head gave a high-frequency shriek that made Palmer's nose bleed, and returned the attack in kind, scissoring off the ear nearest its mouth. Cowed, Seward's head did not attempt any further interference.

The ax-murderer's head leered at Palmer and lifted the ax-hand higher, until it almost brushed the ceiling. Palmer was not sure if the creature standing before him was flesh and blood or composed of ectoplasm, but it was evident the ax, at least, was solid enough to do its job. Palmer stared at the fiend advancing on him like a steer awaiting the butcher's knife.

Just as the ax was ready to fall, a bright light appeared between Palmer and the two-headed thing. The creature balked, uncertainty crossing the ax-murderer's face. Seward's head seemed to take strength from the light and plunged the fingers of its right hand into the ax-murderer's eyes. The beast shrieked even louder than before and Palmer felt blood seep from his ears.

The two-headed thing was gone. In its place stood a woman dressed in clothing better suited to an Ibsen play, her back to Palmer.

"Oh, thank God! Lady? Lady, I need your help . . ."

The woman turned to face Palmer, her left eye swinging loose from its socket.

Palmer screamed and ran. He had to find his way out of the House of Horrors. He'd been too long at the fair. It was time to go home. He bolted from the death-room and headed down a corridor lined with doors of varying shapes and sizes, the sound of his own shouts for help filling his ears.

Suddenly one of the doors opened outward and a golf club cut the air with a wicked slicing sound.

The last thing Palmer saw before the darkness claimed him was the word *Dunlop*.

20

"Home again, home again, jiggety-jig," Sonja muttered as she stepped from the secret passage into the suite of rooms Fell had once called home.

"I never knew this corridor existed. I don't think Morgan or the renfields did, either," Fell marveled.

"I suspect it was left over from when the carpenters were working on the house. It's only natural for a place like this to have secret passages. The building's probably lousy with them."

Fell picked up a paperback from its resting place on the table next to Anise's old easy chair. He fanned the pages and put it back down.

"It's hard for me to believe that she's really gone. I can still smell her . . ."

"Fell, don't."

"Don't what?"

"Torture yourself."

He didn't seem to hear her. Leaning his forearms against the mantelpiece, he studied the room's reflection in the mirror that hung over the fireplace, as if trying to catch a glimpse of the past in its depths.

"Do you know what the last thing she said to me was?" he asked, nodding at the room in the looking glass. "She told me this was a *cage*. A prison. She was right, of course. I can see the bars, now. But for a short while, this was the happiest place on earth. I . . ." He shook his head, refusing to look his companion in the face. "Damn you, Sonja! Why did you have to come into our lives? Why did you force this knowledge on us?"

"I wish I could say I did it because truth is freedom, and living in ignorance is the same as living in slavery. But that would be a lie. I did it because I wanted to ruin Morgan's plans. I wanted to hurt him where he'd feel it. And I wanted you for myself."

Fell frowned. "Me?"

"And Anise. And the baby. I—I've been alone for a long, long time, Fell. I was hungry for the company of my own kind. Sometimes loneliness makes you do things that are selfish. Forgive me."

"What's there to forgive? Besides, even if your reasons weren't altruistic, what you said about ignorance and slavery is still the truth."

"I hate to bring this up, but we can't waste any more time talking about our feelings. I know coming back here is painful for you, but we've got to dispatch Morgan as soon as possible. He's here, somewhere in the house. I can feel him."

"I can feel him, too." Fell's mouth pulled into a grimace. "I'm gonna fix that bastard but good."

Sonja placed a firm hand on his shoulder. "Kid, it's good that you hate Morgan. But be careful with your anger. Don't let it get out of control. Vampires feed on powerful emotions like hate and rage. It makes them stronger. Remember what happened at the bar? You've got to shield yourself from Morgan. I can't do it for you. It will be your will against his. You have to be strong, Fell. As strong as Morgan—if not stronger."

"I know. I may be inexperienced, but I'm not stupid."

* * *

She was here. He sensed her presence in the house the way a spider monitors the strands of its web. How could he have slept, unaware, when first she walked these halls? How could he have been insensate to anything so exquisitely lethal?

At first he'd refused to believe she could be one of his by-blows. But now he knew it to be true. His hand had sown this dragon's tooth. In a perverse way, he was proud of her. Even from a distance there was no mistaking her potential strength. She was a thing of fatal beauty, to be feared and admired, like an unsheathed samurai sword. To know that he had played a role in creating such a fearsome and deadly creature was flattering. Such a pity she must be destroyed.

The breeder, Fell, was with her; his presence nearly overshadowed by the female's. Interesting. There seemed to be something added to the youth's psychic echo; a trace of will, similar to that in the rogue. But it was only a hint, nothing more. Most interesting. If the breeders and their gets harbored potential similar to the rogue's, then Howell's sabotage had, in the end, been in Morgan's favor. What was the advantage to siring a new race of vampires, only to have them destroy him along with his enemies?

Morgan rose from the ornately carved rosewood chair in his study and opened the antique chiffarobe with the blacked-out mirror. If this was to be a formal confrontation, the least he could do was dress for the occasion.

"Who are you? I don't recognize you as being one of Morgan's lickspittle servitors. Answer me! I didn't hit you with the golf club *that* hard!"

Palmer opened his right eye. He tried to open the left, but it was swollen shut. His left cheek rested on rough wooden floorboards. He moaned as he struggled to sit up.

"Wh-where?"

"Never mind where you are! *Who* are you?" A wan, balding man dressed in a grimy lab technician's coat, a stethoscope looped around his neck like a pet boa constrictor, thrust his unsmiling face into Palmer's field of vision. The stranger's forehead bulged slightly, as if his forebrain was slightly too large for his skull. His eyes, amplified by coke-bottle glasses, regarded Palmer with a detached, insectile interest. There was something familiar about the stranger Palmer could not quite place.

"I'm not one of Morgan's renfields, if that's what you're thinking."

The moon-faced stranger grunted in distaste and swiftly shoved his hand inside Palmer's trench coat, removing his wallet and scanning the identification inside. His eyebrows lifted slightly at the sight of Palmer's private investigator's license.

"Hey! Whattaya think you're doing?" Palmer reached for his gun, only to find the holster empty.

"Looking for this?" The stranger extracted Palmer's Luger from one of the oversized pockets of his lab coat. "I might not be a private detective, Mr. William Calumet Palmer, but I know enough to disarm a potential enemy." He snorted and tossed the wallet into Palmer's lap.

"I'd rather you not mention the 'Calumet' part, whoever you are," Palmer sighed, cradling his bleeding head. He peered up at the smirking man leaning against the metal table littered with glass beakers and bunsen burners. "I told you who I am, now who the fuck are *you* and why did you smack me in the head with a golf club?"

"I am Dr. Howell, late of his diabolical majesty Lord Morgan's service." He bowed at the waist with the heel-clicking propriety of a Prussian nobleman. "Forgive me for introducing myself in such a fashion, but I had no way of knowing you weren't one of Morgan's minions."

Suddenly Palmer realized where he'd seen Howell's face before. "I saw you looking out of one of the windows the other day while I was surveying the house!"

"Interesting. And not impossible. But why are you here, Mr. Palmer? This is hardly a place for sightseeing."

"I'm trying to find someone."

"Indeed. Who might that be?"

"A friend. A woman."

Howell's smile widened as his eyes narrowed. "The same woman who entered the house earlier? Don't look so surprised—there's little that goes on in Ghost Trap I don't know about. So, you *are* a renfield!"

"Stop calling me that!" Palmer snapped. "I'm my own man, damn it! Unlike some!" He groaned as he got to his feet. Howell watched him cautiously, but did not threaten him with the gun. "Now, will you help me or—*Jesus Christ!*"

Resting next to Howell's elbow was a ten-gallon jar full of a clear liquid, in which was suspended the monster-fetus Palmer had seen Anise give birth to— and kill—earlier that same evening, its umbilical cord attached to a pulpy yolk sac. The sight of the little bastard made Palmer's leg ache.

"Ah! You've noticed my friend, have you? How do you like him, hmmm?" Howell leaned forward, eyeing the monstrosity in the glass jar with something resembling affection. "He was the prototype for a parasitic twin I succeeded in sneaking into sweet Anise's unhallowed womb." He removed a syringe from one of his pockets and tapped the side of the jar with it. To Palmer's amazement, the fetus opened its eyes, revealing the cold, needful stare of an insect.

The sight of Howell's face, distorted by the glass and the synthetic amniotic fluids that sustained it, caused the fetus to pucker and extend its hideous tube-like mouth. Howell chuckled indulgently. "How cute! It thinks it's feeding time!"

"You're responsible for that—that *thing* Anise gave birth to?"

Howell gave Palmer a sharp glance. "You saw it?"

"We met." Palmer grimaced, rubbing his wounded calf.

"Hideous as it may be, it was my attempt to make amends for betraying my race. I bio-engineered the creature from the breeders' own sperm and ovum, so there would be little chance of rejection, then implanted it in Anise during a pre-natal exam. I performed the operation under Morgan's very nose!" Howell's face twisted into a rueful grimace. "He may be wise in the ways of the supernatural world, but when it comes to science and the technologies, he's no more than a potato-munching peasant, fearful of the shaman's magic.

"The parasite was supposed to devour the original and take its place. However, at my last pre-natal checkup, there were still two heartbeats. If necessary, I was prepared to take care of the little Antichrist myself during its delivery." He leaned forward, eyeing Palmer intently. "You were there, weren't you? At the birth? The child *is* dead, is it not?"

"Yes. It's dead," Palmer lied.

Howell smiled grimly. "Good! Good! Should the breeders' child have thrived, mankind's future would have been seriously endangered!"

"How so?"

"The breeders can only reproduce with others of their kind, which are—mercifully—rare. But their child would have the ability to mate with normal humans and still breed true. Morgan—the preening fool—had no idea of what he was unleashing!"

"And your changeling was an improvement?"

Howell shrugged. "The creatures are designed in such a way that they have no means of eliminating wastes, once severed from the umbilical cord. The pathetic little monsters are destined to die of uremic poisoning within a day or so of their birth."

Palmer shook his head in an attempt to clear the ringing from it. He groaned as his vision swam.

Howell clucked his tongue in disapproval. "I wouldn't bother trying to get a better grip on your senses if I were you. It won't do you any good. This room—my 'secret laboratory' if you will—is located in Ghost Trap's attic, at a intersection of several architectural impossibilities. The barriers separating the space-time continuum are very thin here, weighing the probability factors for my experiments in my favor. Morgan and his loathsome renfields shun this place. I like it. It helps me think. Here I'm free to plot my vengeance against Morgan."

"Vengeance?"

Howell smiled a junkie's smile. "I mean to see the bastard stew in his own juices! I want to see him broken like Dresden china in a trash dump! I want to see the look on his face when he realizes his dreams of godhood have been ground to paste! Just as he destroyed *my* hopes and dreams so many years ago. The monster sorely misjudged me, and now he's paying for it. He and his loathsome little skull-peepers find my thoughts opaque. I confuse them by thinking in terms of formulae. And thanks to the interference generated by certain . . . inhibiting factors induced into my bloodstream, my thought processes are hard to decipher. Surrounded by a nest of telepaths, I've kept my thoughts to myself for over five years!"

"But you're working for this guy, aren't you? You helped him create Anise and Fell."

Howell frowned. "I am Dr. Brainard Howell. Does the name mean anything to you?"

"Uh, well, I . . ."

"Well, *does* it?"

"No."

"And why *should* it?! For years I've been under Morgan's thrall, locked away from my fellow scientists. Unable to communicate my discoveries. Kept incommunicado while slaving to find a way to restructure human DNA into that of a vampire's without the use of actual venom. In the little time I've succeeded in stealing for myself, I've worked *miracles*!"

He pointed to a shelf lined with glass jars similar to the one that housed the changeling. Palmer could dimly make out the forms of tiny triceratops, tyrannosaurs, and stegosaurs curled inside the jars like chicken embryos.

"And there is no one to see! No one to nominate me for a Nobel prize! No one to make sure my name goes down in the history books along with Pasteur! Einstein! Salk!"

"You left out Frankenstein, Mengele, and Benway."

Howell jabbed a finger at him. "Don't get smart, Palmer! I could stick you with a hypo full of miracle juice that would make your amino acids squaredance. 'Swing your partner! Do-si-do! He's got three eyes and no more nose!' How'd you like *that*, Mr. 'I'm My Own Man'?!" The scientist's pupils contracted into pinpricks.

"Calm down, Doc! I didn't mean anything by it! Honest!" Palmer lifted his hands in deference. "But if you hate Morgan so much, how come you're working for him?"

"Human weakness—something creatures of Morgan's ilk are adept at exploiting. I was working at a minor research facility in Colorado when I first made Morgan's . . . acquaintance. I had acquired a fondness for certain . . . chemicals . . . during my postgraduate studies. I found that heroin and other opiates helped to stimulate and focus my thought processes. They enhanced my powers of concentration, much like Sherlock Holmes and his infamous seven percent solution. Genius, Mr. Palmer, has its price.

"Somehow, Morgan learned of my . . . foible. He came to me and threatened to expose my secret vice to my superiors if I didn't agree to work for him. I still had no idea of who—or what—he truly was. Even though he'd essentially blackmailed me into his employ, I did not find much to dislike about my situation. I was paid three times my previous salary and given access to the most technologically advanced—and expensive—equipment available in the field. Plus, my new employer provided a steady supply of narcotics for my personal use. What was there *not* to like?

"It wasn't until I was relocated to this place that I learned what he *really* was! That was five years ago. I have been a virtual prisoner in this house ever since. During that time I have been an unwilling participant in his plan to create a race of living vampires. It took five hundred experimental subjects before I perfected the serum used on the test group that produced Anise and Fell. Five hundred. Even then, the mortality rate was still eighty percent."

"You sound real calm about that."

"Do I?" Howell sighed, rolling up the sleeve of his coat, exposing a pale, surprisingly hairy arm. The inside of his left elbow looked like a pincushion. He took a small plastic bag of white powder from his breast pocket and mixed it with distilled water into a small beaker suspended over a flickering bunsen burner. "Appearances can be deceiving, Mr. Palmer," he murmured, wrapping a length of rubber tubing above his elbow. "Very deceiving."

Sonja scanned the downstairs, finding no traces of renfield activity. Not that she expected any. For some reason, Morgan had effectively slaughtered his few remaining servants by commanding them into the outer house. That still left the oriental she'd seen back at the Shadow Box; the one Fell claimed was Morgan's heavy gun. High-calibre renfields weren't exactly easy to come by, and Morgan sure as hell wouldn't waste one by marching it into a meat grinder like the Ghost Trap.

Fell drifted after her, gazing in fascination at the sections of the house he'd never been permitted to enter. Besides the three rooms that had served as Anise and Fell's suite, the downstairs consisted of a retro-fitted country kitchen, several large, disused parlors full of dusty Victorian loveseats and moth-eaten mounted fox heads, and what had once been a conservatory before the panes had been bricked in.

They paused at the foot of the staircase that led to the second and third floors, Sonja leaning on the bannister. "What's upstairs?"

"Dr. Howell's laboratory and Morgan's library study. I'm not sure what else. The renfields' quarters are on the third floor. I—" He frowned and fell silent, as if listening to distant music. "Did you hear that?"

"What?"

"Someone called my name. It sounded like— There it goes again!"

Sonja scowled. "Kid, I don't hear a damned thing."

Fell trembled like a foal trying out its legs for the first time. "Oh my God, it's her! It's Anise!"

Sonja grabbed Fell's elbow, shaking him in time to her words. "Fell! Listen me to me! It's a *trick*! Anise is *dead*! This is Morgan's doing!"

Fell's face twisted into a grimace as he jerked his arm free of her grip. "How do you know she's dead? Were you there? Did you see her die?"

"No, but—"

"Then how can you be so *sure* she's dead?" He peered into the darkness at the top of the stairs. "Anise? Is that you, darling?" He smiled and turned to his companion, pointing toward the second-story landing. "You heard her that time, didn't you? She's alive, Sonja! Alive!" He began sprinting up the stairs three at a time.

"Fell, no! Don't!" Sonja grabbed his wrist, trying her best to hold him back without resorting to force. "It's not Anise! It *can't* be!"

Fell spun about, his fangs bared and eyes glinting red, and punched her in squarely on the jaw. Sonja hadn't been expecting it and there was nothing to do but roll with the blow. She counted ten risers before the back of her head made contact with the flagstones at the foot of the stairs, then things went black.

"Anise? Anise, where are you, sweetheart?"

I'm upstairs, dearest. Waiting for you.

"Are you all right? Sonja said you were dead. So did Morgan."

I'm fine, sweet one. I've missed you so! I'm sorry about all those nasty things I said the last time we were together! I just wasn't myself. That evil woman filled my head with all kinds of horrid nonsense. I was such a naughty girl to believe her!

"Where are you, darling?" Fell stood at the top of the second-floor stairs, trying to catch a glimpse of her.

In the library, silly. Where else?

As he heard the words inside his head, the door to Morgan's study swung open.

"But what about Morgan?"

He's gone, Fell. Gone for good. We'll never have to worry about him again.

Fell didn't bother to question his luck; it was enough that his lover had returned to him and his enemy had fled. He hurried into the darkened library.

"Anise?"

She was standing in front of the marble mantelpiece that adorned the library's huge fireplace, watching him with a coy, teasing smile on her lips. Her figure had returned to the trim proportions it had possessed before the pregnancy. She was beautiful and sexy and, best of all, she was *alive*. Anise held out her arms to him and Fell threw himself into her embrace.

"Anise! Oh thank God, it wasn't true! You're alive! You're *alive*!"

"Fell, you're squeezing me."

He stepped back to feast his eyes on her precious face, only to see Wretched Fly, the right half of his head swaddled in fresh bandages, returning his gaze. Fell backed away from the renfield, shaking his head in denial.

"No! She's alive! I *heard* her! I heard her call my name!"

"You heard what you wanted to hear, my dear boy. You are still human in *that* regard!"

Fell stared at the figure dressed in immaculate evening wear seated behind the massive marbletop desk. Morgan leaned forward and rested his chin on his steepled fingers, smiling affably at his erstwhile patient.

"Ah, the prodigal son returns!"

"Fuck you, Morgan!"

The vampire lifted an elegantly arched eyebrow. "It seems you've been exposed to the same corrosive influence as your poor sister. Tsk-tsk! One night away from home and you're already falling in with a bad crowd."

Fell's anger was quickly eating away at his caution. "You *used* me, Morgan! Or is it Caron? I came to you for help and you fuckin' used me as a guinea pig!" He jabbed an accusatory finger at the other. "You looked inside me and took out things that had no right being outside my head, and twisted them around so I'd be *happy* playing out your Dracula *über alles* ego trip!"

Morgan tilted back in his chair, studying Fell with a detached interest Fell recognized from Tim Sorrell's therapy sessions. Sonja had warned him about going up alone against the vampire lord, but who was this leech that *he* should be afraid of him?

Fell's hate swelled inside him like a storm, invigorating as an amphetamine cocktail with a speedball chaser. He felt like he could kick Morgan's butt to the moon and back. He was immortal and invulnerable, a child of the night to be feared by all that dared cross his path.

Fell planted his palms on Morgan's desk top and leaned forward, thrusting out his lower jaw in defiance. "You fucked with me! And worse, you fucked with someone I *loved*, asshole! I mean to get satisfaction. I'm going to flay you alive and grill your nuts on a hibachi!"

"Indeed." The vampire smiled. "Then why don't you take your best shot?" Morgan stood and stepped out from behind the desk in one smooth, seamless motion, his arms held away from his sides. "Go ahead. Be my guest."

Fell snatched up an obsidian letter opener from the desk's blotter and moved forward, ready to plunge the knife into one of the vampire's eyes. As he lifted the blade, his eyes met Morgan's and the room began to spin around as if it had suddenly been transformed into a centrifuge. He cried out in pain as an unseen hand forced his fingers back from the letter opener's hilt. The obsidian knife dropped to the carpet at Fell's feet.

Morgan watched his protégé's agony with undisguised amusement. "What's the matter, Fell? Got a cramp?"

Fell growled and looked away from Morgan's taunting smirk.

"Look at me when I speak to you, boy!" the vampire lord snapped.

Fell continued to glower at the floor.

"I said *look* at me, *boy!*" Morgan's words echoed in Fell's skull like thunder.

The youth cried out as invisible fingers yanked at the muscles in his neck, forcing him to meet Morgan's wine-dark gaze.

"Good. Now show me who's boss."

Fell collapsed to the floor, groveling at Morgan's feet like a dog desperate to ingratiate itself. He lay on his back, belly exposed, like a cub submitting to the dominant male in a wolf pack. A thin, nasal whine escaped his constricted throat, increasing in intensity as he pissed himself.

Morgan gazed down at Fell with cold disdain. "Ah, the recklessness of youth!" He knelt beside the writhing young man and caressed Fell's cheek with the ball of his thumb as he spoke. "Ready to snap the leash and bound, unhindered, into the world, as spry and eager as a pup at play! Is that what you want, child? Freedom?"

Fell tried to speak, but all that came from his mouth was a bubble of bloody froth.

"You don't have to answer me—I can see it in your eyes. You're still human enough to believe in such garbage, I fear. And it's contaminated you beyond redemption." Morgan shook his head sadly. "What is freedom but a chance to starve to death? To die at the hands of those who fear you? If you went to the zoo and threw open the doors of the tiger's cage, would it leap free of its prison and run wild in the streets, snacking on infants snatched from their perambulators before catching a policeman's bullet between its eyes? Or would it simply yawn and go back to sleep, the concept of freedom— indeed, of life beyond the confines of its cage—completely without meaning?"

Morgan kissed Fell's sweaty brow gently, like a father bidding his young son good night. "You should have stayed in the cage, Fell," he murmured. "You are now no longer of use to me. Pity. You showed such promise in therapy."

Morgan picked up the letter opener Fell had dropped, turning it about between his agile fingers. He ran his thumb down the length of the obsidian blade, watching his blood boil forth like brackish water. His thumb sealed itself before the thick, foul-smelling liquid had time to stain the carpet.

"Give me your hand."

The command was quiet, almost gentle. Fell gritted his teeth and tried to keep his right arm from unfolding. Although his muscles groaned like rotten mooring ropes, there was no escaping the vampire lord's will.

Morgan placed the letter opener in Fell's rigid,

trembling hand, wrapping the youth's fingers around the hilt.

"You know what to do," whispered Morgan as he stood, his eyes fixed on the boy stretched out at his feet.

Fell ground his teeth together even harder, heedless of the blood filling his mouth as his fangs shredded what was left of his lower lip. He tried to twist his head away from the slowly approaching knifepoint, but it was no use. His body was no longer his to control. He ordered his left hand to claw at his right hand, to try and knock the letter opener from its grasp, but it remained paralyzed. He screamed, but all that escaped his constricted larynx was a tight, dog-like whine.

When the point of the blade punctured his right eye like an overripe grape, he managed a short, muffled shout of pain. Then, to his horror, his left hand rose of its own volition and took the obsidian letter opener from his bloodstained right hand. The left hand was faster than the right, piercing his remaining eye within a few seconds.

The darkness was total, the pain beyond anything Fell had ever known in any life. Then he felt the sharp edge of the blade as his left hand began rhythmically sawing away at his neck. He continued trying to scream long after he'd severed his own larynx.

Anise, I failed you. I failed Sonja. I failed Lethe. Forgive me, please. Forgive—

"What is this! There is a child?"

In his agony, Fell had forgotten that Morgan was in his mind as well as his body.

Morgan straddled the dying man's body, slapping the letter opener from Fell's grip. Morgan grabbed Fell by his bloodied shirt front, making sure not to shake him so hard his head would fall off.

"It was a trick, wasn't it? The child *didn't* die! It's

still alive, somewhere! Tell me where, breeder! Tell me!"

Fell opened his mouth, but all that came out was a large, black bubble of blood. His head tilted to the right at a sharp angle, the spinal cord nearly severed. He could feel Morgan rooting inside his dying brain, searching for the memories concerning Lethe's whereabouts. Blind and partially paralyzed, it was like being alone in a dark house with a rabid, hungry animal.

"Tell me where it is, breeder, and I'll kill you fast!"

Fell raised his right hand, the fingers closing on his long, blonde hair. He'd fucked up big time, and now he was paying for being a stupid jerk. He'd waltzed into Morgan's trap like the world's biggest fool. He'd gotten a taste of being superhuman and it had made him foolhardy. He was dying, but he'd be doubly damned if he'd betray his own daughter to this monster. But Morgan was stronger, both physically and mentally, and accustomed to getting what he wanted.

"*Tell me*, breeder!"

Fell wanted to say "fuck you," but since his larynx was severed, the best he could do was grab a fistful of his own hair and give it one good, final yank.

Morgan yowled in rage as Fell's head dropped to the floor, coming to rest on the stained Persian carpet. He let go of the body, kicking it a few times in frustration. The sound of ribs snapping did little to assuage his anger. Wretched Fly watched his master nervously.

"Send the pyrotic after Howell. Unplug its television and tell it there will be no more *Gilligan's Island* or *S.W.A.T.* until it brings the good doctor back to me! When I'm through, it can use his corpse for a host."

"Very well, milord. And the rogue?"

"She's mine."

Sonja sat up, rubbing the back of her head. Her fingers came away sticky with blood. She grunted and wiped her hand on her jacket. The kid was stronger than she'd suspected.

She got to her feet, leaning heavily on the bannister. Blue-black fireworks bouquets exploded behind her eyelids. Had she been human, the fall she'd taken would have killed her. As it was, she'd suffered an insult to the brain that was far from problematic. But that could wait. She had to find Fell. Make sure he was all right. What did the young fool think he was doing, running off like that?

"Fell!" Her voice sounded weak in her ears, like that of an old woman. "Fell, where *are* you?"

Her answer came in the form of a footfall at the top of the landing.

"Fell? Kid, are you okay?"

Fell lurched into sight, his tread heavy and unsteady.

Sonja shook her head, as if somehow denying what stood before her would change it.

Fell's clothes were so black with blood they looked like someone had doused him with a five-gallon can of paint at point-blank range. The corpse lifted its stiffening right arm to display Fell's head, dangling by its long, yellow hair. The eyes had been gouged out and the nose sliced off.

Dead fingers spasmed as the body went limp, collapsing on the landing. The head bounced and rolled its way to the foot of the stairs, staring up at Sonja with its ruined sockets.

Her grief was so deep, so painful, it numbed her. Alone again. After so many years of loneliness, she'd finally found others to share her life, her knowledge with, only to have them snatched away from her within the span of a day. It wasn't fair.

From the darkness on the second floor came the sound of laughter.

She knew that laugh. She'd last heard it in London, over twenty years ago.

"I'm coming for you, bastard!" she whispered under her breath, her fingers closing on the folded switchblade in her pocket. "And I'm gonna make you pay!"

She comes. And my hands shake in anticipation. Her aura precedes her, lighting her way like foxfire. Did I create this magnificent creature? That I could have succeeded by accident where my carefully laid plans failed so horribly is both fascinating and humbling.

I must destroy her. Her very existence is a threat to my continuance. Yet I can not help but stand in awe of her—worship her.

She comes. And my hands burn when I think of her blood.

Palmer pressed his hand to his forehead, shielding his eyes from the things eeling in and out of his field of vision. They looked something like centipedes, except that they were transparent and swam about in mid-air. If Howell saw them, he didn't seem to mind; he was too busy checking his syringe for air bubbles to worry about extra-dimensional hell-creatures in the rafters.

"Uh, look, Doc—If you're worried about getting away from Morgan, I'm sure Sonja will be more than happy to help you in that area . . ."

"My dear Mr. Palmer," Howell sighed, slapping the inside of his elbow with his index and middle fingers as he tried to raise a vein. "I have spent over five years in the grip of one vampire. What makes you think I'd want to hand myself over to yet another one?"

"Sonja's not like Morgan."

"And rattlesnakes are nothing like gila monsters." Howell deftly jabbed the loaded hypo into his arm.

Watching Howell shoot up made Palmer want a cigarette. He winced and averted his gaze.

Howell smiled wryly. "Go ahead and look away. I don't mind. Mainlining isn't a pretty sight, not even to junkies. You could jump me right now. Why don't you?"

Palmer shrugged. "I don't know." It was the truth.

Howell quickly untied the rubber tubing and flexed his elbow a few times. He turned to face Palmer, his eyes dilating as the heroin rushed through his bloodstream. It suddenly occurred to Palmer that, despite his appearance, Howell was only a couple of years older than himself.

Howell removed the Luger from his pocket. Palmer tensed. The guy was a loon and, as if that wasn't enough, a junkie to boot. There was no telling what he might decide to do.

"I'm not proud of the things I have done in Morgan's service. But it's too late to pretend they didn't happen or that I had no choice in the matter. I must admit that the work challenged me, unlike anything else I've even done in the private sector." Howell handed the Luger back to Palmer, butt first. The detective muttered his thanks and quickly returned it to his shoulder holster.

"I dug my grave years ago, Mr. Palmer. I am a dead man. The only question is when my heart will stop beating. I do not expect to live terribly much longer. In fact, I'd be surprised if I survive to see the dawn. But I warn you, do not trust your champion simply because she is a woman. The females are even worse than the males."

"Sonja's different—she's not like the others." He frowned as he listened to himself. What he was saying sounded stupid, even deluded, but it was the truth. How could he explain it to someone like Howell?

"You love her." The scientist's voice was flat, almost dead sounding, reminding Palmer of Chaz's equally lifeless pronouncement.

"Yes. Yes, I do." He was surprised to hear himself admitting it out loud.

"They always love their masters. That's what makes them so loyal." Howell paused, sniffing the air. "Is it my imagination, or do I smell barbecue?"

21

Sonja followed the trail of blood to the library, where Morgan was waiting for her. She felt him as a siamese twin senses its sibling's moods and health. It was a dreadful, unwanted intimacy, and it made her want to retch.

"My child."

The library door opened of its own volition and a strange, flickering light the color of a ripe bruise spilled into the hallway.

"Come forward, child. So I may look at you."

The voice was familiar, although it lacked the upper-class British accent it had possessed when she'd first heard it in 1969.

She took a hesitant step into the purple-black light, shielding herself as best as she could from the siren-call of his personality.

Morgan stood in front of a mammoth fireplace, dressed in a neatly tailored dinner jacket and matching pants. His hair was bound in a ponytail by a black velvet cord. His smile was brilliant as he studied her over the top of his aviator glasses.

The Other's voice hissed a warning from its place inside her head: *Don't be fooled by the surface. You're no longer a sixteen-year-old debutante. Look beyond the illusion. See him for what he truly is!*

Sonja's vision flickered as she shifted spectrums and Morgan's image warped and twisted like a piece of cellophane held too close to a lightbulb. His flesh lost its sun-worshipper's glow, fading until it resembled a mushroom coated with tallow. His fingernails were long and curled, like those of a Mandarin, and his features bloated by the gases of cellular decay. The smell that emanated from him reminded her of the dead mouse she'd once found lodged in an old sofa-bed. The very thought of this putrescent monstrosity thrusting its rancid member into her was enough to make her gorge rise, twenty years after the fact.

The Other thought that it would be a really good idea to pluck Morgan's eyes out and use his head for a bowling ball. Sonja agreed, but continued to fight the rage boiling inside her. She hated the leering monster who'd raped and tortured her so many years ago—in truth, she'd cultivated that hate in order to face her day-to-day existence—but this was not the time to indulge her loathing.

Sonja knew the immensity of her hate, knew what it could do once unleashed. She had sworn she'd never allow herself to lose control again. Not like last year. She could never forget the lives she'd destroyed and the souls she'd shattered that night.

"Should I say 'so, we meet at last,' and get the cliches out of the way?" suggested Morgan, his handsome, debonair visage once more securely in place.

"Do you know who I am?" She had to fight to keep the tremor from her voice.

"I know that you call yourself Sonja Blue. Or perhaps you mean, do I recognize you?" Morgan's lips curled into a cruel smile. "Do you have any idea how many hapless, silly human girls I have seduced in the last six hundred years, my dear? And you expect me to remember *one* out of that multitude?"

"My . . . *her* name was Denise Thorne. London, 1969."

The vampire nodded, as if this answered something. "Ah, yes! The heiress! You were actually missed. Careless of me. Even more careless that I didn't make sure you were truly dead when I disposed of you. I blame the sixties *zeitgeist* for that. It was such a happy-go-lucky, irresponsible era! I found it quite contagious. Didn't you?"

"Cut the routine, dead boy! You know why I'm here."

Morgan sighed and studied his fingernails. "I know! I know! You're here to kill me. How tedious. Tell me, child, what exactly would my demise prove?"

"That I'm not like you."

"Indeed? If you are not like me, how have you survived these past few decades, little one? How have you kept yourself fed?"

"I—I have my ways."

"Caches of bottled plasma, no doubt. But that is hardly enough, is it? You can't lie to me, child. I know how *bland* prepackaged blood can be. Have you killed, my pet?"

"I—"

"Answer me true, child."

"Yes."

Morgan smiled a slow, sly smile. Sonja fought the urge to rip it off his face. "How many have you taken down? Dozens? Scores? Hundreds? *Thousands*?"

"It doesn't matter."

"Ha!" Morgan laughed, the smile widening into a smirk. "And you say you aren't like me!"

"I am not one of your kind!"

"That is true. You aren't like us. Nor are you, in

many ways, like your dear, departed siblings. If only Fell and Anise had turned out half as well as yourself. But perhaps that's what I get for choosing flawed templates. Still, it's a shame to destroy something so . . . unique. You remind me of something I once saw in a vision, fifty years ago—"

"—in a Gestapo torture-house in occupied Amsterdam."

Morgan's look of smug self-assurance faltered. "How do you know of that?"

Sonja smiled mockingly, pleased by the look of confusion on his face. "There are places where the future and the past blur—provided one has the eyes to see. The window worked both ways, Morgan. I saw you, dressed in your SS colonel's uniform. And you saw your death, separated from you by time and space."

He was inside her head, fast as a striking cobra. Sonja tensed as Morgan's will crashed against her own, like a wave breaking against a high cliff. As the pressure inside her skull increased, she was dimly aware of something warm and sticky flowing from her nostrils. Impressed by her show of strength, Morgan withdrew with a low, bemused chuckle. He tilted his head to one side, studying her closely from behind his aviator shades.

"Why are we fighting, child? Is this how father and daughter greet one another?"

Sonja wiped at the blood oozing from her nose and mouth. "You're *not* my father!" she spat.

"I *Made* you, child! You are shaped in my image! We are bonded! There is no denying me! We are much alike, you and I. You have more in common with me than you ever did with Anise and Fell. They were weak. Flawed. Unworthy vessels. They could not surrender the illusion of humanity."

He held up his left hand, dragging the nail of his

right thumb across his palm. A black, polluted liquid gushed forth. "Honor thy father, Sonja! Look into yourself and you'll find me there—it's in the blood!"

She felt it then; the relentless pressure of his will, bearing down on her like a leaden weight. It was as if she'd been suddenly transported to the bottom of the ocean floor. The temptation to capitulate was intense. It would be so easy to surrender and allow him to fill the void inside her. She dropped to her knees, her arms wrapped around her abdomen. Blackish-purple solar systems went nova behind her eyes.

Breathe! Breathe, damn you! shrieked the Other.

Morgan moved closer, smiling down at her like a punishing parent. "You are beautiful. I like beautiful things." His handsome, male model features shivered, ran, turned into a worm-eaten ruin. "You are also very, very dangerous. I like that, too. In you I see elements of my younger self—angry, volatile, scheming, defiant. I find this similarity . . . arousing." He gestured with one corpse-like hand to the knot in his pants.

"Humans are always prattling on about love. I know nothing of that. I *do* know of hunger, need, *want*. You have awakened a hunger in me, my beauty. The hunger of a moth for a flame, the mongoose for the cobra. I have spent centuries exploiting the weaknesses of others, only to discover a frailty in myself. I cannot allow this. It imperils my continuance. But, still, I can not help but be fascinated . . ."

The vampire lifted a hand smelling of graveyard mold and touched her cheek. His skin was dead and cold against her own. Sonja closed her eyes and saw a young girl, naked and bleeding, struggling to wriggle free of the red-eyed demon pinning her to the back seat of the car. She heard her screams as he emptied burning semen into her battered womb.

She heard him laugh as the girl's pulse fluttered and dimmed under his cold, cold hands.

The Other's sibilant voice snarled in her inner ear:

Twenty years! You've been hunting this bastard for twenty years, living just to kill him! To pay him back for what he did to you! And what are you doing? You're cringing like a damned whipped dog offering up its throat! You came all this way to die at his hands? Let me out! Let me out, woman, before he kills us all!

"You're trembling . . ." His voice was a husky whisper, close to her ear. His breath billowed out in a mildewed cloud.

"Don't *touch* me!" The switchblade was in her hand as she struck him, slicing air and decayed flesh in a single, powerful arc.

Morgan shrieked and recoiled from her, clutching the left side of his face. A thick, yellowish fluid welled from between his fingers. "Silver! *Silver!*" His voice cracked, climbing the register. "You *hurt* me!" He sounded like a petulant toddler.

The sight of her enemy's pain was good. Very good. "I'm not one of your pedigreed lap dogs, Morgan! I was born in the gutter and raised on the street! And I *like* raw meat!"

There was a hysterical gleam in Morgan's remaining eye. How long? How long had it been since he'd known pain? Not the temporary discomfort of snapped limbs and ruptured tissue, but *real* pain? The kind only immortal flesh is heir to. The realization that he'd been badly—and permanently— scarred both angered and thrilled him.

"I *was* going to let you live, changeling!" he hissed. "Maimed and lobotomized, true. But still alive. Not now, bitch!" His voice dropped, becoming an inhuman growl. "Not now!"

Morgan threw wide his arms and his remaining eye rolled back in its socket. Although she'd never battled a Noble before, Sonja recognized the ritual stance used in psychic combat. She followed suit, falling inside herself in time to meet Morgan on a field of battle known only as the Place Between Places.

There was darkness and light, and at the same time, neither. There was up and down in all directions. Morgan's imago hung suspended in mid-air, its features unmarred, dressed in the flowing silks and samite of a medieval Florentine prince. His eyes burned like polished garnet and flames licked from between his lips. His hands were turned palm-upward, each cupping a ball of black energy that smoldered like malignant St. Elmo's Fire.

"Is that the best you can do, prodigal?" he sneered contemptuously, motioning to his opponent's self-image.

Sonja looked down at herself. Except for her leather jacket looking brand-new, there was no appreciable difference between her imago and her physical self. *"What matter does it make? We're all naked inside our heads."*

As if in reply, a tiger with three heads and the tail of a scorpion jumped out of Morgan's chest. Sparks flew from its myriad sets of gnashing teeth as it roared in unison. It pounced, knocking Sonja onto her back.

As the chimera's fangs closed on its victim's face, the Other began to laugh.

Howell and Palmer watched as the lock on laboratory door began to glow, becoming white-hot within a heartbeat. The odor of roasting pork was strong enough to make Palmer's gut growl.

"Is there another way out of here?" he snapped at Howell.

The scientist nodded, unable to take his eyes from the door. "There's a trapdoor that leads to the nucleus." He motioned to the dissection table pushed against the wall.

"Then what are we waiting on?" Palmer grabbed Howell's arm. "If that's what I think it is, you don't want to be here to tell it hello!"

Howell pulled away from Palmer, shaking his head. "No! Like I told you, I'm a dead man. Better for me to die facing one of Morgan's servants than to end up in his hands."

Before Palmer could argue any further, the door flew open, its lock and handle reduced to warm taffy. The pyrotic stepped into the room, sizzling in its own fat. Although it had the same boiled lobster complexion and dead white eyes as the elemental he'd confronted in San Francisco, Palmer doubted it was the same body. The one guarding Morgan's Pacific Heights residence would have been a puddle by now.

"So, the renfields sent you in their stead, eh?" Howell picked up a large, wickedly curved knife from the tray of instruments next to the dissecting table. "It'll do him no good! I'm not going back! You're going to have to kill me!"

The pyrotic did not seem to hear, much less understand, Howell's statement. It moved closer, smoke issuing from its ears and nostrils like party streamers.

Palmer didn't waste any more words. If the scientist wanted to purge his sins in a one-sided battle with the pyrotic, that was his business. Palmer dove under the dissection table and peered down the trapdoor; all he could see was a rickety ladder disappearing into the darkness below. Hardly the stairway to heaven, but it would do.

"No! No, stay away from that, you idiot! It's not a television! I said, *no*!" There was the sound of glass breaking and Howell screamed something unintelligible.

The changeling fetus lay on the floor, surrounded

by shards of splintered glass. Its skin was the same bright, blistered pink of a boiled shrimp. The changeling emitted a plaintive mewling sound as it flopped helplessly about on the floorboards like a landed baby shark.

Palmer looked up in time to see Dr. Howell, shouting curses at the top of his voice, drive his blade into the pyrotic's stomach, slitting it from crotch to throat as easily as he would carve a holiday turkey. The pyrotic opened its mouth to scream, but all that came out was the hiss of live steam. Napalm spilled from the pyrotic's wound, splashing Howell.

The hapless scientist screeched as he was consumed by a column of flame, trampling the dying changeling under his heels. Howell's screams grew as he waved his blazing arms over his head like a small boy beset by angry hornets.

A sinuous serpent-shape made of smoke and fire, like the bearded dragons wrapped about Chinatown's luck gate, uncoiled from the pyrotic's slit gullet, twining its way through the air in search of another host.

Palmer slammed the trapdoor shut behind him and quickly descended the ladder. Whatever dangers Ghost Trap might hold below, they were preferable to being turned into a human cherries jubilee.

Sonja calmly studied the chimera squatting atop her chest, with its poison-laden stinger and triple set of jaws. The chimera thrashed, roaring its confusion, as it began to sink into its erstwhile victim's chest. She got to her feet, the chimera's oversized scorpion's tail still whipping madly about in the middle of her stomach. Her eyelids fluttered as she was transfixed by a surge of intense pleasure.

Morgan's unmarked face began to drip pearls of blood as something that looked like an ape with long, spidery arms, pulled itself free of his torso. The ape-thing had fungus-gray fur, compound eyes, and a ragged, lamprey-like maw. With a high-pitched squeal, the avatar launched itself at its master's foe, sinking a claw into her face.

The ape-thing emitted an ultrasonic shriek as first its wrist, then its elbow, was absorbed. The avatar jettisoned its right arm and leapt free, screeching like a bat. Clutching the stump of its right shoulder, the beast loped back to Morgan and cowered at his feet. Scowling, the vampire quickly gathered the avatar back into himself.

"You surprise me, changeling! I knew you were powerful, but I had not dreamed you possessed such will! It's been a long time since I've been challenged this way! It's almost enough to make me doubt my superiority. Almost."

A tentacle burst from Morgan's chest, whipping about his head like a lariat. Two more emerged from his sides, quickly wrapping themselves around Sonja's waist, arms, and legs. She hissed as the coils tightened, the hiss becoming a yowl as thousands of tiny needle-filled mouths began working at her dream-flesh.

And she was back in the physical world, curled into a fetal ball on the library floor. Or was she? She was still aware of herself, trapped in the Place Between Places, but at the same time she could feel the nap of the rug against her cheek. Morgan's shell squatted over her, hunched forward like a gargoyle perched on the cornice of a cathedral. His remaining eye was rolled so far back in his head it looked like a marble.

Damn it, don't just lay there snorting dust bunnies! Kill him! Kill him before he realizes he's only trapped part of us! The Other's voice sounded weaker, somehow.

Part of us? What did it mean by 'part of us'?

Stop worrying about the duality of nature and stab the motherfucker!

Sonja's fingers were numb as she fumbled in her pockets for her switchblade. Where was it? Where?

*   *   *

Morgan tightened his grip on his enemy's imago, grinding the illusion of bone and flesh together to generate very real pain.

"Do you know what happens to a body once its imago is destroyed, little one? It's not unlike performing a lobotomy on one's soul."

The Other spat a streamer of blood into Morgan's face. "Choke on it!"

She spied the switchblade lying where she'd dropped it during her first seizure. Morgan's control over her body had lessened, but her arms still felt as if the marrow in her bones had been replaced with lead. She forced her right fist to unclench and slowly, painfully, inch its way toward the open switchblade.

Pain the color of an exploding sun filled the Other's eyes and ears. The more it struggled, the tighter the coils became, but the Other refused to lie still. It was not in its nature to surrender.

Morgan drew his appendages in, tilting his captive so that she dangled inches from his reconstituted face. In the real world, the jagged knife wound she had dealt him earlier would permanently render his smile into a joker's leer. But here, in the Place Between Places, such inconveniences could be ignored.

"You are beautiful, and oh so sweetly lethal, my dear! It has been amusing, and I will bear a reminder of your murderous affection for centuries to come." He touched his cheek as if savoring a parting kiss. "I really must end our little affair . . . but not before you tell me where you've hidden the breeder's get."

"Get bent."

*   *   *

It was no good. She couldn't uncramp her fingers enough to reach the blade. They were going to die. So close. She'd come so *close*.

Something the size of a man's hand separated itself from the shadows and scuttled toward the switch-blade lying just outside of Sonja's reach. As it drew nearer, she realized it *was* a man's hand, albeitly six-fingered.

"That's funny, I don't remember you falling out of my pocket . . ." Sonja murmured.

The Hand of Glory nudged the switchblade with its fingers, pushing it in the direction of her own outstretched hand.

"Good girl, Lassie!"

"Tell me where the child is, changeling! Tell me!"

Blood gouted from the Other's nostrils, tear ducts, mouth, and eardrums. The tentacles knotted themselves even tighter, grinding its internal organs into paste.

"I don't know." It wasn't exactly a lie.

"Come now, prodigal daughter! You can do better than that!"

"Why do you want the baby?"

"Because it is mine. It was my idea to create the thing— a man is entitled to the fruit of his endeavor. I intend to use the breeders' young to build a new society of living vampires."

The Other laughed, spraying Morgan's face with blood. "You stupid fuck! You don't even know what you created!"

"What do you mean by that?"

"The baby isn't a vampire, you dolt! It's seraphim!"

"You lie!"

The Other started laughing again, only harder. "You should have gotten a load of your face when I said that! What's the matter, dead boy? You soil your pants?"

"Shut up! Shut up, damn you! Stop laughing at me!"

"Make me!"

"Damn your eyes, Sonja Blue! I was willing to show you mercy, but now I won't be satisfied until you're flayed to the bone!"

The Other's blood-smeared face split into a sharp, white grin. "What makes you think I'm Sonja?"

Wretched Fly dashed into the library, wringing his hands in agitation. "Milord! *Milord*!"

Lord Morgan remained hunched, immobile and silent, over the rogue's body. Wretched Fly reached out and shook his master's shoulder. Morgan's right eye rolled back down, fixing Wretched Fly with a hard, angry stare.

"What *is* it? Can't you see I'm busy?"

"Milord, the pyrotic's disincorported! It's set the house afire!"

"What?!"

"It's spreading everywhere! The south wing's sixth and fifth floors have already collapsed! Milord, the sun's rising! We *have* to abandon the premises before the entire building goes up!"

"What about Howell?"

"I can only assume the doctor and the others are dead, milord. I can not find any trace of them on wide scan."

"Very well, go and prepare the Rolls. I'll be there momentarily, after I tend to my errant . . . daughter."

"Like hell you will, dead boy!" Sonja spat, thrusting her weapon's silver blade into Morgan's unprotected chest.

Morgan screamed like a old woman as he leapt to his feet, tearing at his expensive clothes. The edges of his wound were already turning black and withering away from contact with the silver. "Poison! Poison! You horrible, nasty creature!"

Morgan wept as he ripped the rotting tissue from his chest with his bare hands, desperately trying to keep the taint from spreading to the rest of his body. "Unclean! Unclean!"

Sonja staggered to her feet, her muscles shrieking as circulation was restored. She made another swipe at Morgan, but her aim was blurred by the smoke filling the room. Wretched Fly grabbed his master and hurried him from the room.

Sonja tried to follow him, but her head was hurting real bad. She took a few steps and dropped to her knees, gagging on smoke. Morgan was escaping. She had to stop him. Kill him. Get it over with, once and for all. If she died under tons of flaming timber, what difference did it make? Who would be left to mourn—or even notice—her passing?

As her body was wracked by a coughing fit, it suddenly occurred to her how *quiet* it was inside her head. The Other's needling voice, her constant companion for nearly two decades, was strangely silent.

She moved cautiously, searching for signs of the Other as if probing a sore tooth with her tongue. Could it be that Morgan had somehow managed to kill it, while sparing her?

You're not rid of me, yet.

No, the Other was not dead. But it *was* hurt. It seemed weaker than it'd been in over a decade.

You owe me one.

She was back in the burning house, struggling to pull oxygen from the smoke-filled room. She glimpsed the Hand of Glory laying on its back, fingers curled in on themselves like the legs of a dead spider. The hand suddenly twitched and righted itself, scurrying across the antique Persian carpet and out the door into the hall.

Sonja dragged herself to her feet, coughing violently as she inhaled a lungfull of dense white smoke. She staggered into the hallway, now almost obscured by billowing smoke. She could hear the not-so-distant roar of fire and the laughter of children.

The house shook as Ghost Trap's west wing collapsed into its cellar, knocking Sonja to the floor. She lay there, dazed, and wondered whether she was going to suffocate or burn to death first. The sound of laughing children grew louder.

A boy and girl, dressed in clothing fashionable before Mary Pickford was America's sweetheart, emerged from the swirling smoke. Sonja recognized the little girl as the ghost-child she'd met earlier. The children grabbed her hands and lifted her from the floor. Sonja decided she was too weak to fight them; besides, they seemed to know where they were going.

The Seward children lead her through smoke-obscured rooms into a dark passage. Sonja heard their long-dead, insectile voices buzzing in her ear, but could not make out what they were saying. Soon they were back within the tortured architecture of Ghost Trap's outer house. As the Seward children continued to escort her, Sonja dimly realized her feet were no longer touching the floor.

Suddenly there was a desperate banshee wail, and their way was blocked by a hulking grotesque with two heads. The ghost-children deftly yanked their dazed charge out of the path of the large, blood-spattered ax the two-headed apparition swung in their direction. Sonja tried to break free of the dead childrens' grasp, but they refused to let go.

The gibbering two-headed ax-murderer wrenched its weapon free from the splintered floorboards and prepared to lift it a second time. Then came the sound of a woman's laughter—light, merry, free—echoing through the empty rooms.

The creature paused to listen, its twisted, bat-snouted face grimacing.

Mrs. Seward's ghost materialized beside that of her killer. She suddenly grabbed her husband's head by its hair and began to *pull*. The ax-murderer squealed like a frightened piglet and flailed ineffectively at Mrs. Seward with its ax-hand. There was a muffled sucking sound, like someone pulling their foot free of thick mud, and the shoulders and torso of the late Creighton Seward emerged from the ax-murderer's leprous skin.

The ax-murderer shrieked even louder than before, its clawed feet drumming against the bare boards like those of a petulant child throwing a tantrum, but Mrs. Seward was not to be denied the reclamation of her husband. With a final, mighty tug, she freed Seward's naked body of its demonic twin. Robbed of its unwilling symbiote, the demon collapsed like a gutted scarecrow, its corpus returning to formless ectoplasm.

The dead man shivered like a newborn foal and threw his arms around his murdered wife, his face pressed against her bosom. Sonja stared dully at the embracing couple, reunited for the first time since that horrible night in 1907, when Creighton Seward, in a moment of weakness, made an unwise bargain in a bid for artistic genius.

Mrs. Seward, her face no longer mutilated, leaned forward and brushed her translucent lips against Sonja's cheek.

Sonja found herself lifted into the air, hurtling through room after room as if shot from a cannon, the rumble of walls crashing and floors collapsing echoing in her ears. She saw the window a split-second before she was catapulted through it into the tangled, thorny embrace of an overgrown rosebush.

Sonja dragged herself a few yards before collapsing. She dimly registered the sound of yet another of one of Ghost Trap's chimneys tumbling down in a thunderclap of bricks and mortar. She knew she was in extreme danger of the exterior wall collapsing on her, but somehow it didn't seem to matter.

He had escaped. After all those years spent tracking him through the cities of the civilized world, she'd had him, felt his blood, felt his pain . . . only to have him escape. She'd been so close . . .

"Sonja! Thank God I found you!"

She squinted up at the figure kneeling over her. "Palmer?"

He looked like he'd been whacked with a golf club, his face was smeared with soot, he reeked of smoke, and he was the most beautiful thing she'd ever seen.

"It ain't the Easter Bunny, baby!" He kissed her blood-smeared brow and helped her to her feet. After they were safely away from the house, they turned to watch its death throes. Ghost Trap glowed like the rising sun.

"Look," whispered Palmer, pointing at the smoke and sparks drifting heavenward.

Sonja watched as the pellucid outlines of the Seward family ascended the currents, accompanied by an equally pale and familiar figure with long, flowing hair and the shade of a moon-faced man in a flapping white coat, a deformed infant cradled in his arms. Within seconds of her sighting them, they were gone, lost amongst the smoke and soot and lightening sky.

"I'm not going to ask why you're not on a plane to Yucatan. I'm glad you're here, Palmer." She leaned her forehead on his shoulder. "You up to driving? I've got the keys . . ."

"It doesn't matter, Sonja. The rental's buried under a couple tons of fireplace. It looks like we're going to have to hoof it into town and catch the bus into San Francisco."

She groaned and took his hand. "I guess we better start walkin', huh?"

As they made their way to the county road, Palmer heard the crunch of tires behind them. He turned in time to see a vintage Rolls with heavily tinted windows bearing down on them, an oriental man, his head swaddled in sooty bandages, behind the wheel. Without thinking, he grabbed Sonja and dove into a nearby ditch. The Rolls rocketed by, spewing gravel in its wake.

Palmer and Sonja clambered back onto the shoulder and watched the limousine's tail lights disappear in the early morning mist.

Morgan lay on the floor of the Rolls, wrapped in blankets and curled in a fetal position. His chest still burned, but he was certain he'd removed every trace of the silver-tainted tissue before the toxin had a chance to infiltrate his central nervous system. His chest would heal. It might not even scar. The same could not be said of his face, however.

Morgan touched his left cheek and moaned. Wounds dealt by silver weapons never truly healed, and they always left ugly scars. But that was not the worst part. The mutilation of his flesh was a minor thing, compared to what that bitch had done to him.

Lord Morgan moaned again and huddled even deeper into his blankets. Broken bones would mend, damaged organs regenerate, even severed limbs regrow, in time. But there would be no healing for the wounds she'd inflicted on his psyche, only a gradual spread of infection.

Lord Morgan, late of the Inquisition and the Gestapo, lay on the floor of his car and contemplated the dreadful sickness that humans called Love.

EPILOGUE: MERIDA, YUCATAN

A man's mind, stretched by new ideas, can never go back to its original dimensions.
—Oliver Wendell Holmes

Palmer was hammering together a wooden crate on the porch of his *hacienda* when the mailman blew his whistle.

"Tweet, Daddy! Tweet!" squealed Lethe, rounding the corner of the house as fast as her baggy diapers would allow. Her Barbar the Elephant play-shirt was smeared with mud, and judging from the dirty tablespoon she was waving, she'd been digging up the back patio again.

"Whoa, droopy drawers!" Palmer laughed, catching the toddler in his outstretched arms, flipping her upside down. Lethe giggled and wriggled in his grip like a puppy. Not bad for a nine-month-old. "You know you're not supposed to go near the road!"

Palmer deposited the child in the macramé hammock he kept strung on the porch and trotted down to the mailbox at the foot of the hill. He made a mental note to take the Landrover into the city and buy some fencing material. Lethe was advanced for her age, but he still had problems with her wanting to run out onto the road every time the mailman made his rounds. Lethe loved getting mail.

A dark, ragged form emerged from the *hacienda* and joined Lethe in the hammock. The little girl's giggles were soon joined by the peals of crystal chimes and the yattering of dolphins.

Palmer sorted through the letters as he walked back up the path to the house. Two were from boutiques in California and New York, ordering three more crates apiece of Day of the Dead tableaux, stuffed toad Mariachi bands, and handpainted paper maché carnival masks. There was also a package addressed to Lethe with a fistful of Asian stamps plastered across it, and a postcard from Sonja.

"Look, honey! Aunt Boo sent you a present!" Palmer handed the package to Lethe, still curled in the seraphim's lap. Within seconds, the porch was littered with tatters of brown paper and Lethe was playing with a ragdoll dressed in a tiny blue cotton kimono, its dyed cornsilk hair pulled into an elaborate geisha's coiffure.

Palmer glanced at the front of the picture postcard— a panoramic view of downtown Tokyo at night— then flipped it over to read the message. There was no salutation or signature. There never were.

Still no sign of M. But I'm getting closer. The chimera is very excited. It smells its old master. The scar makes it harder for M to change identities. There are rumors of atrocities in Mainland. M? Hope to be home for Xmas. Miss you.

Palmer looked up from the card to find the seraphim staring at him with its pupil-less golden eyes.

"No news, Fido. Same old things." The seraphim nodded, although Palmer had his doubts as to how much the creature understood. "Lethe, sweetie, why don't you go play with Fido on the patio? I've got work to do."

Lethe nodded her tiny dark head, her golden eyes flashing in the afternoon light, and hopped out of the hammock, leading the grizzled seraphim by the hand. Palmer smiled as the unlikely twosome, nut-brown nature-child and bedraggled street-person, disappeared around the corner of the house—Fido shambling after Lethe like a trained bear.

Even after all these months, he still had a hard time accepting it all. A year ago he'd been looking a twenty-to-life sentence in the face. Now he was living the life of an expatriate *yanqui*, making a decent living selling Mexican and Central American folk art to painfully chic boutiques and galleries north of the border. He'd also discovered, to his surprise, he was a damn good father. Yeah, a lot of things can change in the space of a year, he mused, fingering his jade ear plug.

Lethe had reappeared a couple of weeks after he and Sonja had set up housekeeping in Yucatan. One minute the patio had been empty, the next Lethe and the seraphim were there. Although the baby was not yet a month old, she was already crawling and babbling.

When it became evident the seraphim was not going to leave, Sonja decided it was time for her to continue on her hunt. Palmer knew the seraphim made her nervous. It had taken him a few weeks to get used to the creature's presence, himself. But after he started calling it Fido, he began to relax. Somehow "Fido" seemed an appropriate moniker.

Every so often Sonja would appear on the doorstep, unannounced but always welcome, loaded down with exotic toys for her "niece." Although she adored Lethe, Sonja could not tolerate being around Fido for more than a few days.

During her brief visits, she and Palmer lay curled together in the hammock and listened to the nightbirds call. In its own strange way, their relationship was idyllic.

The last time Sonja had come home she'd been amused to discover the ritual tattoo on his chest.

"What's this? Have you decided to go modern primitive on me?" She giggled, running her hands over the raised markings covering his pectorals.

"I—I decided to get a tattoo to hide the scar from my surgery."

"Really?"

"Kind of. Besides, it matches the scars you leave on my back."

She was silent for a few minutes. "Do you still have the dreams?"

"Sometimes. They've gotten stronger since the hand came back . . ."

"The *hand?*"

"Yeah, I know it sounds crazy, but a couple weeks ago something tapping at the windowscreen woke me up. At first I thought it might have been a bird. Then I saw it, squatting on the ledge outside the window. It was the hand Li Lijing gave you, scratching to be let in!"

"What'd you do?"

"I let it in."

"Weren't you scared?"

Palmer shrugged. "I've heard stories about dogs traveling cross-country to rejoin their families, so why not a six-fingered hand? Besides, it doesn't do anything except hide under the couch. My mom used to have a chihuahua like that. And if I had to make a choice, I'd rather have an animated amputated hand than a chihuahua."

"Can't argue with you there. So what is this tattoo supposed to represent?"

"The old Mayan guy who did it says it used to be the seal of the *Chan Balam*, the Jaguar Lords."

However, he hadn't bothered to tell her that while his Spanish remained hopelessly retarded, he could now speak fluent Lancandon, the tongue of the children of Quetzicoatl, and that he'd stopped smoking his precious Shermans in favor of the burrito-sized hallucinogenic cigars favored by the Mayans. That had been three months ago. He wondered what she'd have to say about his earrings.

Palmer resumed his work on the packing crate, pausing every now and again to sip from a pitcher of lemonade. He noticed a *campesino* trudging his way along the unpaved road that ran past the house, headed in the direction of the paved highway three miles away where a rattle-trap bus carried locals into the city.

Palmer stiffened at the sight of the stooped, unwashed man dressed in the traditional loose-fitting white cotton pants and tunic, a machete hanging from his belt. He scanned the *campesino*, briefly sampling his thoughts and measuring his aura for traces of Pretender taint.

Luckily for the *campesino*, he was exactly what he looked like—a peasant on his way to town. He would live to ride the bus to Merida. Palmer allowed himself a sigh of relief. He disliked killing, even Pretenders. But he knew he could not allow his vigilance to slacken, even for a moment. For as every good parent knows, the jungle is full of jaguars hungry for the blood of children.

About the Author

Nancy A. Collins is the oldest of four children born and raised in rural Arkansas. Her first novel, SUNGLASSES AFTER DARK, won the 1989 Horror Writers of America's Bram Stoker Award for Outstanding First Novel, and the British Fantasy Society's Icarus Award for Best Newcomer. She is also the writer for DC Comics' SWAMP THING series. She currently lives in New Orleans.